Praise for *The House of Whispers*

'A creepy, chilling story . . . Another Anna Mazzola triumph'
JENNIFER SAINT

'Chilling and compelling, with echoes of Daphne du
Maurier's *Rebecca*, this is a thrilling mystery with many eerie
twists and turns to keep you hooked all through the night'
ESSIE FOX

'Darkly atmospheric and dripping with menace.
Anna Mazzola is a twisted genius'
TAMMY COHEN

'Powerful, spine-tingling and beautifully penned,
this is gothic historical fiction at its very best'
ABIR MUKHERJEE

'Beautiful, chilling, and darkly enchanting. Anna Mazzola
is a truly gifted storyteller'
CHRIS WHITAKER

'Eerie and unsettling, but perhaps Anna Mazzola's superbly
realised depiction of a nation gripped by the horrors of
fascism is the most terrifying thing of all'
KATE GRIFFIN

'Absolutely brilliant. Gripping, beautifully written and
properly chilling'
CAROLINE GREEN

'Robert Harris meets M.R. James in an evocative gothic
tale set in a Rome on the edge of catastrophe . . . Mazzola's
dazzling imagination is at its very peak'
DAVID HEWSON

'The sense of place is impeccable, the sense of danger truly chilling'
SINÉAD CROWLEY

'The thrilling tale of a woman caught between the pressures of pre-war Italy and the more mysterious manifestations of something amiss in her own household'
ALISON LITTLEWOOD

'A delicately told ghost story set in the bright heat of 1930s Italy. Claustrophobic and compelling'
AMANDA MASON

'Packed with political and emotional intrigue . . . historically rich and deeply unsettling'
SARAH HILARY

'Gothic, immersive and very, very scary . . . Set in 1939 Rome against the rise of fascism, injecting a powerful sense of dread'
ALLY WILKES

'A gripping, thrilling story which had me hooked from the start, as the terrifying reality of fascism in pre-war Italy is increasingly entwined in an anguished marriage'
MARY CHAMBERLAIN

'Tense historical fiction like no other . . . Dark and mysterious with whispers of a buried past hidden in the walls. I cannot recommend *The House of Whispers* highly enough'
AJ WEST

THE HOUSE OF WHISPERS

ANNA MAZZOLA

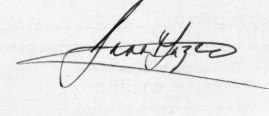

ORION

First published in Great Britain in 2023 by Orion Fiction,
an imprint of the Orion Publishing Group Ltd
Carmelite House, 50 Victoria Embankment
London EC4Y 0DZ

An Hachette UK Company

1 3 5 7 9 10 8 6 4 2

A CIP catalogue record for this book
is available from the British Library.

ISBN (Hardback) 978 1 3987 0383 4
ISBN (Trade Paperback) 978 1 3987 0384 1
ISBN (eBook) 978 1 3987 0386 5
ISBN (Audio) 978 1 3987 0387 2

Typeset by Deltatype Ltd, Birkenhead, Merseyside

Printed in Great Britain by Clays Ltd, Elcograf S.p.A.

www.orionbooks.co.uk

For my father (please don't read the sex scenes).

'Our irrational, darker selves demand familiars.'
– *Elizabeth Bowen*

Part One

Part One

I

I dreamt again of the burning. The first one, when I was seven years old, the sky above Piazza Oberdan stained blood-red, the flames hissing, the men in black shirts dancing and shouting, 'Viva! Viva!' as though the fire were a product of their demented energy, a strange creature come alive to drive the Slavs out of Trieste. I saw again the faces of the people at the open windows and on the balconies – rows and rows of them in the tall white building of the Narodni Dom, the Slovene national home. I heard the jeers of the mob, the scream of the sirens, smelt the smoke that filled the evening sky.

Only, in my dream, I was no longer a child clutching my mother's hand, but the young woman I am now: solid, sensible, apparently capable. Yet I made no movement to help, no attempt to stop the *squadristi* as they poured on petrol, barred the doors; no attempt to make the police do something, to yell in their faces, to beg them to help, to clear a way for the firefighters who were blocked by the baying Blackshirts. I stood as I did then, transfixed, horrified – only now, as an adult, I understood what they were doing and I knew what would come next. I longed to cry out, to scream, to stop them, but my mouth was clamped shut and my feet refused to move so that I remained helpless, shaking, as powerless as a child. I woke then, relieved to find myself in my narrow bed, but disturbed that the dream had come again.

People say I couldn't possibly remember as much as I do, as I was only a child when the *squadristi* burned the Slovene cultural centre, a symbol of all that they hated: the foreigners who contaminated *la città Italianissima*, the most Italian city. But memory is a strange and fluid thing. Sometimes we remember everything precisely. Sometimes we remember nothing at all. The memory of that night is captured for me in time as a fly in amber — the sound of the glass in the windows shattering; the desperate cries of the people in the apartments, the cafe, the restaurant, the theatre, as they realised the doors were locked from the outside and that they would have to jump; the pathetic sound of my own mother's muted and baleful weeping. I re-member it all because that was the moment I understood that everything I knew was about to be destroyed, and that I would have to hide who I was. That was the beginning of my journey to becoming an all-Italian girl. It was how I became not Iva Valentich, but Eva Valenti.

But it's not that fire I wanted to tell you about. It is the second one.

4

2

Rome, 1938

I will begin the story on the day I first saw him. It was the day that Hitler came to Rome.

We'd spent the morning in one of the great, echoing music rooms of the school where Ettore and I worked. Supposedly we were practising, but in fact we were most mostly smoking, talking, joking, as we often did in those days. Mirella, Ettore and I had met at teacher training school some years before and formed a trio, more for the companionship than for anything else. We were all, in our way, outsiders, though I wouldn't have accepted that then.

The door to the room opened and Allegra, another of the teachers, peered in: 'What on earth are you laughing about in here?'

'Eva has a new admirer: the dashing Signor Malinconico!'

Ettore and Mirella were almost besides themselves by this point. Signor Malinconico – Mr Melancholy – was their name for one of the maths teachers: a spindly-legged man with a drooping face who seemed always to be out of luck.

'You're awful, the pair of you. He merely asked me to dinner. The poor man is probably lonely.'

Allegra sat on one of the metal chairs, crossed her stock-inged legs and lit a cigarette. 'Poor Mr Melancholy. He's such a strange fellow, isn't he? What on earth did you say to him, Eva?'

'Well, I couldn't say no, could I?'

Another convulsion of laughter from Mirella and Ettore. 'Of course you could say no! What, are you really going to go out for dinner with that funny little man? Please say you aren't!'

'It's all very well for you to laugh; you're not the ones who are in this situation.'

'Oh Eva,' Mirella said. She was my best friend in Rome, in the whole world. 'You *are* funny. You're always so worried about upsetting people that you end up in these scrapes. You'll have to make up an excuse. Tell him you have a new boyfriend who's terribly possessive, or something.'

'I can't say that. He won't believe me.' I had no boyfriend; hadn't had a relationship for over a year, and the ones before that were hardly anything to write home about. Not that I really wrote home anymore. Only the occasional postcard to my aunt in Trieste.

'Then we'll have to tell him you've passed away,' Ettore said, straight-faced. 'Poor Eva, she died as she lived: running from unsuitable suitors.'

Another gale of laughter and I shut the lid of the piano. 'Right, that's it. I'm going home! Mirella, are you coming?' We shared an apartment in the Trastevere district: us and a talking bird.

'Later. I said I'd call in on Amalia first. She's going to lend me some of her records.'

Still chatting, we packed up our instruments, heading along the musty corridors, past the ceramic cross on the wall and the portraits of Il Duce and the King, and emerging into the bright spring sunlight, Mirella blowing us a kiss as she left.

As the three of us walked down the Via di Monserrato, we could hear the sound of a brass band playing a military march. All of us knew, of course, about the parade, the visit. We couldn't *not* have known. For over a week, black swastikas had been crawling over the walls like spiders, appearing on signs and on the flags that streamed beside the Italian tricolour. For months, the newspapers had been full of the nations' growing friendship, and the Germans' admiration for Il Duce – our great leader – and our beautiful, vibrant nation. It gave me an underlying sense of nervousness that I tried my best to suppress. Though we were largely insulated from news of the outside world, I'd heard what Hitler said of Slavs and the Jews, and Mirella was, among many other things, Jewish.

'You'd think he was coming here on honeymoon,' Ettore murmured to me as we walked. 'Not on a state visit.'

Rome did look fine in May, with the chestnut trees and oleanders in blossom, the sunshine turning the stone buildings and statues to brilliant white and gold: the carved lions and wolves triumphant. People were strolling the piazzas and parks dressed in beautifully tailored suits with little hats, small dogs and children on their best behaviour. Anything deemed unsightly had been hidden away. Houses had been razed and apartment blocks bulldozed, better to display the glories of ancient Rome; the city's beggars had been cleared from the repaved streets; shabby shops had been repainted or shut.

'Ettore, don't be so cynical,' Allegra said, catching his comment. 'It's a national holiday – a moment of national pride. We should try to enjoy it!'

I raised an eyebrow at Ettore, but I didn't say anything. At that time, it was always best not to speak, or to speak only in whispers. You never knew who might be listening, or how your words might be twisted against you. In any event, what could I, an insignificant young woman, do about it all? That was how I thought about things in those days. It was how so many people thought. My parents had taught me to save my energies for the things that mattered: family, work, learning, God. Leave the politics to those that knew better. My life had often been a struggle, my mind at one time unstable, and my focus then was on establishing myself, earning enough, doing my best to belong.

As we approached the Piazza Farnese, we could hear the boom of a man's voice over a loudspeaker, his the familiar tone of the ardent party member. Across the wall, splashed in white paint, was the familiar slogan, '*Il Duce ha sempre ragione!*' Il Duce is always right.

'It is with the same faith and with the same will that the German and Italian nations have fought against the corrupt old ideologies to create this vital new regime of the people!'

A crowd had amassed in the piazza and rows of children stood in the centre on a platform wearing the black and grey uniforms of the Fascist youth organisations: the *Balilla* and the older *Avanguardisti* boys behind, the *Piccole Italiane* and the *Giovani Italiane* at the front. Some held banners, others musical instruments. It was one of many parades prepared for the arrival of the Führer, one of the myriad of entertainments the government had laid on as though to give the impression that Italy was always decked out like this; as if people had nothing better to do with their days than sing and march and clap.

'National Socialist Germany and Fascist Italy are both great forces,' the man shouted, 'embodying and powered by the energies of the new generation!'

Ettore scoffed. 'Both are vampires, more like,' he said to me in a low voice, 'feeding and growing on the blood of the young.'

I looked away from him and towards the crowd, searching the faces of the people to see if anyone had heard him, if any might be a *Questura* agent on the lookout for any sign of subversion. It was dangerous to talk, however quietly, in a public place like this. We'd all heard about the arrests that had preceded this visit – the hotel guests awoken and interrogated in their rooms, the hundreds of houses searched for dissenters. Ettore, though, was always the most vocal, always the most daring, even though he had the most to hide.

'Let's head towards the front,' Allegra said, pulling me by the arm. 'I want to see who's speaking. I want to see who's there.'

We made our way nearer to the centre of the piazza where a stage had been constructed and, beside it, rows of chairs on which numerous military and official types sat. Closer up, I could see that the children were sweating in their heavy uniforms, and that some of the smaller boys were scratching at their legs or crotches where the coarse material rubbed. They must have been standing out here for hours.

The speaker was a squat, pallid man in full military regalia, perspiration running down his face. The loudspeaker squealed. 'In honour of the young of our nations, let us now sing "*Giovinezza*"! Youth!'

The drums started up, then the brass, and the people in the seated area took to their feet.

> '*Giovinezza, giovinezza,*
> *Primavera di bellezza,*
> *Della vita, nell'asprezza*
> *Il tuo canto squilla e va!*
> *E per Benito Mussolini,*
> *Eja eja alalà.*
> *E per la nostra Patria bella,*
> *Eja eja alalà.*'

I watched the faces of the audience, seemingly rapt as they sang loudly and clearly of 'our beautiful Fatherland' and I wished as I had before that I could be properly part of it: have that sense of belonging, that certainty that I was part of a community, a nation. I sang along, of course, sang the words of the song that had become a second national anthem, sung by the men who marched on Rome, sung by the troops who conquered Abyssinia to enrich the Roman empire. But I sensed that I did not have that fire in my heart that would have made me properly Italian. I worried that, despite my best efforts at camouflage, some might recognise me as one of the 'allogeni', as the Slovenes had been called when I was young: the people from outside. I followed the words and I followed the rules, but I feared that people would see through that to the foreigner within. Standing there in that crowd, I was never more aware that in order to survive I would need to burrow deeper: to become faultlessly, unassailably Italian.

'Look, that man there.' Allegra had hold of my arm and was pointing. 'The one in the dark blue suit with the two children near him. Near the middle. You see? That's Signor Cavallera. I teach the daughter, Chiara.'

I scanned the rows of people who were still standing, clapping, and caught sight of a dark-haired girl, maybe fifteen or sixteen, in a peach-coloured dress. She stood next to a polished-looking man in a midnight-blue suit, a tall boy on his other side.

'She's the one whose mother died a few months ago,' Allegra continued. 'Remember, I told you? A brain haemorrhage.'

'Yes, I remember. Terrible.' Allegra had described it all at some length: the sudden death, the pursuant drama, the exquisite, expensive funeral.

'The girl, though, Chiara, she plays very well.'

I shielded my face from the sun with my hand so that I

might see them better. Both father and son were slim and tanned, black-browed. The man was saying something to his son, who wore the uniform of the *Balilla*. The daughter was paler, but no less handsome, her hair a dark cloud around her face. She stood motionless, paying no attention to her father and brother, her hands behind her back. She was, I noticed, the only person in the row who wasn't smiling.

'Come on, let's go.' It was Ettore. 'There'll be a lot more of this today.' He motioned for us to follow him and began to make his way through the crowd towards the shady side of the street.

I looked back at the girl in the peach dress, the man with the shined hair. They looked, I thought, like the perfect Italian family, only incomplete.

3

I didn't see the Cavallera family again until near the end of the summer. I'd returned to Trieste in July for the funeral of my aunt Agata, my mother's sister, whose death had unsettled me more than I'd thought it would. I hadn't much wanted to go back, for it wasn't a place I associated with happiness. The city, once an open and cosmopolitan place, had, by the time I was old enough to form proper memories, become a testing ground for prejudice and hatred. The Great War had crushed Trieste, with bombs and starvation and fear. Many of those who returned from the front were, like my father, filled with bitter disappointment and rage, consumed with the idea of 'la vittoria mutilata' – the mutilated victory, a national humiliation. Amid the wreckage, black-shirted *squadristi* thrived, threatening and attacking the Slovenian community from which my parents came. Where once we'd been welcome, we were now intruders, to be italianised by force, to never speak our own language. Youth and cultural associations were closed down, political parties banned, a free press consigned to the past. Those who disagreed could chose prison, exile or perhaps to be beaten and shot. We'd relocated to Puglia only because we

12

were ordered to, and I'd little wish to return to a place that had wanted me gone.

I needed to attend the funeral, though. I owed it to my mother, dead five years earlier, and to Agata herself, not dissimilar to my mother: self-effacing, long-suffering, kind. It had been she who'd encouraged me to move to Rome after both my parents died; make myself afresh, pursue my long-held ambition to teach music. Her death shook me to the core, I suppose because she'd been the only relative with whom I'd kept up much contact, the only one with whom I'd felt any real connection, and now I was all alone. With Agata's passing came a strange feeling of being left alone to float adrift. There was no one with whom I could really talk any longer about my childhood, my parents, the events that had exiled us from Trieste. But perhaps that was best, I told myself: end that whole era, shed my old skin. Now there was only Italy. I felt a blur of guilt at the edges of my consciousness, and an ache of sadness at what was lost, but I did my best to push those feelings away. There was little point in looking back.

Returning to Rome, I found that the mood had shifted, darkened, with an almost tangible increase in anxiety. Food supplies were diminishing and prices were rising; queues snaked around grocery stores. And though Hitler was no longer a physical presence, his shadow loomed over Rome. In July, the newspapers that had for months been running stories about the dangers of intermarriage with blacks and the conspiracies of 'Foreign Jews' published a 'Manifesto of the Racial Scientists'. This document set out in very clear terms what the Italian race should and could be: it did not, it said, include the Jews. Many did their best to dismiss it. It was a sop, people said, to Germany. Nothing more than that. So was the creation of the new General Office of Demography and Race – *Demorazza* for short. These were all merely words. After all, Il Duce had never been anti-Semitic. He'd always said Jews were a key part of Italian society and the Fascist party. Didn't he even have a Jewish mistress? Margarita Sarfatti. No, all this was just lip service to the Germans; a show of solidarity that was necessary now but would fade in time. So I heard again and again from friends and other teachers and the women in the shops and I tried my best to believe them, but a queasy uneasiness lodged in my stomach. What would it mean for Mirella?

'You'll be late!' she shouted now from outside my bedroom. 'What on earth are you doing in there? Praying?'

I opened my bedroom door and stood before her in my blue cotton dress. 'What do you think? Too formal?'

'No. Perfect and beautiful. They'll love you.' She kissed me on the cheek and she smelt of lavender and the resin she used on her bow. 'I'll go to the market while you're out. Get us something for supper.'

'You're an angel.'

'Apparently no, I'm a devil. You clearly haven't been reading the papers.'

'Oh, Mirella. Ignore the newspapers.'

But, of course, that was impossible.

I left our little apartment and took the stairs down to the lobby, the dingy corridors giving off their familiar odour of cooked onions and cigarette smoke. I thought of what Allegra had said before she left Rome: 'You shouldn't worry too much about it all. It'll all blow over, just as it did back in 1934. You remember? The supposed Jewish anti-fascist plot? All those arrests? It came to nothing, didn't it? It'll be the same soon enough. You'll see.'

Although Allegra and I had not been close, I did not like that she was moving away. It added to my sense that everything was in flux; that everyone was leaving me. She was returning to Sienna to look after her mother, now bedridden. 'There's

14

no one else to look after her. My brother won't, of course. Not his job. That's our lives, eh? Caring for children, caring for parents.'

She had recommended me to take over the teaching of some of her private piano pupils. The Cavallera girl, Chiara, was one of them and I'd known at once that I would take the job, remembering the pale-faced girl without a smile, her handsome father and brother next to her.

'You needn't feel you have to, you know,' Allegra had told me. 'Like I said, she's a gifted pupil, but not a happy one.'

'All the more reason for her to have a good tutor, surely.'

'Yes, she's a sweet girl. And Signor Cavallera is very charming. But it's a peculiar house, a peculiar energy, if you know what I mean.'

'Well, it's a house in mourning, isn't it?'

'Yes.' Allegra paused. 'Yes, maybe it's that. I don't know. But I don't want you to feel you have to.'

'I *do* have to take all the work I can get, though, Allegra. They've told me I'll have fewer music classes at the school from September. I'll need to take on more private pupils, so this is a good start.'

Things were much harder for me financially than they had been a year ago, just as they were for many in Italy. The international sanctions brought in following Il Duce's conquest of Abyssinia had started to bite. This wasn't the time to turn work down. It wasn't only that, though. I felt drawn to the family in a way I couldn't fully understand. I thought – though this would seem ridiculous later – that I might be able to help them.

Their house was on Via Giulia: a Roman *palazzina*, painted primrose yellow with white stucco work, a great wooden door with brass knockers in the shape of angry lions, and lemon trees in pots outside the doorway. I stood staring at the lions' faces, waiting for the door to be opened, a fluttering inside my chest. I could hear a dog barking and the sound of a male voice.

I'd half-expected a servant to answer, but it was Cavallera himself, fighting to restrain an excitable Italian greyhound. 'Signorina Valenti, yes? I must apologise for this brute. He thinks it's time for his walk, but then he always thinks it's time for his walk. Zefiro! Back! Where are your manners?'

Once he'd managed to close the door, Cavallera shook my hand and smiled widely.

'Thank you for coming. What a welcome. Who would have a dog?'

I smiled back, not quite sure what to say, and stepped into a stone vestibule where the scent of lemons gave way to that of polish. The dog had begun to whine.

'Let me take your jacket. Please, come through to the sitting room. No, not you, Zefiro!'

The dog was undeterred and followed us into a large, green-walled salon with a highly shined wooden floor and a gleaming black piano. Above a dark marble fireplace hung the obligatory portraits: the Duce and our diminutive King. His Royal Short Arse, Ettore called him.

'Have a seat. Some water?'

'Oh yes, please.' I sat, overly rigid, in one of the striped, stiff-backed armchairs while Cavallera picked up a cut-glass decanter filled with ice and fruit and poured me a glass of water. Closer up, I saw that he was older than I'd first thought, perhaps forty-five, with a lined, bronzed face. He smelt of eau de cologne mixed with cigarettes. His dog, too, was fine-looking, with a glossy dark grey coat.

'You're a friend of Allegra's, then? She said you were an excellent player.'

'Allegra is generous. I'm a decent pianist but nothing special.

I do, though, love to teach.' That was true: it made me feel useful and energised. It had been a music teacher who'd changed my life, and I wanted to bring that happiness to other children – give them something no one could take away.

He smiled. 'Oh, I'm sure you're being modest. I wish I had the patience to teach, and indeed to learn to play properly. I'm afraid I've no ear for music at all – perfectly useless.' A pause, he rubbed the dog's head. 'My wife was an extraordinary musician. Allegra may have told you.'

I hesitated. 'She did, yes. She said she loved to hear her play.' Allegra had in fact said little about the woman's musical abilities, but much about the manner of her death, the terrible tragedy of it all, and her many beautiful dresses ('Adelina. Always elegant and contained. Always immaculate. And the house! Well, you'll see for yourself.')

Cavallera was still stroking the dog, absently. 'It's odd not to hear her playing anymore, you know. I'm still getting used to it. We all are, aren't we, Zefiro?' The dog cocked his head. 'Poor beast. He still goes looking for her, you know.' Cavallera laughed in the way men sometimes do when they're attempting to mask their feelings and I felt a surge of warmth towards him.

'Allegra said your daughter played very well.'

'Yes, she too has talent, I think, but she needs encouragement. She's rather lacking in confidence.'

'I'll do my best, Signor Cavallera.'

'Dante, please. Call me Dante. I won't always be here for the lessons – I'm often working – but you must keep me informed of how she progresses. You'll let me know if there are any difficulties?'

'Of course. Although I'm sure there won't be.'

He nodded, appraising me with his dark brown eyes, and I felt suddenly inadequate in my plain blue dress that I'd worn

17

and washed too many times and with my scuffed leather shoes that no longer shone.

'It's been difficult for her, with her mother gone,' he said quietly. 'Sixteen isn't a good age to lose one's mother.'

'No, I'm sure.' I didn't mention that I'd lost my own mother five years before and that I wasn't convinced there was ever a good age to lose a parent. 'I was very sorry to hear of your loss. Allegra told me about it at the time.'

'Thank you. She was... well, she was everything to us.'

'Of course.' I had to appear to understand, but in fact I had never loved anyone entirely, absolutely. I'd always held myself back. The only relationship I'd witnessed up close was my parents', and I had no wish to emulate that. I longed for closeness, longed to be loved, but I had no idea how to achieve it.

'Anyway, I'll call Chiara now,' he said, standing up. 'You've just missed Alessandro, Chiara's younger brother, but you'll meet him next time, no doubt.'

'Your son: does he play too?'

Dante laughed again, properly this time. 'No, no, he has no time for that sort of thing, my Alessandro. He's thirteen years old. It's all marching and guns and parades. You know how it is with boys that age!'

I nodded, but I didn't know, not really. Most of my pupils were girls and I'd never had a brother, only a sister who'd died when she was very small. Ettore had been the closest thing I'd had to a brother and certainly he was not one for marching and guns. His love, like mine, was music, for it was a place to lose yourself.

I heard Dante calling to his daughter and a minute later she arrived, entering the room slowly, keeping close to the wall. She wore a pinafore over a silk blouse with a cardigan pulled tightly around her. Her gaze was cast down.

'This is your new piano teacher, Signorina Valenti. Signorina

Valenti, this is of course Chiara. I trust she'll be a good pupil for you.'

'Oh, I'm sure she will. A pleasure to meet you, Chiara.'

'*Piacere*,' the girl said, but her gaze remained on the floor. She was, as I'd remembered, a pretty thing with long dark eyelashes and a dark halo of hair circling a delicate face.

'Chiara, my darling, please greet our visitor properly. It's not as if she's going to bite you.'

'Yes, Father.' The girl finally met my gaze and I almost wished she hadn't, for her eyes were so full of pain.

'Well, I'll leave you to begin your lesson. Signorina Valenti, do call for our housekeeper if there's anything you need. I look forward to seeing you again.' And with that, he gave me a wide smile and departed, Zefiro the dog trailing after him.

I smiled brightly at his daughter. 'Well, let's get started, shall we, Chiara? Show me what you've been playing.'

The girl's father had been right – she had talent, far more than most of the pupils I taught at the school. But then she'd been privately tutored since she was seven, Allegra had told me, and had often played with her accomplished mother. Chiara showed me a Scarlatti sonata first, her fingers gliding effortlessly across the keys; then began Bach's 'Fantasia in C Minor'.

'Thank you, Chiara. That was lovely. I can see you've already reached quite a standard. There are things we can work on, however, and various ways in which I can help you.'

The girl looked up for a moment, eyes wide, and I thought she was going to say something, but she only pulled her cardigan sleeves down towards her hands. Why had Allegra not told me her pupil was so anxious? Or was it me that was making her nervous? I was determined to win her over.

'Are there any pieces you're particularly keen to learn?'

'You should ask my father.'

'Well,' I smiled, 'I'm asking you. What do you like?'

A pause, and then: 'Gershwin. I should like to learn some Gershwin.'

A surprising choice for such a traditional-looking girl. Maybe there was more to her. 'Well, then we shall get you his songbook, yes?'

Finally, she smiled. 'Yes, I'd like that.'

'Excellent. For now, let's get you started on some exercises to loosen the tension in your wrists and arms. Here, let me show you.' I pulled my stool closer to the piano and embarked on a series of scales and arpeggios.

Chiara grew less anxious as the lesson progressed, and after half an hour I'd even managed to coax a laugh from her, telling her about Bruno, our pet bird – how he sometimes sang along while I played, or made rude remarks about the quality. 'He's taken to calling us all stupid, recently, and he just won't be made to stop.'

Leafing through her sheet music, which was carefully ordered, I found Fauré's 'Dolly Suite' and suggested we play it together. We'd reached '*Le Jardin de Dolly*', and were, I thought, making a decent go of it, but then a wrong note was struck and abruptly Chiara moved her hands away from the keyboard.

'Why did you stop, Chiara? You were playing very well.'

Her breathing was shallow, her chest rising and falling. 'I can't. Not now.'

I noticed that there was a pencil marking on the page. Someone – it must have been her mother – had written, '*Both hands!*' in small, neat script.

'Of course,' I said. 'Perhaps we've done enough for today.' I cursed myself for an idiot. She must have played the duets with her mother. That must be why she'd become upset.

★

When I made to leave, I saw that a grey-haired woman in an apron was feeding the goldfish that swam in a large glass bowl.

She smiled in greeting and introduced herself as Greta, the housekeeper. 'I keep things running as best as I can, so anything you need, you let me know. I'll get your coat for you, shall I?'

'Yes, if you wouldn't mind.'

She had a kindly face, I thought, but tired, the mouth drooping at the edges, and I noticed she walked with a limp. I followed her into the hallway where coats and hats were hung neatly upon a wooden stand and she handed me my jacket and my straw hat, the one I'd been wearing now for years.

'You'll be coming every week like the last girl, will you?'

'Yes, every Thursday, just like Allegra.'

'Gone to look after her mother,' she said. 'Now, there's a good girl. I doubt my daughter would do the same for me.'

'Oh, I'm sure she would,' I replied awkwardly. For what did I know of her daughter? She might hate her mother, or fear her as I had my father.

'No, no, she's *una pigra*, an ingrate. I don't know what I did wrong with that one. You'd think she'd been dragged up by wolves, not a God-fearing mother like myself. Write to me, I say, and what does she write to me but postcards asking for money?'

As Greta complained about her ungrateful daughter and her many needy grandchildren, my eyes were drawn to the silver-framed photographs on the hall table: one of two young dark-haired children, beribboned and unsmiling; the second of a slender woman with short wavy hair looking into the camera, shading her eyes from the sun.

The housekeeper noticed me staring. 'Adelina. Their mother.'

'Yes, of course.' The woman was beautiful. Elegant in a way I would never be, in a drop-waisted dress with a sash.

'It's getting on for six months now since she passed.'

'Awful for the family. For all of you.'

Greta nodded, still looking at the photograph. 'Yes. The house has been very different, I can tell you.'

'I'm sure. Well, it was good to have met you. I'll see you all next week.'

I gave her a smile as I left, but she only half-smiled back, seeming lost in thought. After a moment, she closed the door.

It was nearly seven o'clock by the time I returned to our apartment block, a shabby place in Trastevere, off the Piazza Mastai. Gazing up, I could see the pots of basil and oregano, the cooking pans left on windowsills, the underwear hung out to dry. A woman I didn't know was shaking a mat from a window, dirt falling to the cobbles beneath.

When I opened the door to our apartment, I could hear Mirella in the kitchen and found her heating water on the little stove.

'There are you are. Do you want a *caffè d'orzo*? I'm just making some.'

'No, I want some real coffee!'

'Fat chance.'

'In that case, give me your disgusting brew.' I took off my coat and shoes and walked barefoot to the tiny balcony, where Bruno, our mynah bird, was calling my name. 'You, you ridiculous bird. Have you missed me?'

He stared at me with his yellow eye and squawked: 'Stupid!'

'Oh, well, thank you, you horrible brute. No pumpkins seeds for you.'

I gazed out onto the interior courtyard below. Two grubby children were pushing a third in a cart. A dog was nosing about the bins. From one of the flats, a radio blared; from another, an infant squalled.

'Here,' Mirella said. 'There are some coffee beans in it, but we'd best get used to the taste of chicory.' She passed me the tiny cup and saucer and then began forming *pastasciutta* on the flour-covered table. 'So, how was your new pupil?'

'What a sad little girl. Beautiful house, though, in the Via Giulia.' And a handsome father whom I was still thinking about, but I wouldn't mention that.

Mirella sipped her coffee and grimaced. 'All right for some. Anyway, I got us something nice, though you can't eat or drink it. Come. Listen to this.'

It was a Duke Ellington record, only slightly battered. She put it on the gramophone and we danced about our little kitchen, her taking the part of the man, both of us howling with laughter, until Margareta in the next apartment started shouting at us to turn it down – did we not know she was trying to get a baby to sleep? Had we no sense in our young heads at all?

'Sorry, Margareta!' Mirella called back, raising her eyebrows at me and stopping the needle on the gramophone. 'How many children does that woman have now? Is she starting her own football team?'

I laughed. 'Where did you get the record?'

'Some woman at the market was selling them second-hand. Oh, I know, I know: I shouldn't have spent the money, but we're owed a little happiness, aren't we?'

'Of course we are, and money isn't so tight as all that.'

Her face fell. 'I've been meaning to talk to you about that, actually. Bad news from Mamma Gioiosa, I'm afraid.' Mamma Gioiosa was our name for the landlady, a woman entirely devoid of joy. 'She's putting the rent up.'

'No! Again?'

'She says the rates have risen. The cost of living and so on.'

'As if we don't know.'

23

'Exactly. Good thing you have some new pupils. I'd try to find some myself, but nobody wants a Jew.'

'Oh, Mirella. I can't believe that's true.'

'Well, believe it.' She pulled away from me and walked over to the sink, all her former lightness gone. 'I've fewer pupils now than I've ever had. You're telling me that's a coincidence? That it's nothing to do with that Defence of the Race magazine and this government's crazy theories?'

I didn't know how to respond to that. I didn't have the emotional vocabulary. My family had never discussed politics, never engaged with it, never acknowledged the violence done to them. But I'd seen the magazine in the newsstands over the past month, with its false and incendiary headlines. I'd read Mussolini's *Manifesto della Razza* with its definitions of who counted as Italian. 'I can pay more of the rent, Mirella.' It seemed the only thing I *could* do.

'For now, maybe. What happens when it goes up again? What happens when I lose all of my work altogether?'

'You won't.'

'No? Even so-called Aryan girls will be struggling for work when the government regulations come in. You know, don't you, that they're limiting women's work? We're supposed to be off having babies like miserable Margareta. And then today, you know what they sent me?' She went to the table by the front door and brought back an envelope with a Fascist party stamp. My stomach clenched with dread. 'The census,' Mirella said. 'They sent me the census. They want to know my "race". Not just my religion, my "race". What is this now? This is how we're defined: not as people, not even as a religion, but as a breed they don't want. Did they send it to you? No. They only want to know about Jews.'

The false coffee soured in my mouth. Since August, they'd been sending this document requiring people to name their religion, their origins. 'The other teachers at school say it's just a formality.'

Mirella shook her head. 'Who knows what it is, but I won't answer it.'

'And then what happens?'

'I don't know.'

Some part of me knew, though, I think, even then. Because I'd seen what had happened in Trieste: how Slovenes and Croats had been cut off from their culture, their occupations, their organisations, how any dissenters were crushed or killed. 'Couldn't you just... lie? Say you were Catholic? Surely that's what lots of people have done.'

Mirella stared at me. 'And why should I do that? Why should I deny who I am?'

Into my mind came a memory of my mother, standing in her apron and slippers, crying. It was the day the minister of the church had been shot for refusing to preach in Italian. 'Because it's easier that way,' I said to Mirella. 'You'll be safer.'

She frowned at me. 'Easier? Easier to pretend Jewish people don't exist, aren't entitled to be here, in Italy? Maybe Bruno was right; sometimes, Eva, you can be stupid.'

'That's not what I meant.'

'I'm not hiding, Eva. I'm not ashamed of who I am!' She turned her back to me. 'Anyway, I'm going over to see Ettore and Pietro. You'll have to finish supper yourself.'

'Mirella, wait, I'm sorry. It was a silly thing to suggest. I just worry about you, that's all. I worry about all of it. Please: you must stay here and eat.'

'*Ci vediamo.*' The door slammed and I heard her footsteps descending the stairs. Within a minute, she emerged onto the piazza, walking quickly, and she did not look back at me to wave as she usually did.

I was left with a horrible curdling sensation in my stomach.

I leant over and looked at Bruno. 'Stupid. Am I really stupid? I just want her to be all right.'

Was it foolish to mask your origins if that's what it took to live a decent life? I wasn't sure. As I finished forming the *pastasciutta* and heated the oil in the pan, I thought of my little schoolgirl self, standing at the front of a classroom, the blast of pain as the cane came down on my hands. 'Here, we only speak Italian. You are forbidden to speak your Slav.' I still remembered the shame of it now: it was like needlepoints of fire in my mind. I'd tried to explain to the teacher that I hadn't meant to talk in Slovene. I'd answered my friend in my own language by accident, forgetting in that instant that we were no longer so speak it in school, nor in church, nor anywhere. We were to be little Italian children, or we were to leave. Many Slovenes and Croats chose the latter option, abandoning the land that had now been declared Italian even though it was where they and their families had long lived, opting instead for Yugoslavia or even South America where they could at least speak their language, keep their own names, retain their own traditions. Not in Trieste. In Trieste, we only spoke Italian. We no longer used Slovene even at home, though my mother and I sometimes spoke it in whispers.

'It's best,' my father decreed, 'that we adapt, try to fit in. There's nothing for it now.' He'd even volunteered to Italianise our names, as teachers had been asked to do, to show an example to the rest. No more Valentich. We were now the family Valenti.

At the time, I'd accepted that he must be right, because he was my father, he was the one who decided everything in our household, the one who ruled our meagre lives. I internalised the shame and the pain and assumed, as children always do, that the bad feelings were my own fault. Only later did it occur to me to wonder what my mother had thought: my mother who made paper dolls and hung them about my bed, who carefully painted eggs at Easter and left them in the henhouse so that I might have a little magic in my life. Had she agreed with this plan, or had she gone along with it because she was too frightened to challenge the man who made the rules in our house and who was never to be crossed? I knew some of her friends had left – sold their little homes and moved to Yugoslavia. Did she ever want to go with them? She'd never said so, or at least not to me, and I knew she wouldn't have dared say it to Father.

She was a pretty, quiet woman who did her best to make herself invisible and hope her husband and the Blackshirts would leave her alone. She taught me how to sew and how to heal, for she'd been a nurse in the Great War. She also taught me that it was best to keep myself small: to alter my behaviour to ensure that nobody hurt me. Her real name was Mila, but her family had called her Miška: Mouse, and, when the italianisation of names had begun, my father had decided she should be Mia instead. She didn't abandon everything, though. Even after we left Trieste, she still made *kipferln*, Slovene crescent biscuits: small acts of culinary resistance.

I never cooked Slovene food, though I still remembered the taste. I ate only good Italian meals, like the pasta I prepared for myself now. Olive oil, tomato sauce, pecorino cheese. You are, they say, what you eat.

Over the years, my father's conviction that we should be Italian – *were* Italian – grew, morphing from an instinct to survive to a fervent belief in nationhood. After all, had he not fought for Italy in the Great War? Had he not been maimed in the name of this nation?

When the government removed him from his job in Trieste and dictated that he should become a teacher in a school in Puglia – a region we'd never been to before, where we knew no one – he didn't see it as an attempt to remove him from his homeland, but as a sign that he'd been accepted; that we were truly Italian. By then, I was fourteen years old. I did my best to believe him, because he was my father and, according to the church and the law, fathers are always right. But part of me knew, part of me saw, and when we arrived in Ostuni, a maze-like white city, the children spelt it out for me clearly. They often called me '*forestiera*': stranger. I was an outsider there, despite my new name, my meticulous Italian, my desperate attempts to please. The difference was, I was no longer really Slovene either.

My early teenage years were rather lonely things, in which music became my escape: the only place where I could truly be myself. It was at that time – perhaps because of my splintered identity, perhaps because of the suppressed pain – that my mind began to play games on me, imagining things that could not be there. But I don't like to think of that. When I was nineteen, my father died (his heart, long congealed, finally stopped) and, a year later, my mother followed him, as she seemed to do in everything. I had hoped for more time with her alone.

I left Ostuni then and came to Rome, a much bigger city, where the layers of stone and marble had been worn away by centuries of kings and popes and peasants and soldiers and where I'd believed my difference, my otherness, could be smoothed carefully away. When in Rome, one does what the others do and that will make you safe. It didn't appear to be keeping Mirella safe, though, even though Jews were as assimilated as they could be, even though until a few months ago the fact of her being Jewish had been only one facet of her, no more important than her being a musician, a woman, a friend, a teacher.

I mixed the ragù in with the pasta, thinking of what I could do to protect myself, what I could do to protect Mirella. When I finally sat down at the table to eat, I found that I was not very hungry.

4

As I arrived at the Cavallera house the following week, Chiara's brother, Alessandro, was getting ready to go out, sitting on the stairs, pulling on black leather boots to complete his Balilla uniform.

'A real gun, you see?' he said with relish, showing me his rifle. 'The same as the troops have, only smaller.' He, in fact, looked very much like a smaller, younger version of his father, but he didn't have Dante's charm, and I wasn't sure what to say to him.

'*Imbecille!* Signorina Valenti doesn't want to hear about your pistol,' Greta snapped at him. 'Boys and their little weapons,' she muttered to me. 'They always think we want to see them, eh? *Via*, Alessandro! Hurry up, or you'll be late.'

Chiara was standing against the wall with her arms folded, watching her younger brother.

He met her eye. 'What? Want a go yourself?' He made his fingers into the shape of pistol and fired them at her, laughing.

'You're too stupid to have a gun.'

'You're too ugly to have a boyfriend.'

'Who says I want a boyfriend?'

'That's what all girls want.'

'What would you know? Nothing. You know nothing about girls. You're barely out of short trousers. Just shut your silly mouth.'

'*Ragazzi! Basta!* In front of Signorina Valenti as well. What would your father say? He'd say you were a pair of animals, that's what he'd say, and he'd be right.'

Brother and sister glared at one another in silence.

'You go play piano while I go prepare for war,' Alessandro said.

'What war? There is no war.'

'Of course there's war. War in Abyssinia, war in Spain. There will be another big war, too, just you wait. Il Duce will conquer the world!'

War, war. I hated the word. It was war that had led to Trieste being handed to Italy like a bag of sweets, war that had crippled my father, killed others, destroyed faces and limbs and lives, leaving twenty million dead. It was war that was killing good people in Spain, Ettore's friends among them. There would not be another proper war. There couldn't be. Perhaps Chiara, despite her youth, understood some of that, as she turned away from Alessandro and walked towards the piano room. Then again, perhaps she simply found her brother annoying in the way that many girls did. I followed with my case of sheet music.

'*Ciao!*' Alessandro shouted and then the door banged. I could hear Greta grumbling as she returned to the kitchen, a mixture of dialect and expletives.

When we'd sat down at the piano, I pulled out the Gershwin songbook that I had borrowed from Ettore and the girl gave a delighted laugh: a glimpse, perhaps, of the old Chiara.

'You found one!' She grabbed the book and began to turn the pages, then set it above the piano keyboard. 'Can I try?'

'Of course!'

I showed her the fingering and within a few minutes she had mastered the right hand and begun to put it together with the left. The girl was certainly a fast learner, but then we all knew the song.

'Here,' I said. 'Like this,' and played the chorus myself.

When Chiara tried again, she made a good hand at it. As she played, I could hear the words of the song in my head – *It ain't necessarily so* – and for a moment I was back in the jazz club where I'd first heard it, watching a beautiful black singer swaying her hips as she sang. It must have been two years ago or so, when things were easier and more open. When we weren't always afraid. *The things that you're liable, to read in the Bible.*

I moved my chair and joined in, an octave up, beginning to enjoy myself.

David was small but oh my,
He shot Goliath—

A cracking sound, startlingly loud, from behind us.

We turned to locate the source. I realised almost immediately what it was because I could see the water running from the vase to the table, and then the whole thing came apart as though the glass had been split with a saw, the water streaming to the ground and the fresh-cut flowers slithering along the table towards the floor.

'*Mio dio*,' I said. 'How on earth?'

'Greta!' Chiara's voice had a sharp note of panic. She jumped up and tried to hold the vase together, but it was no use. The water had already soaked the tablecloth and carpet.

There came the sound of hurried footsteps and the housekeeper appeared. She and Chiara stared at one another.

'It just broke,' Chiara said.

'I'll get the mop, don't you worry. Leave that.'

I came over to stand next to Chiara, looking down at the

broken crystal and discarded flowers. 'How peculiar,' I said. 'It must have had a crack running down it, I suppose.'

She didn't say anything, simply stared at the glass and I saw that there was blood staining her blouse.

'Chiara, your hand!'

The girl looked down at her hands and turned them over, exposing a shard of glass, embedded in the skin, a line of red blooming across the white.

'Quickly, let's get you to a sink.' I took her through to the bathroom and ran water over the cut, removing the shard with care, as my mother had trained me to do. I let the water wash away the blood and then used a towel to dry it.

Chiara had gone very pale and I made her sit for a moment on the edge of the marble bath.

'There. You'll be fine. It isn't too deep. I don't think it needs stitches. You've bandages somewhere, have you?

'In the cabinet.'

I opened the mirrored cabinet and found it meticulously ordered: rows of balms and dressings and pills, carefully labelled: catarrh syrup, calomel, methylene blue. I supposed Adelina had prepared it all like this. It was strange seeing her small, neat handwriting on the labels. The same writing as I'd seen on the sheet music.

There was a bottle of tincture of iodine which I used to clean the wound, and a roll of gauze, which I wound around the girl's palm, fastening it with a safety pin. 'Your poor hand. Well, no more lesson for you today, I think!'

I was sitting on the bath next to her by that stage and I could almost feel the distress rising from her. I thought she was going to cry, but she just sat, very still, very quiet, seeming to hold it all in.

'What a strange thing.' I forced a smile. 'But you mustn't worry about it. You'll be all right.'

'Thank you,' Chiara managed after a moment. 'For trying to help.'

'Don't be silly. It's no bother.' I felt a surge of pity for this young girl, having to navigate this time of her life, this time in the world, without a mother. I squeezed her shoulder and stood up. 'I'll go and see how Greta is getting on.'

When I walked back into the piano room, the housekeeper was squatting on the ground near the table, collecting the fallen and sodden flowers.

'Do be careful with the glass. Poor Chiara has cut her hand,' I said to her. 'I've done the best I can, but maybe you could take a look at it a bit later. I don't think it's bad.'

With some difficulty, Greta stood up and faced me. She too looked drained. 'Thank you, Signorina.'

'There must have been a fault in the glass, I suppose,' I said. 'Or had something hit it, damaged it. The dog, perhaps?'

The housekeeper stared at the spot where the vase had been. 'No, not the dog.'

I thought she might say something else – about how queer it was – but she just bent down again to continue with her cleaning.

When I returned to the bathroom, Chiara was standing, staring at the labelled jars. She turned to face me, her dark eyes very large in her pale face. 'You'll tell him, won't you, that it wasn't my fault? That I didn't do anything? He doesn't like mess.'

'Well, of course. But I'm sure your father won't blame you. No one will. It was just a peculiar thing.'

I smiled and she gave an odd half-smile back at me. 'Thank you, Signorina Valenti. I'm glad you were here, or no one would have believed it.'

For an instant, then, my mind flashed back to my illness years before, to the things I'd experienced that could not have been real: the angry murmur of voices, the sensation of stretching skin.

'Well,' I said to Chiara, 'these things do happen. Now, you'd better change your blouse.'

I might have thought more about it all – the vase, Greta's comments, my long-ago malady – but I was very busy over the next few days, teaching and interviewing for new positions, for I knew I had to take on all the new pupils I could.

Before I left one middle-class house in the Prati district, the girl's father – a fat man with a thin moustache and a gold Fascist lapel pin – had stared at me and my long dark hair and said: 'You'll forgive me for asking, Signorina, but you're not Jewish, are you?'

Flustered, I'd answered that, no, I wasn't, and he'd said, 'Good, good. Always pays to be sure. You understand why I have to check.'

I'd left the house with a sick feeling in my stomach, wishing I'd said something else, something more. The newspapers were talking by then of a new law that would prevent Jewish people from teaching in schools. Still, though, I couldn't quite believe it would happen; that the government would be so foolish.

Mirella herself was barely able to grasp it. Her father was an academic, a tutor. Would this law apply to him too? Everything they'd strived for was being torn away and there wasn't even a reason for it. It was an awful suffocating feeling of tightening dread. I tried to comfort Mirella, I cooked her nice things to eat, but there was no real assurance I could give her, as none of us knew what would happen. I clung to the hope that it was all some kind of mistake, some bureaucratic error. 'It must be,' others said. 'It must be. Italy is not anti-Semitic.' Saying it did not make it true, however. Though I tried at the time to believe it, I knew, of course, that there had always been

34

anti-Semitism in Italy, cultivated by the Catholic Church.

Mirella and I hadn't talked again about the census, but I saw that the large white envelope had gone from the table. I prayed that she'd thrown it in with the rubbish, but I feared she'd told them the truth, and I feared for what that meant. We had some notion by then of what was happening in Germany, though, in fact, it was only a fraction of the true horror. We'd heard that the state was stripping the Jews of their money and possessions and sending them out into the unknown. We'd heard that the other European countries had failed to form a plan to help them. No one wanted more immigrants, not after they'd been parted from their money; each country's priority was to protect their own citizens. It had been the same, I thought, when the Slovene teachers were removed from their jobs, even when rural schools had been firebombed. Generally, people had not rallied around the persecuted, but retreated into their own dens and hoped that the hurricane would pass; that, somehow, it would not touch them. There were exceptions, and there were resisters and anarchists, but they were few in number and they were brutally put down. It never occurred to me that I could be one of them.

When I next went to the Cavallera house, Dante was at home, Zefiro at his heels, and I was ashamed to feel the heat rise to my face at seeing him. I was little better than the dog.

'Ah, our little nurse. Thank you so much for looking after Chiara last week.'

'Really, it was nothing. Is she all right?'

'Fine, fine. Just a surface wound, though she could only begin playing again three days ago. At least, that was her excuse! You must come and take coffee with me once you've finished your lesson. I'll get Greta to make us espresso.'

I couldn't refuse. His attitude didn't permit it, and besides,

35

it had been weeks since I'd had proper coffee. I let myself think that was mainly the reason that I'd accepted, but over the course of the lesson, I found myself increasingly distracted and at one point Chiara had to repeat her question to me: 'Did your parents play the piano?'

'Oh, no. Neither of my parents played.' I hesitated. Chiara had assumed that I was like her and that my parents had been like hers – educated, cultured, monied. I thought of my rough-handed father and his bitterness towards those who'd been born with more. I thought of his resentment when I'd begun to play. 'It was a teacher who got me started, and who taught me on the school piano for many years.' Miss Pintar. A force of nature who'd seen that music meant something to me before I'd even understood it myself; who had fought my corner for me. 'She even made my father buy a piano in the end, you know. Found him one at such a low price that it was impossible for him to claim we couldn't afford it.'

Chiara was staring at me and I found myself adding: 'We weren't poor, though. Not by the standards of the village. My father was just very careful with money.' Mean. He was mean. Mean with my mother, mean with me. What he was saving his money for, I have no idea, but every penny had to be wrenched out of him – every pair of shoes had to be begged for, every additional shopping item justified. It was all about control. I don't know how my mother managed it. 'But, no, in answer to your question: my parents didn't play the piano. Didn't play any instrument. I don't think any of my family did. My mother had a beautiful voice, though.' I remembered her singing when my father was out, humming as she hung up the washing. I remembered her singing me a Slovene lullaby on the nights I was too upset to sleep.

Lipa zelenela je tam v dišečem gaju. Green grows the linden tree.

36

'My mother played every day,' Chiara said quietly. 'Except one time when she hurt her hand. I would hear her playing when I woke up in the mornings. She would sit here in her dressing gown and slippers.' She paused. 'Sometimes, in my dreams, I hear her playing.'

That chilled me. I could imagine Adelina quite clearly, elegant in a silk morning wrap, her hair freshly curled. 'It must take a lot of getting used to, not having her here anymore.'

Chiara looked at me but didn't say anything. Instead, she began again to play.

By the time our hour was nearly up, I could smell the scent of toasted coffee in the air: rich and delicious.

Dante appeared and insisted I join him in the kitchen, where Greta was pouring the syrupy liquid from the stovetop coffee maker into tiny china cups, and where Zefiro lay in his basket. Greta brought the cups over to the counter, together with the sugar pot and small silver spoons.

'*Grazie*, Greta,' Dante said. 'Please, Signorina Valenti. Help yourself to sugar. It sounds as though Chiara is making good progress?'

I swallowed and prayed he couldn't see how nervous I was. 'Yes, I think she is. She's an excellent student – far easier to teach than many of the young people I see.' Unhappy, terribly unhappy, but I didn't feel I could say that to him.

'You have lots of pupils, then?'

'A fair few, yes.' I explained to him about my work teaching music at the school, my private pupils. I worried that conversation would soon dry up and that I'd have nothing to say, but Dante exuded a confidence that proved intoxicating. He drew me into talking about where and when I'd trained and why I'd wanted to teach, then moved with ease to talking about his own work as a lawyer for the town council, his ambitions to obtain promotion. He asked me about what I myself hoped to achieve, where I lived and who I lived with. He seemed genuinely interested in my responses. I told him about Mirella, but not about my concerns. We didn't discuss politics or current affairs at all. People didn't then, not unless they knew each other very well. It was too dangerous and considered rude. Of course, I could see that Dante toed the party line – the portrait of Il Duce in the living room, the children who attended Fascist Saturday school. But then everyone did those things back then. If you *didn't* do them, it meant you must be an anti-fascist, and then woe betide you, because you'd be ostracised, demoted at work, quite possibly beaten. Your children, if you didn't sign them up to the Fascist youth organisations, would be given poor marks at school and not allowed to progress the year. And if you went so far as to be vocally anti-fascist – to actively resist – the punishments were far harsher, vaguer, more frightening. 'If you're not with us, you're against us' – that was the Fascist motto, and very few dared to speak out of turn. Which is why what happened happened.

'Well,' Dante said, 'I imagine that women living together are far neater and more organised than bachelors. Lord, before I married, I lived with two friends from university in some godawful flat in the Piazza San Silvestro. The place was an utter pigsty.'

I couldn't quite imagine it, somehow: this polished and handsome man living in squalor. I'd noticed that his hands, holding the coffee cup, were white and smooth, the nails neatly filed. His hair was perfectly trimmed and slicked back with brilliantine. He was a man who took good care of himself. And why shouldn't he, I supposed, but it made me nervous, conscious of my own bitten nails and minimal make-up. I wished I was as polished as he.

Dante was still talking of his bachelor apartment, of how

they would rarely do the washing up, but would instead buy new crockery, and how the place became infested with mice. 'My wife, as she later became, couldn't wait to get me away from there.'

'Well, your house here is very beautiful.'

'Thank you. That was mostly her doing, I confess: the decorating, the furnishings. She had a wonderful eye for such things, though, unfortunately, Zefiro here has a tendency to ruin them, don't you, you wretched hound?' Zefiro sat up at the sound of his name and ambled over towards us.

I thought at once of the crystal vase, the water running to the ground. 'The vase,' I said. 'Did you work out why it had broken? It seemed such a curious thing for it suddenly to split apart!'

Dante spread out his hands to indicate the mystery of it all. 'Probably Alessandro damaged it and wouldn't admit to it. That would be typical of him.'

'Really?' The boy had struck me as awkward, perhaps arrogant, but not necessarily destructive.

'Yes, things always seem to break in his presence. You know, when he was a little boy, we had these two porcelain dog figurines. Hideous things, if you ask me, but my wife loved her ornaments and it was she who decorated the whole house. So we have these two delicate little spaniels, or whatever they are, on either side of the fireplace. One day, one of the little dogs disappears.' He raised his eyebrow at me. 'No one can say where it's got to. Greta says she has no idea, the children deny all knowledge. It has simply... vanished. We'd had a party a few days before and we decided maybe someone had taken it – a child, most probably. Or maybe someone had broken it and was too embarrassed to tell us.'

I smiled to indicate I was enjoying this story, as he was clearly enjoying the telling of it, though I thought I could guess the

39

ending. I noticed that Greta, who'd been quietly washing up at the sink, had half-turned to watch us.

'Anyway, weeks go by, we forget about the dog. One day, we decide to go to the seaside – to Ostia. My wife goes to the laundry cupboard to get the bathing suits and towels. And that's when she finds it: the dog. Only it has no head! It looks like it has been hacked off! Alessandro denied it was him, but we knew of course that it was. Who else would remove the head of a china dog and then hide it in a cupboard? I punished him, as any good father must punish his sons, but to this day – to this very day – he claims he was innocent. Framed!' Dante laughed – a flash of white teeth. 'Children. They certainly keep us on our toes.'

I was still smiling. 'Yes, indeed.'

Greta met my eye, then turned back to the sink.

'You want children, of course,' Dante said. It was not a question. It was assumed that all women would have children. Il Duce had decreed that we were to produce babies for the fatherland, a myriad of them. Women were rewarded for producing enormous broods: some had eight or even nine.

'Oh, yes,' I said. 'Well, that is… in time. I am not married.' What a stupid thing to say. It was perfectly obvious I was on my own. My loneliness was almost palpable.

'You're still young yet.'

'Not so young.'

'You can't be more than twenty-two, surely.'

'Twenty-five, in fact.'

'No! You do not look it.'

'You're too kind.' I'd flushed a deep crimson, I was sure of it. I searched for something to say to him, but he'd already moved on to talking about how they had spent the summer at Lago di Bolsena and had I ever been. No, I confessed – I had not.

'Well, you must go. It's delightful in the summer. Wonderful for children. Boating, fishing. Of course, without their mother, it was rather different, but I think they enjoyed it nonetheless. My parents used to take me there when I was a boy. Yours never took you?'

'Sadly, no. Too far. I grew up mainly near Trieste.'

'Ah, lovely Trieste. I confess I've not been in, what, ten years? You go back now and again, I assume, to see your family?'

'Occasionally, yes. We moved to Puglia when I was fourteen and I've been very poor at keeping in touch with friends there.' Friends. Were there ever really friends? 'My uncle and cousins still live just outside Trieste, but I don't visit often.' Now that Agata was dead, I doubted that I'd go back for years.

'Oh well, I'm sure your family will welcome you back whenever you chose to visit. Italians are like that, aren't they? Family is always family.'

Italian. He'd assumed I was Italian and my instinct was to be flattered. I should have corrected him then and there – told him my parents had been Slovene – but I didn't. It was too awkward. In any event, I was, I told myself, predominantly Italian now. Had I not suffered as a child – torn from my friends, beaten for speaking the language of my parents, choked with ash from our burnt town hall – in order to become one of them? So I didn't say anything. If I had, it might all have turned out very different.

Greta walked over to us. 'You want me to boil the water for more coffee, Signor?'

Dante looked at me. 'Signorina Valenti, you'll have another?'

'Eva, please. And no, that's very kind, but I must be getting to my next lesson.' This was a lie. There was no next lesson, only the damp apartment where we had no real coffee, but I felt suddenly uncomfortable and nervous. 'The coffee was delicious, thank you.'

41

He frowned and smiled at the same time. 'Next time, you must indulge me and stay a little longer. Let me see you to the door. Greta, another for me, please. I've a long night of work ahead.'

Over the next few weeks, we settled into a sort of routine, the Cavallera family and I. It was a reassuring pattern at a time when the world seemed to be sliding into chaos. I would arrive at five o'clock every Thursday to give Chiara her lesson, and then, at around six, I would join Dante for a coffee. I came to look forward to these meetings more and more, for Dante always did his best to put me at my ease and made me feel that everything I said was interesting, though really I had little to say. His self-confidence was infectious, invigorating. He made me laugh. I never wanted our conversations to end.

I'd previously thought I was incapable of speaking to men, of forming any real relationship, but Dante seemed entirely different to the boys I'd encountered before. So different too to my father, with his silences and bursts of temper. And although Dante and I only ever talked at that stage of superficial things – of our work and our friends, music, films and books – I felt that there was something between us, something bright and hopeful when everything else seemed to be going awry.

We were never left alone, exactly. Zefiro was always there, insisting on attention or walks or snacks. Sometimes while we were speaking, Alessandro would barge in to share with us some exploit or to show us the scrapbook he kept with photographs of Il Duce and the troops, with pages and pages of guns and military equipment. I wasn't sure how to feel about Alessandro at that time. Though his manner could be a little abrasive, I felt for him, for he was clearly so anxious to please his father and to live up to what he thought were his father's ideals, and those of Fascist manhood: heroism, obedience, strength.

Chiara, for the most part, remained fairly quiet over those weeks, but she opened up a little, occasionally telling me about her lessons at school where she was taught how to change and bathe a baby, or showing me patterns of dresses she intended to make. Adelina had evidently been a gifted seamstress as well as a musician, and had taught her daughter to sew.

Greta, too, began to talk more to me, mainly about the aches and pains she suffered in her hips and back, the difficulties she had with the children squabbling, her supposed ingrate of a daughter, whom she referred to as 'Quella malignazza Sophia!' But, occasionally, when Dante was not there, she would say something quite different. 'I tell you, Signorina Valenti, it can't all be explained away, what happens in this house. It's like there's someone going about behind my back making messes as soon as I've tidied.'

I dismissed what she said as nonsense because it didn't fit with what I perceived. The Cavallera house seemed my place of sanctuary against the growing fury outside.

One day in September, Mirella and I agreed to meet Ettore with his friend Pietro, a dark-complexioned, intense and wiry journalist with whom Ettore had lived for many months. We'd decided to go to the bar near the apartment where we often drank. Only, when we arrived, there was a new sign on the door: 'ARYAN CUSTOMERS ONLY.'

I felt ill, seeing that. There'd been more and more talk of the 'race laws' and restricting the rights of Jews, but I hadn't wanted to believe any of it would happen. This, though, was solid and real: something undeniable. I put my arm around Mirella, felt the stiffness of her shoulders.

'We should smash the windows,' Pietro said, furious. 'How dare they?'

'Well, you can still go in,' Mirella said, her voice tight. 'Perfect Aryans that you are.'

'Of course we won't, Mirella.'

I glanced at Ettore and he held my gaze for a moment with his light brown eyes. He and I had never discussed it, but both of us knew that neither of us were the Italian citizens Il Duce wanted in his country. Not us, not the brown-skinned, not the Roma, the Evangelicals or prostitutes or anyone who was in any way 'other'.

'None of us are ever going in here again,' Ettore said. 'I'll tell Beppe as much right now.' He and Pietro disappeared together into the smoke-filled bar.

Mirella detached herself from my arm. 'You see? This is why I shouldn't hang around with non-Jews anymore.'

'Please don't say that, Mirella. You know how much we love you.'

She'd been spending an increasing amount of time with other Jewish people, discussing what was happening. She'd never previously sought out their company very much. Most of Rome's Jewish population lived in or near the old ghetto area, making a living as itinerant peddlers, rag pickers, salesmen, tailors and shopkeepers. Now, though, she'd made an effort to seek people out, attending meetings, visiting the synagogue, working out what on earth they could do. 'What did people expect?' Mirella had told me the previous day. 'If you attack us as Jews, we'll defend ourselves as Jews. Apparently that's my sole identity now.'

When the boys re-emerged, Ettore's expression was sombre. 'Come on, let's get away from this *cesso*.'

We went instead to a quiet bar near Portico d'Ottavia at the entrance to the ghetto. Its walls had been torn down fifty years before, but it was difficult to feel that they weren't rising up again. The place was small and barely furnished – a zinc-topped

44

bar, five tables covered with white paper napkins. Along a wall, a line of bottles and a poster advertising trips to Venice. We ordered Camparis with soda.

'It was a pokey little place, anyway,' I said. 'We only went there because it was cheap.'

'What did Beppe say?' Mirella asked, ignoring me.

Ettore lit a cigarette. 'The usual *cavolata*. That he was sorry but that was the way things were going. That he had to make a living, and that meant acting the model citizen, blah, blah, blah.' He blew out a trail of smoke.

'Why are people like this?' Pietro said quietly, looking into Ettore's eyes. I understood what their relationship was, but we never spoke about it.

Ettore leant forward. 'Because they want to believe things are simple, black and white, all the more so when their lives feel chaotic.'

And things were chaotic: we all had a clear sense that the situation was worsening, intensifying, not just in Italy but across Europe. It was always difficult to work out from our newspapers exactly what was going on as they were banned from publishing any news that might affect the morale of the people (suicides were to be brushed over, homicides hidden). Even they, however, talked of a 'Sudetan crisis' and 'serious incidents' in Czechoslovakia, people shot dead. Hitler's territorial demands were ramping up, boiling over into violence. Everywhere, there were whispers of war.

'People want to believe that they're on the right side,' Ettore continued, 'and that if they do enough to fit in, the bad times won't come for them. It's the same reason people think *he* will save them. Someone clear and strong who'll take responsibility for the mess the world is in — sort it all out, stop them having to think for themselves.'

I felt a deep unease at his words, because he was probing at my own assumptions. We'd grown up being told Il Duce was always right. It was the slogan written or chiselled on walls, pavements, banners. He'd produced the evidence for it too: the trains we were told of, the wide empty autostrada, the smashing of the mafia, the killing of malaria, the draining of the Pontine Marshes. Didn't that show us that he never failed and that we were not to question his judgement? Did a good daughter question her father's decisions when he was only trying to protect her? For the past sixteen years, the country, myself included, had been taught the importance of toeing the line, of not resisting, not even questioning. And on the surface, at least, the situation wasn't so bad that people felt they had to take a stand. As Carmela, one of the younger teachers at the school said, 'It's not as though they're doing anything awful like they are in Germany. Oh, I know it's not very nice to be told "you're not really Italian" and "you mustn't work in this or that job", but it's not as though they're hurting anyone or killing anyone.'

No, not yet. But even I, who hadn't wanted to acknowledge it at first, could see what it was like for Mirella when people who'd previously said '*Buongiorno*' to her in the street now looked the other way; I could see the newsstands that'd previously stocked only newspapers now showing in prime position the vile covers of *Defence of the Race* with their ghoulish caricatures of the evil Jew.

'I won't be able to stay here,' Mirella said suddenly.

'What do you mean?'

'I mean they'll make it impossible for us to live here. They're doing it bit by bit. They're not even brave enough to do it outright like the Germans have. No, they must pretend that these measures – taking people's incomes, stopping them from mixing with non-Jews, preventing them from holding certain jobs – these are all necessary and reasonable measures for protecting the Italians. Which, apparently, we Jews no longer are. Instead, we're the internal enemy.' She ground out her cigarette.

'No one here really hates Jewish people, though,' I said. 'That's just vitriol that the newspapers spout.' I think I knew as I spoke how thin it sounded.

'Newspapers that people read and read and don't question until finally they begin to accept what they're saying: which is that Jews are the privileged outsiders. They're the traitors the Catholic Church always said they were. They're the reason their own lives are hard. So they'll put up a sign in their bar and drive them out, bit by bit.'

Pietro nodded and said very quietly: 'Mussolini thinks he has to provide Italians with an enemy to make them believe they have an identity as a nation. He thinks this will make them fighters. And even if people don't really buy all this, they'll toe the line, just like Beppe is, to avoid trouble for themselves.'

'Right,' Mirella said. 'So, measure by measure, people learn to accept that Jews are the main enemy, just as they are in Germany.' She noticed me frowning. 'Well, Eva, have you seen anyone standing up? Shouting about how awful these measures are – how they must be stopped?'

I felt a terrible, creeping shame. 'But no one does, Mirella. About anything.' Because we knew what happened to those who openly resisted. Or rather, we did not know. We knew that bad things happened, but those things were not predict- able or clear. There were tribunals, there were people sent into exile, but there were also people who just disappeared in the night, or who were beaten until parts of them oozed onto the pavement, who were tortured until they were dead.

'No one dares resist,' I said. 'It doesn't mean they agree with what's happening.'

'Some people dare,' Pietro whispered, and I felt coldness

seep down my spine. What had he involved himself with?

'A tiny number,' Mirella said in a low voice. 'A tiny number of brave, brave people. And everyone who doesn't dare? Everyone who stays quiet? The regime takes that to mean they consent.'

I thought of my mother, my mother who rarely disagreed with my father. I thought of the sounds I'd heard at night. Did that mean she had given up, given in, or simply that she'd taken the best course available to her? I wasn't sure. 'There's no use in it, Eva,' she'd said to me once when I'd asked her why she didn't push my father for money. 'It only makes him more angry.' She must have worked out by then that there was no point resisting. It only made things worse for her, for me. She did what she did to survive. That was what I was doing now – it was what all Italians were doing, perhaps all of Europe – burrowing down, protecting our own, hoping we would brave the approaching storm.

That night, lying in bed, I listened on the radio to Il Duce giving a speech in my old home town of Trieste. I shouldn't have listened, but still I clung to the threadbare hope that he must know what he was doing, that he would guide us out of this mess. As a teenaged girl, I'd heard his promises and believed him to be making them to me, the newly Italian Eva. Where my own father was spineless and mean, Il Duce had seemed forceful and effective, pledging to lift people from poverty and restore the prestige of the nation; to make Italy great again.

Like so many, I'd chosen to believe him when he distanced himself from the violence of the *squadristi*, the men who'd scorched a path across Italy, even though it was the path Mussolini himself had used to walk to power. He was the strong man who would save us, who saw the value even in me, who'd bring order where there'd been chaos and ineptitude.

48

Now, though, on the wireless, Mussolini talked in his usual thundering tone of how he'd last spoken in Trieste in 1921, 'when we were tormented by a mediocre and crippled peace, while Triestine squadrists energetically and heroically cleansed your city of the relics of the old regime'.

Energetically cleansed. I thought of the blackened shell of the Narodni Dom, the dismay and fear I'd felt on seeing it. That was not a cleansing, it was a killing of a culture. I think I'd understood some of that even at seven, yet somehow, the lesson it had taught my parents, and so me, was not to fight back, but instead to try to be accepted, not as a Slovene but as one of them. And now Il Duce was explicitly condoning it; saying these men were not vandals but heroes. I felt a sure sickness, then, at my own naivety, at my parents' stupidity. Why had they bowed to a man like him?

When my attention returned to the speech, Il Duce was talking about Hitler's claims upon Czechoslovakia. 'If there are two camps, for and against Prague, let it be known that Italy has chosen its side.' I felt very cold, hearing that. He meant, I understood, that Italy would side with Germany if war came. I'd heard Hitler's hysterical, hypnotic ranting on the radio, against Slavs, against Jews, against 'the enemy'. I knew he'd annexed Austria by force: the so-called Anschluss. If Il Duce was to throw his lot in with this man, would anti-Slav sentiment rise again as it had when I was a child? Would he drag us all down to the bottom with him?

The audience in Trieste, however, cheered these words as they'd always cheered Mussolini, because hadn't he always looked out for what was best for us, his children? I'd been in one of those crowds once, one of the thousands gathered at the Palazzo Venezia, two years before, when he'd emerged onto the balcony of the red *palazzo*, chest puffed out, and raised his voice above the chants of the throng to announce the conquest of Abyssinia and the beginning of the new Italian empire. I'd seen all those people – housewives, grandfathers, clerks, soldiers – gazing at him in admiration like flowers drawn towards the sun. *Du-ce! Du-ce! Du-ce!* The shouts and the cries and the bright, upturned faces. Fathers hoisting children onto their shoulders so that they could see their leader at this astonishing moment in Italy's history: the moment where we turned back the tide on the shame heaped on us after the war and began to rebuild our nation. How had we all been so blind?

Il Duce was continuing his Trieste speech: 'For prestige, it is necessary to have a clear, severe racial consciousness, that establishes not only the differences, but also very clear superiorities. The Jewish problem is only one aspect of this phenomenon. World Jewry has been, for sixteen years, despite our policy, an irreconcilable enemy of Fascism.'

Jews as the enemy. Mirella had been right.

I switched off the radio, wanting it all to go away, and lay awake for a long time in the darkness.

5

Four gashes, quite deep, as though someone had dragged their nails across the flesh of her arm, or as though she'd been clawed at by some beast. I saw them as Chiara was playing and her blouse slipped up her arm. In a heartbeat, she'd pulled the sleeve back down to cover her wrist, but I'd seen the marks clearly. I just didn't know what they were.

When the time came for my evening coffee with Dante, my usual anticipation was shot through with anxiety. Should I say something? If so, how to broach it? As the weeks had progressed, I'd been increasingly drawn to him, like a moth to a light. It had become, I suppose, an infatuation, for he was not only physically desirable but confident, eloquent, and of a higher status than the men with whom I generally mixed. Our discussions, though, were still fairly light: the chatter of a courting couple, not about our true hopes and fears. Dante was, I recall, talking about his old flatmate, Massimo, who now lived nearby and who'd always been entirely luckless with women. 'He talks to them about the most peculiar of subjects. There was one occasion where I had to rescue a girl from a monologue he was giving about how to get rid of vermin.'

He paused and looked at me. 'Eva, you're rather quiet this evening. Is something the matter? Good lord, I'm as bad as Massimo, aren't I, rattling on? Though at least I've not been talking about rats.'

'No,' I laughed, 'it's nothing you've said, and nothing wrong, exactly.' I hesitated. 'It's only that I'm a little worried about Chiara.'

He gazed at me, nodded, and quietly went to close the kitchen door. '*Dicca me*,' he said when he was sitting down again. 'Tell me.'

I set down my espresso cup. 'I've noticed that Chiara has scratches or cuts, here, on her arm.' I showed him my own unmarked arm.

For a moment, he was silent. 'Did you ask her how she got them?'

'No.' I had a horrible feeling I'd overstepped the mark.

'It's probably Alessandro's doing,' Dante said lightly. 'He can be a little overexcitable at times. I've known him hurt her before.'

'You have?'

'Oh, you know – pinching, slapping, that sort of thing. I've told him to grow up, act more like a man. He probably scratched her in a fight.'

'Perhaps,' I said, though they hadn't looked like injuries from a children's scuffle. I'd been thinking of another unhappy girl I'd known when I was at school – a girl whose arms and legs were striped white with scars. They'd never been explained either. 'Only… I hope you don't mind my saying, but Chiara often seems deeply unhappy. I wondered whether there was something I could do.'

For a long moment, Dante said nothing at all and I was afraid that I'd angered him, or made him angry with Chiara. He always spoke firmly to his children, brooking no dissent. I thought little of it at that time, as that was how many fathers were then, and it was a good deal better than my own father.

At last, Dante said: 'You're right, of course. She's been terribly unhappy since her mother's death, almost a different person entirely. My wife was a wonderful, patient mother to Chiara. Since she died... I confess I don't know what to do.' He squeezed his eyes shut, as though trying to shut out the pain.

I felt a tremendous rush of warmth towards him. 'I'm so sorry, Dante, I didn't mean to intrude.'

'No, no. It is I who should apologise.' He coughed, took another sip of his coffee. 'Good god, you'd think I was a child, not a man of forty-three! And there's me telling Alessandro to be more manly.'

Masculine, brave, strong. It was what was expected of all our men, it was what Il Duce personified.

'You lost your wife. Their children lost their mother. That would be difficult for anyone.'

'Thank you, Eva. You've been very kind, to me, to Chiara, to all of us. You arrived rather in the aftermath, I'm afraid. I think we were all numb for the first couple of months, and now it all comes out, in different ways. Alessandro's been in trouble at school for all manner of things. Fighting with other boys is perfectly normal in my book, but now he's scratching his own sister. And Chiara, well, you've seen what she's like, how withdrawn she is. I've tried to reach out to her, but honestly, I've no idea how to speak to a shy young girl like her. None at all. It was always my wife who dealt with Chiara's anxieties. I suppose it's my own fault for not getting to know my own daughter better when she was younger.'

'Oh, I'm sure it's not your fault. I'm sure you tried.' Tried better, at least, than my own father, who'd treated me not as a child but an encumbrance, a drain on his resources.

Dante spread his hands. 'I tried yes, but I failed. I'm still failing now. I've tried to understand her grief, her sadness, but I have so much of my own. I admit that at times I've felt frustrated with her.' He looked at me and gave a brief laugh. '*Mio dio*, you didn't ask for all this unburdening when you agreed to have coffee with me this evening! Let's at least have a proper drink.'

He went to the drinks cabinet and brought us back a tumbler each of vermouth. 'She needs a woman's touch, that's the thing. Someone who understands and can bring her out of herself; not an oaf like me. And you've seen what Alessandro is like – full of life but not exactly full of compassion. Most of the time he just annoys her and sometimes he's downright mean. It hasn't been easy for him either, of course, but he needs to buck up. So do I, in fact.' He downed his drink and poured another. 'I'll talk to him about this scratching business.'

I sipped my drink, deciding it was best to just let him speak, but I wasn't sure it could all be so easily dismissed. If it was Alessandro, then it had been a vicious, nasty attack, an indication of some behavioural problem. And if it wasn't Alessandro, then what could have caused such marks? Though I tried not to, I thought all too clearly of how, at the height of my illness, I'd clawed at my own skin, believing it to be crawling with beetles. Was it possible Chiara had experienced the same? That she too had been gripped by visions? Could grief bring such things on?

Dante was talking now of how they never really discussed his wife's death at home, and how perhaps that had made things worse. 'It just seemed better to try to move on. I didn't want to think about it.'

I hesitated. 'How did she die exactly, Dante? I hope you don't mind my asking. Allegra said it was some kind of haemorrhage.'

'Yes, that's what the doctor concluded. She'd been having terrible headaches for days, dizziness, hearing peculiar things in the house. Well, we thought it was just that: headaches. I feel so stupid now for not having called in a doctor earlier. I should have known.'

'But how would you have known? You really can't blame yourself.'

'Oh, trust me, I can. I keep going over it in my mind. What if I'd listened to her properly? What if I'd just called up Dottor Falluci, got him to check her over? What if I'd stayed at home that day? What if, what if, what if?'

'You can't think like that. You mustn't.' I knew I should have left him alone, but I wanted to know more about Adelina – much more. It was as if I couldn't help myself. 'And she just collapsed?'

'Yes. Or at least we suppose so. None of us were there. I came home and found her lying on the floor, already cold.' He rubbed his face and I thought he was trying not to break down.

'I'm so sorry, Dante. I should never have asked you to talk about it.' I cursed myself for my ghoulish curiosity. What on earth had come over me?

'It's all right. It helps to talk, to be honest, and I haven't really had anyone to talk to, is the sad reality of it. My parents died a few years back; in any event, we weren't close. And it's not the sort of thing one discusses with your colleagues. Anyway, they found a swelling in the brain – a haemorrhage. It happens sometimes. Rarely. We were incredibly unlucky, I suppose. Well, now we're owed a damn bit of good luck, I'd say. Certainly the children are.' He took another gulp of his drink.

I was quiet for a moment, still thinking of the marks on Chiara's arm, imagining Adelina sitting at the piano, writing notes for her daughter on the music. My own mother hadn't had the skill to do that, but she'd listened. She would sit quietly and listen to me play and I knew I'd done something to make her happy. I had a certain burst of longing for her then, as I did from time to time. 'You know, there's a concert next week. Carlo Zecchi, the pianist, is back in Rome. If I could get tickets, perhaps I could take Chiara with me. Try to draw her out a little, work out what's going on in her head. What do you think? She might talk more when she's out of the house. Things will seem different then.'

Dante toyed with his glass. 'You might be right. Things do feel a little claustrophobic here sometimes, and, of course, there's so much of her here. So much to remind us.' He set his glass down. 'Yes, now that I think about it, I think that's a marvellous idea. Chiara would like that.' He looked at me and smiled. 'Maybe we have had some good luck, Eva. Maybe it's you.'

I felt the heat rush to my face. 'Oh, I don't know about that. I've barely done anything at all.'

'Well, you listened to me this evening and for that I'm very grateful. You know, I've a feeling things are going to get better.'

I smiled back at him, a little shy. So much did I want it to be true that I began, in fact, to believe it.

Chiara was more enthusiastic about the piano concert than I'd anticipated. What exactly would Zecchi play? she wanted to know. And what should she wear? She rarely socialised, I realised, which saddened me. She should have been out in the evenings playing table tennis with friends, giggling, as even I — the *straniera,* the *forestiera* — occasionally had at her age. It seemed that in the aftermath of her mother's death she'd entirely shut herself off. I would have to coax her out of her shell.

On the evening of the concert, she seemed nervous, but she

smiled to see me and didn't resist linking arms as we walked up cobblestoned Via Giulia and along the Ponte Sant'Angelo towards Teatro Adriano. The evening was jasmine-scented and hopeful, lights appearing in the windows. There were the usual catcalls as we walked, which I ignored, pretending not to notice the men who nudged each other, the Blackshirts who stared boldly after us. I felt highly protective of Chiara. It wasn't only her age: there was a vulnerability about her, an oddness. She was a younger version of myself, but one I had a chance to help.

The theatre was done out beautifully, a huge chandelier hanging from the high ceiling of the concert hall, banners running around the stalls. The place hummed with the sound of conversation, the tinkling of glasses, polite laughter. The audience was mostly older than us (middle-aged women in velvet dresses and veiled hats, rotund men strapped into tailored suits), but there were some younger, more glamorous people at whom Chiara gazed, taking in the women's sequined jackets, slim skirts and thinly plucked brows, their silky, straight-seamed stockings. We took our seats and waited for the final guests to arrive, then for the music to begin.

With the opening notes, the reality of our tormented world receded. Zecchi was as good as I'd remembered – better – the floor reverberating with the notes of the piano, the music swelling to the ceiling. Gradually, I felt my body relax, felt myself sucked into the music, became not Eva or Iva, but something floating free, content. When I remembered to glance at Chiara, I saw that she too was watching intently, her eyes glistening. Perhaps, for her, as for me, music was a means of escape, of fleeing one's identity. When the interval came, she clasped my hand. 'Oh Eva, he's quite brilliant. I'm so glad we came.'

'So am I, Chiara. Let's go and get a drink.'

We headed to one of the bars where I bought us both a

cordial and led Chiara to a little table by the wall, away from the chattering audience. 'You've been here before?'

'Yes, with my mother, several times. It's lovely to be back. Strange, but lovely.'

'Then I'm very pleased we came.' We sat for a minute watching the other people: women in pillbox hats and furs, the barman pouring drink after drink: Negronis, Martinis, Milano-Torinos.

'You know, it's silly,' Chiara said, 'but I thought maybe I'd lost my interest in music.'

'That's not silly. Not after everything you've been through.'

She wiped her mouth. 'Things have seemed less important, somehow far away. Do you know what I mean?'

'I think so.' I'd felt strangely detached in the weeks after my own mother died, sapped of energy. 'It's natural to feel like that after you've lost someone. It's how I felt, at any rate.'

Chiara sipped at her cordial but didn't say anything else. An older couple took the table next to us, the man opening a silver lighter to ignite his wife's cigarette.

'Do you still think of her a lot?' I asked at length.

'I try not to. I'm not sure it helps. Alessandro gets very upset if I talk about her. It was more difficult for him, maybe, being younger and a boy. He didn't really know how to grieve – thought somehow he shouldn't – and I think it's damaged him more than it has me.' A long pause. Chiara stared at the grain of the table. 'But I have... I have the most vivid dreams.' She said it almost in a whisper. 'Violent, terrible nightmares. It's almost as if they're real.'

'Well, it must have been such a dreadful shock.'

'Yes.'

'Does your father know? About the nightmares?'

'No,' she said quickly. 'I haven't said anything. I don't want to bother him.'

58

'You wouldn't be bothering him. He cares about you greatly, I can see that.'

She eyed me levelly. 'Yes, he's a very good father, very protective of us, but I wouldn't want him to know. I wouldn't want him to think there was something wrong with me.'

I nodded. 'I understand.' And I did. It was why I'd concealed from my mother my own nightmares and visions, until they became such that I couldn't separate them from reality and I'd ended up in a psychiatric hospital where they attempted to affect a cure. I remembered little of those weeks. I did not wish to remember. I preferred to think of that person as somebody else. 'Well, you can tell me about them, Chiara, if you'd like to. It's nothing to be ashamed of, you know – having nightmares. It's our mind processing what's happened to us, and given what's happened, how your life has changed, it's perfectly understandable that you should be upset, even angry.' I thought again of the red scratches on her arms.

The bell rang signalling the second half of the concert was to begin.

'Do you think, Eva, that there will be war?'

'War?' The question seemed to come out of nowhere. 'Oh Chiara, I hope not.' I noticed the man and woman next to us had turned their heads. I should have spoken more quietly.

'I don't want Alessandro to have to go,' Chiara said in an almost whisper. 'He would go because he thinks that's what Father wants of him, what the country wants of him. But he's only a boy, and he wouldn't cope. He's far more fragile than he lets on.'

I leant forward. 'I can't believe there will be war. You don't remember what it was like after the Great War, but I do. Your father does.'

She shook her head. 'My father doesn't think like that.

59

Anyway, hadn't we best return to our seats?' She whispered: 'That nosy couple are watching us.'

I felt a lurch of anxiety. You never knew who might be government spies, or who might take it upon themselves to report anything that seemed unpatriotic. Perhaps because of that I didn't stop to question what Chiara meant when she said her father didn't think as we did. I merely led us back to our seats.

In the third week of September, Mirella arrived back at the apartment in the middle of the day when I was writing up some notes, her face swollen and red, her eyes empty. There was a new circular. Jews could no longer go to school. Nor could they be employed in any capacity in any Italian education, from nursery to university. She no longer had a job.

'No. I can't believe it. How?' Despite the newspaper articles, the broadcasts, I'd refused to accept it would happen. 'Oh, Mirella.'

I sat her down at the kitchen table, held her hand. Her face was blank, as though the life had drained away from her.

'This is madness,' I said. 'Pure madness. It was only, what, two years ago, that Il Duce was claiming Italy wasn't anti-Semitic – that anti-Semitism was a stupid idea.'

'Well,' she said dully, 'he changed his mind. And it seems people in this country will be whatever their government wants them to be, whatever the newspapers tell them.'

I knew she was right and I didn't know what to say. I could only lean forward so that our heads were nearly touching. 'I'm so sorry, Mirella.'

'The children,' she said softly. 'Little Gabriele and his sister, Eleanora Ottavia. They told them to leave. They sent them home. Just like that.'

I closed my eyes for a moment. 'What will they do?'

'I don't know. Set up their own schools, I suppose. Or leave. If they can.'

'You won't leave, will you?' I felt a pang of fear.

'I don't know, Chiara. This is my home. It's always been my home. But I'm no longer welcome here.'

'You are. This insanity can't last. It won't.'

'Of course it can. You know it can, Eva. You've seen it happen before.'

My heart dipped. I watched Bruno pecking at seeds in his cage. I remembered the day my father had arrived home, having been told he could no longer teach in the Slovenian school where he'd worked for years. There were to be no Slovenian teachers, not in Trieste. They must leave and they must teach – if they were to teach at all – in Italian, far away from where they'd grown up. 'That is how it must be,' my father had said. 'We must see it as an opportunity.'

Only later would I understand that this is how you begin to destroy people: you take away their jobs, their identity, their culture. You make them question who they are. I saw again the flickering fire of the Narodni Dom, the blank horror on my mother's face. It was happening again, but I couldn't leave again. This was the only place I'd ever felt at home. The only way out, I decided, was to burrow further in. Only that way could I be safe.

6

Now that I'm telling the story, I find it hard to understand how I couldn't have seen it all coming, but I didn't then. I was a different person, I suppose: younger, more naive, more hopeful, more desperate to be accepted and loved.

I saw some of it, though; I couldn't help but see it. Even from our suppressed news channels and overly bright newspapers, I could sense that the darkness was spreading across the entire continent, perhaps the entire world, like an inkpot left to spill across a page. On the radio, we heard Hitler's demented, terrifying raging as he threatened war with the Czechs. By late September, it seemed that the whole of Europe was holding its breath, waiting for what would come next. Statesmen assembled in Munich to try to smooth over Hitler's demands. The Italian papers talked of the great role Il Duce was taking at the conference, as the arbiter of peace. But this was the man who for years had spoken of making a nation of soldiers, a man waging war against his own people, a man who only dressed in military uniform. It hardly seemed hopeful. Would there really be another great war, despite the enduring pain of the last? It was the question that was whispered in bars and dining rooms across the city. 'Of course there'll be war,' Ettore told me. 'It's just a matter of when.'

Then, in the Cavallera household, something peculiar happened. One Thursday when I arrived to give Chiara her lesson, I heard male voices upstairs and Chiara told me that one of Dante's friends was visiting. We continued with her lesson as usual, and I hoped that in the meantime this friend would leave so that I could have my usual drink with Dante. He did not leave, however. Instead, Dante brought him into the piano room at the end of our lesson to introduce him, Zefiro following after them.

He was a tall man with gingery hair and moustaches, a broad, white face and pale eyes. I instinctively disliked him, though I couldn't really say why. Perhaps it was the close way he looked at me, or perhaps I just saw him as an intruder on our privacy. I was very polite, however, standing smiling as Dante explained to him who I was and told me that this was Massimo, his old housemate who lived close by, the friend whom he'd mentioned before.

'Let me get us all an *aperitivo*,' Dante said, and disappeared to the kitchen, leaving Chiara, Massimo and me to attempt conversation. Not, in fact, that Chiara spoke very much at all. Indeed, she didn't even look at the man and I wondered if she too disliked him for some reason, or if this was her general demeanour around strangers.

'Well, I must say I've been enjoying listening to your lesson. What's that piece you were playing at the end, there? Very catchy indeed.'

'It's Gershwin,' I said, when Chiara made no answer. 'It's from *Porgy and Bess*.'

'Ah yes, Gershwin. I used to play a little myself, you know,' he continued, 'but I was never much good. You, I understand, are very talented, Signorina Valenti.'

'Oh, I don't know about that.' I had the uncomfortable feeling that he was assessing me, judging me.

Dante reappeared with a bottle of Campari and a bottle of Vermouth. 'I've asked Greta to prepare us some food. Come, sit down.'

The men talked then of the work Massimo was engaged in at the Ministry of Education, Massimo explaining that they were reviewing the music programme in schools and what did I think should be covered? What were Chiara's views on what she was taught at school? She answered his questions quietly and deferentially, keeping her gaze down. I did my best to keep the conversation going and to make helpful observations.

A few minutes later, Greta entered the room bearing a tray of *supplì* – rice croquettes with tomato sauce and mozzarella. '*Eco!* Help yourselves.'

She couldn't have whipped these up in a few minutes, I thought. She must have known she'd be expected to provide refreshments. I felt a little as though I'd been ambushed. Indeed, looking about the room, I saw that it was even cleaner and brighter than usual, a large bunch of hydrangeas carefully arranged in the new crystal vase.

Dante moved the conversation on to Munich and to the reports that Il Duce was the hero of the hour – the only man who spoke all the requisite languages, the only one who really knew how to deal with Hitler. It was the first time he'd talked openly of our leader and I wondered how much of it was to impress his friend, and how much he truly felt. Could he not see, as I was at last beginning to, that as a nation, we'd been duped?

All at once, there was a darkening of the sky outside and a hum like that of a great machine. Only it was not a machine: it was insects, hundreds and hundreds – maybe thousands – of them, and they were swarming though the open window and

64

into the room. Wasps. They were wasps. It was Chiara who screamed first.

'What on earth?' Dante shouted. And then we were all yelling and screaming, Zefiro barking insanely, because the wasps were in the room and around our faces, like a black cloud, and they were stinging, stinging, stinging.

'Get out!' Dante yelled to us. 'Into the corridor! Eva, take Chiara!'

I dragged Chiara with me out of the living room and towards the bathroom, slapping at my arms and legs to fight off the wasps that crawled over me. I turned back for a moment and saw Dante shutting the living-room door and Massimo shouting at the insects that were flying out into the corridor, hitting them over and over again with a rolled-up newspaper.

Alessandro had appeared on the stairs. 'What's happening? What is it?'

'Wasps,' I told him. 'A huge swarm of them. Get back into your room. Shut the door. Greta, help us. We need something for the stings.'

She had her hands to her face. 'Yes. Come.'

In the bathroom, I ransacked the meticulous cabinet and found lotion, which I spread on Chiara's blistering arms and neck and on my own. Greta was crossing herself and muttering something about the house.

A moment later, I heard Dante shout: 'Eva! Greta!'

I ran back and saw that Massimo was leaning against the wall, his hand to his throat, his face bloated and pale. 'It's the damndest thing. I feel like my throat is closing up.'

'It's a reaction to the stings,' I said. 'It must be. We need to get the doctor at once.'

Dante stared at me. 'I'll get Alessandro to run to Dottor Falluci immediately.'

'Massimo, you must sit down.' I tried to lead him towards a

chair in the hallway, but his legs buckled beneath him and the next thing he was sprawled upon the ground.

'Dear God,' his words were peculiar and swollen, barely words at all.

I got him into the recovery position, as my mother had taught me, but there he seemed to lose consciousness altogether.

Meanwhile, the wasps that had escaped the living room were still buzzing furiously and Greta was hitting at them with a towel, shouting at them: '*Mascalzoni! Brutti! Vai al diavolo!*'

I looked at Massimo's face, his eyes wide, the pupils slid upwards, the skin around the eyes puffed out, and I felt sick with fear. He looked like a man possessed by some malignant force. Over the next few minutes, his face continued to swell, becoming a grotesque white mask, and I could hear the breath wheezing through his lungs, the sound growing ever more repugnant. I looked up at Chiara, who was standing outside the bathroom with a wet towel pressed to her neck. Her face, I saw – her lovely face – was covered in stings, red risings blistering the skin.

'Why did they come for us?' she whispered to me. 'Why did they come here?'

'I don't know, my love. Something must have attracted them. The food, maybe. The light.' But the truth was that I did not know.

The next twenty minutes seemed an eternity. I was terrified that the man would die, as I could hear his breathing growing more congested. Dante, his shirt sweat-soaked, no longer spoke but sat on the step beside his friend simply staring at him. He disappeared for a time – I assumed to smoke – and came back even more agitated. Greta was still fervently crossing herself and murmuring what I assumed were prayers.

And then the doctor was there, a fleshy, bespectacled man

running up the steps surprisingly quickly, Alessandro with him, opening a black leather case and giving the man an injection from a long glass syringe.

'*Dio!*' Alessandro said, staring. 'He looks like he's had it!'

'No, he'll be all right, I think. It's an allergy to the wasps' venom,' the doctor said after he had caught his breath and mopped his face with a handkerchief. 'You did well to find me immediately, or he might indeed have died. I've given him adrenaline to counter it, but we'll need to get him to hospital.'

'Of course,' Dante said, gathering himself. 'I'll drive him. Thank you for coming so quickly.' He was once again the calm, controlled father, the note of hysteria gone. 'And, Eva, thank you for all your help. We were extremely fortunate you were here.'

After they'd left and it was just Greta, the children and me in the house, I listened at the living-room door, but I could hear no buzzing within. It was as though the whole thing had never happened.

Very gently, I pushed the door open a crack. The normally ordered room was now in chaos, the table and chairs knocked over as we'd fought to escape, the food all over the floor, but the insects were seemingly gone. After a moment, however, I sensed movement above me. When I looked up, I saw the wasps were all still here, thousands of them, clinging quietly to the chandelier. They'd entirely covered it so that the whole thing looked like a moving mass of blackness. I had a feeling too that something else was there. Something besides the wasps. I felt it as a wingbeat in my chest.

I retreated to the hallway and closed the door again. Only then did I really feel the pain.

7

By the following day, my stings had largely settled down, but Massimo remained in hospital. I could see the strain of it on Dante's face when I visited. There were dark bruises under his eyes from lack of sleep, and though he spoke in his normal assured manner, I detected anxiety beneath.

'He's in the best possible hands, so I'm not worried, but, of course, it's terribly embarrassing. That it should have happened here. The poor man: I invite him to stay for a drink and he gets attacked by an army of angry insects!' He gave a short laugh. 'Extraordinary. But then, I suppose, we live in extraordinary times.'

'We do.' I still hadn't really talked to him of what was happening in Italy – about the Race Laws, the threat of war, the feeling that events were spiralling. I wanted to. I also wanted to ask him about the things Greta muttered about the house, about the peculiar sense I'd had the previous night. Somehow, though, I didn't dare.

'And you, of course,' he said. 'I feel terrible that you should have witnessed all that. You're not stung too badly, I hope, are you?'

'No, no, not too bad at all,' I said, although I must have had at least ten wasp stings and had slept little myself.

'I confess I'm glad you were here,' he said, his official voice slipping. 'You dealt with it all so quickly and calmly. I'm not sure Greta would have been able to manage on her own. I'm not sure I would either, to be honest.'

'Oh, I didn't do so very much.'

'You did. You knew at once what was wrong and what to do. You calmed Chiara, you calmed me, and for that I'm very grateful.'

The moment hung between us. I considered saying something, about the house, about the sense that things in the outside world were collapsing, but I found that I couldn't. Perhaps I feared I would push him away, this man whom I desired so much. 'How is Chiara this morning?'

'Well, how is she ever these days?' He smiled, shook his head. 'I think she's all right, but it was an awful shock, wasn't it? I've kept her home from school today just to be on the safe side. I think even robust Alessandro was a bit taken aback. I've rarely known him so quiet. Small mercies, perhaps!'

Robust. Was Alessandro robust? His sister had suggested he was vulnerable. I thought back to Alessandro's demeanour the previous day. He had not seemed distressed, I thought, but oddly excited. I increasingly thought he might be disturbed.

'May I see Chiara?'

'Of course, of course. Do go up to her in her room. I'm sure she'll be pleased to see you.'

I turned and climbed the stairs. I knew as I walked he was watching me.

I found Chiara sitting up in bed, a book in her hands, a blank look on her red-blotched face. She had reacted badly to the stings, for they'd risen up on her arms in welts. She smiled, however, to see me.

'How are you feeling?'

She shrugged. 'All right, I suppose. But I can't stand seeing anyone with my face like this. They laugh at me enough as it is.'

'Who laughs at you?'

'The girls at school.'

'Which girls?'

She shrugged. 'Oh, you know, the popular ones. The ones who everyone listens to.'

Yes, I knew all about those sorts of girls. There had been a clique of them at my own school: seeking out anyone that was slightly different, and laughing, hurting, whispering.

'What do they say? Why would they laugh at you?'

She shrugged again. 'They're just like that.'

'Well, maybe we'll set the wasps on them.'

She smiled at that and I wished she'd told me about the girls before. Then she said: 'It had to happen in our house, didn't it? No one else's. Ours.'

I looked away from her. 'It was bad luck, I think, Chiara. The windows were open; there was food inside. They must have been passing and decided the living room seemed a tempting prospect.'

In fact, I was not so sure. I'd asked the science teacher at school, Gianni, whether he'd heard of anything similar happening before and he'd said that they must have been bees because wasps didn't swarm like that, not unless there was a nest. 'Wasps don't just fly around in great hordes attacking houses,' he had claimed. 'I tell you: they must have been bees.' They had not been bees, though. I'd been stung by bees as a child and remembered the fatness of their bodies, the little black stings they left in your skin.

'There's an awful lot of bad luck in this house, then,' Chiara said.

I thought of Adelina's photograph in the hall, the wasps on the chandelier. Was it bad luck, or was it something else? I squeezed Chiara's hand.

She stared at me. 'Will you come back tomorrow?'

'Yes, if you like.'

'If I was you, I wouldn't. I wouldn't come back here ever again.'

'Chiara! Don't be ridiculous. Of course I'll come back.'

'You mustn't feel that you have to.'

'Well, I do. And I will.' I gave her a bemused smile, but she did not smile back. Her eyes were very dark and still. 'I'll come back tomorrow evening, after my classes finish. All right? I've a book you might like to read.'

I could have run from the family at that point. I could have made my excuses, claimed I had too many classes, or pretended that I was moving away from Rome. But I didn't. Instead, that strange episode, the glimpse of Dante's vulnerability, his gratitude, Chiara's fear, made me want to stay, made me want to try to help. I didn't see then that she was warning me.

After the disaster came the semblance of order and calm. We heard that at the Munich conference, France and England had accepted that Hitler should be allowed to annex the Sudetenland, feeding Czechoslovakia to the Führer in the hope it would sate his appetite, and proclaiming 'peace with honour'. It didn't feel like peace, though. It felt like a lull, a break in the storm. The air still hummed with tension.

I visited Chiara several times over those days, just as I'd said I would, until her stings had finally settled down, leaving only small red marks. She seemed grateful for my company, but still very quiet. We played duets together – Haydn's 'Piano

71

Concerto in C', Ravel's 'Ma Mère l'Oye' – sitting very close, and sometimes she would laugh, hinting at the girl she'd once been. Zefiro would often sit with us, listening, his tail thumping against the floor. Alessandro would sometimes watch us too. But it was not like when my mother had listened to me play. It made me feel vaguely uncomfortable. I wasn't sure what he wanted.

I would like to say that I went to the house just for Chiara, but, of course, it was also to see Dante. By that time, it was as though something within me had caught light: I longed to see his dark eyes, his tanned skin, smell the rich tobacco-tinged scent of him. I'd never desired a man in such a way before and it surprised me. It had only ever been silly flirtations with young men my age; relationships that began simply because of their persistence, and which fizzled out when I gave nothing away. Dante seemed so much more than those boys: wiser, cleverer, more self-assured. He was a man who knew what he wanted and what was to be done; he was a man who already had his own home and family, a clear identity and purpose, and that made me feel safe at a time when everything else was in chaos. If I found that he was in the house, which he mostly was, as I visited in the evening after school, I felt the heat flow to my face, sometimes down my body. Stupid, of course, I told myself it was stupid, but that didn't seem to make it any better.

I couldn't tell how Dante felt about me, exactly. He didn't look me over as many men did, their gaze lingering on my breasts, nor did he give excessive and embarrassing compliments. I wouldn't have wanted that, of course, but I would have welcomed some sign of desire and he gave little away. Nevertheless, I sensed that he wanted me there. He always seemed pleased or satisfied to see me and always insisted on me taking a drink with him after I'd been to see Chiara. We'd discuss how she was and how Massimo was faring, which was fortunately a good deal better. He'd been allowed home and seemed comfortable. Dante had insisted on paying his medical bills. 'Hopefully, the old man will forgive me!' The chandelier, he said, had been quite ruined when men came in to destroy the wasps. 'A shame. My wife bought it in Geneva some years ago. I hadn't wanted to let it go.'

I felt a tinge of unease, hearing that, but I decided to push it aside. 'Chiara seems a little better.'

'Seems, yes.'

'What do you mean?'

'She's begun sleepwalking again. She hadn't done that for months.' He blew cigarette smoke out of the corner of his mouth. 'Not that it's so uncommon, of course, but it's unnerving to discover that things have been moved during the night, or to wake up and find your own daughter moving about the house like a wraith.'

'She's definitely asleep?'

'Oh yes. Eyes open, but asleep. I worry that she'll fall down the stairs or injure herself in some way.'

'Have you...' I hesitated, 'spoken to a doctor about her?'

'A psychiatrist or something, you mean? God, no. The girl will snap out of it soon enough, I imagine. It's a difficult age. A difficult age to be motherless.'

A pause. I didn't want to press the issue, but it seemed unlikely Chiara would simply snap out of her disturbed behaviour. I certainly hadn't.

'I think she's unhappy at school as well,' I ventured. 'I think some of the other girls aren't very kind to her.'

'Really? Well, that's girls for you, isn't it? At least boys will have their fights in an openly aggressive way. When Alessandro comes home with a mouth full of blood, as he does rather too often these days, I know exactly what's happened. With girls, it's all so much more insidious and devious; game-playing.'

'Maybe.' I knew what he meant – I'd experienced it myself as a girl and a foreigner – the whispers, the silences, the cruel laughter. 'But boys can be devious too.' Hadn't Dante told me himself that Alessandro had lied about the broken figurine? And there was something disingenuous about him, something askew. Dante wasn't, however, listening.

'I shall talk to the school. They know what she's been through – what we've all been through. Damn it, I should have picked up on this earlier.'

'You can't blame yourself for these things. You've all been doing so very well.'

'Thank you, Eva, but I don't think I've been doing very well at all. Look at the state of my children, one sleepwalking, the other regularly in fights.' He blew his cheeks out. 'It was my wife who made this household, really. Who kept it all going; kept me going. She had this incredible knack of working people out – what they wanted, what they needed.' He lit another cigarette. 'And it's not the time to be a bachelor, not in Il Duce's Italy. I'm no longer the sort of man the Fascist government wants.'

He was talking, I knew, of Mussolini's great idea that Italy should be a nation producing a constant line of children: little soldiers and future mothers.

'It seems as though a lot of people are not the sort of people this government wants.' I said it quietly. It was the most I'd dared say about the situation in Italy. The Race Laws. Mirella. The persecution of anyone who was slightly different.

Dante frowned. 'Well, they say he's building us up for great-ness, reconstructing the nation, and we're all meant to play our part.' He hesitated, perhaps reading my expression. 'But we don't always want to play the part that's chosen for us, do we? We like to feel we have some control.' He met my eye and I felt quite sure then that he understood what my concerns were. More than that, he felt them too.

74

When I left the room, I found Greta standing in the hallway, very still.

'Are you all right, Greta? You gave me quite a scare, there, standing in the half-darkness!'

'It's not the girl moving things at night,' she said quietly.

'I'm sorry?'

'It's not Chiara. She sleepwalks yes, but it's not her that makes things move.'

I felt my stomach plummet.

'Things move during the daytime too,' she whispered. 'He knows that. This past month, I've seen a plate jump off a shelf with my own two eyes. I'm imagining that, am I?'

I remembered my own imaginings – the insects, the noises, the certain sense that my organs were shifting inside me. I knew all too well that what we saw and felt was not necessarily what was there. Nevertheless, I didn't like it.

There came the sound of footsteps.

'Oh good, you're still here.' It was Dante, holding my gloves. 'You left these in the salon and it's a chilly evening. I wouldn't want you to be cold.' He pressed them into my hands and smiled.

Greta had moved away.

I went directly from the Cavallera house to the school where we were meeting to rehearse. When I arrived, Ettore and Mirella were already in their chairs, playing, and they continued as I came in and took my place at the piano, finally joining in. We practised more these days, talked less. Music was easier than reality, an easier way of being together.

Ettore smiled at me as he drew the final stroke with his bow. 'How's your boyfriend, Eva?'

I blushed crimson. 'He isn't my boyfriend!'

'No? Spending a lot of time at his house though, aren't you?' He exchanged a glance with Mirella.

'Poor Signor Malinconico!' They both began to giggle.

'Oh, for goodness sake, you two! I've been helping Chiara.'

'Of course you have,' Ettore said, affecting a serious voice.

'I have! She's not been well and I promised—'

Ettore had launched into a rendition of an Irving Berlin song:

'How much do I love you?

I'll tell you no lie

How deep is the ocean?

How high is the sky?'

The two of them howled with laughter as I sat, arms folded, glowering at them. 'You are both very childish.'

'So,' Ettore said, 'when do we get to meet him?'

'Never?'

'Oh, come on,' said Mirella. 'We need to judge him for ourselves. Assess his handsomeness. Bring him out for dinner with us!'

'Mirella, honestly, I can't. It's not like that.' I wasn't sure I was ready for them to meet Dante. I couldn't trust them not to embarrass me or let slip something about my origins, my past, and, truth be told, I wasn't sure he would like them. He was so much older than us, so much more mature.

'Okay, okay. Let's play the Rachmaninov,' Ettore said.

My fingers played the notes, but my mind strayed to who else in the school was aware of my Slovene family. I hadn't set out to conceal my background, exactly, but in fact very few people knew.

'We're not bad,' Ettore said, as we finished the piece. 'Maybe we should hire ourselves out at weddings and parties. Bring in a little extra cash.'

'Aryans can't employ Jews anymore, remember?' Mirella said

lightly. 'We'd have to play at bar mitzvahs only.' She'd lost all her private work now. Her only income came from teaching music classes in one of the hastily created Jewish schools, where the children who'd been barred from mainstream schools were now receiving an education.

Ettore passed his hand over his face. His attempt at levity had failed. 'How do they think people are going to manage, eh? How are Jewish people meant to support themselves?'

'They're not. They're supposed to leave. And you know what? That's exactly what I'm going to do.'

'Mirella, no.' My heart fell.

'What choice do I have, Eva? Stay here and hide, relying on you to pay all our bills? I can't do that. I don't want to do that.' She began to unwind her bow. 'You know they're taking our names out of the phone books now?' She laughed. 'We're quietly being erased.'

I did know that. I knew too of the clerks, college professors, delivery boys, all dismissed from their jobs because they were Jewish. I'd heard of men who'd thrown themselves from the roofs of their offices after their businesses were taken from them.

'I have to leave now, while I still stand a chance of being accepted by another country. I need to get my parents out too before we end up like those poor German Jews.' By that stage, thousands were fleeing Germany and Austria and being refused entry to other countries. 'The Germans are giving all Jewish citizens new passports with the letter "J" stamped in red. You know why? Sweden and Switzerland asked them to do it so they could easily identify Jews and refuse them entry!'

'It isn't just Jews they're clearing out, you know,' Ettore said. 'It's political opponents, homosexuals.' He lit another cigarette. 'Italy's on the same track.'

I hugged my arms around myself, suddenly cold. 'You don't

77

hear people talking of it that way, though,' I said. 'You never hear people saying we should get rid of people.'

'Not yet, no,' Mirella said quietly.

I got up from the piano and knelt next to her. 'What can we do to help?'

She was crying now. 'You can help me work out how to get out, how to get my parents out. You can stop making me feel bad for not being like you, for not thinking I can just hunker down and hide who I am.'

My stomach contracted. 'If you'd seen what I had ...'

'I know, I know. And you were a child. You did what your parents told you. But you're not a child anymore, Eva.'

I stood up, keeping my gaze on the floor. The silence stretched between us.

'Have you told Cavallera?' Ettore asked me quietly. 'That you're Slovene?'

I didn't reply. I sensed that he and Mirella were looking at each other.

'Eva, you must tell him.'

I snapped my head up. 'And you, Ettore. You tell everyone what you are, who you are, do you? You wear your heart on your sleeve?'

For a long moment, we stared at one another and I felt the shame seep over me for having spoken to him like that. Of course he couldn't reveal who he truly was, because the world was desperately unfair.

I put my hands over my face. 'I'm sorry. Forgive me.'

He stood up, flexed his shoulders. 'No, you're right, I hide who I am too. But not from the people I love. And, unlike you, I'm doing something about what's going on in this country.'

'What do you mean, "doing something"?'

'Doing things. Changing things.' He started unwinding his cello bow.

I felt very afraid. I thought of the men I'd seen strung up on lamp posts, the stories I'd heard of torture cells, airless chambers of death. 'Ettore, I know we all think what's happening is wrong, but—'

'*Thinking* something is wrong is no longer enough, Eva. Look at what's happening here. Look at what's happening all over Europe.'

Mirella too began to pack up her violin. 'I hate this country,' she said very quietly. 'I hate what it's doing to all of us.'

The autumn went on like that, things tightening incrementally, seemingly inevitably, into a stranglehold. In October, as the city prepared for the commemorations of the March on Rome, government agents appeared everywhere – in the banks, in the bars, loitering in the streets. You could recognise them by their thick necks spilling from their shirts, and their heavy black boots, as they scanned the crowds for dissent.

For years, our activities had been observed, our correspondence opened, our names kept on file. For years, we'd been terrified of the shadowy organisation that repressed anti-fascism. OVRA, they called it, like *piovra*, the mythical octopus, its tentacles reaching into our lives, squeezing out any sign of subversion. Now, however, things felt far closer, the belt tightened, the knives sharpened. Everyone had heard of someone who'd been taken away, somebody sent into *confino* – a friend of a friend, an uncle, a former colleague. Everyone was on alert, knowing that any stray comment would be picked up and acted on. Even thinking differently began to feel dangerous.

I hadn't wanted to attend the commemorations at all, but Carmela and Serafina, two of the other teachers from school, were insistent that we should all go together after work. They were about the same age as me, both single, both hopeful, and now that Mirella was less often at home, we were spending more time together. The parade would be full of handsome officers, Carmela promised, and she'd heard that presents would be given out – mementoes, badges, chocolate, cigarettes. 'Come on. We'll just go for a bit.'

The whole affair was far more ordered and elaborate than it had been in previous years, the Piazza del Popolo swathed in flags and banners. Mussolini was, I thought, making a point: Italy was not a country to be ignored; it was on a par with Germany.

We stood on the steps above the square as the parade passed. First came the Fascist Youth movements – the *Balilla* and *Avanguardisti* marching with their flags and boots, their replica guns and their genuine zeal, flanked by blackshirted standard-bearers. Alessandro might well be there, I thought, but I couldn't see him among the hundreds of heavy-booted boys. Then came a huge military band who moved past amid a roar of hand-clapping, vivas and cheers, playing the music to '*Giovinezza*', throwing and catching batons.

My eye was on a twirling silver baton when I saw a flash of something else in the crowd ahead of me – the green of a jacket as someone fell. It was a young man and, with a jolt of horror, I realised he was being dragged along the ground by a group of Blackshirts. I saw flashes of his green jacket and blood-streaked face as he was pulled further from the parade, and I broke away from Carmela and Serafina, following the men as they lugged the man towards a wooded area. Several people turned to look, but no one did anything to help even as the Blackshirts – some with truncheons, some with fists and feet – began to brutally beat the man, who lay curled on the pavement like an injured animal, his arms about his head, shuddering under the blows. For a moment, I stood frozen as I did in my dreams of the Narodni Dom burning, watching as the men kicked and hit and spat, but then something within me propelled me forward. I ran away from the parade and towards the men. God knows what I intended to do, but in any event, I was too late. A van drew up and the man was bundled into it like a rag doll, the Blackshirts climbing in after.

I stood staring as the vehicle pulled away, my heart beating too fast, too hard.

'Eva?' A hand on my arm. 'I thought it was you.' It was Dante, his expression grim. 'Let's get away from here.' He led me up the street and towards the Pincio Gardens, where we sat side by side on a wall. 'Are you all right?'

The man's face was still before me, covered with blood. 'Why were they beating him, Dante?'

'I don't know. An anti-fascist, perhaps.' He lit a cigarette.

For a minute or so, we sat without speaking. I wasn't capable of making conversation. The intensity and suddenness of the violence had horrified me – the sight of his face recurred again and again in my mind. I told myself I should have been used to it, inured to it. Since my childhood, the *squadristi* had been purging and beating any dissenters with their boots and petrol and castor oil. I'd heard enough tales in my time of men beaten and tied to trees or strung upside down from meat hooks. I'd seen patches of blood in the streets. Yet I felt hollowed out. It had been so very close.

'Not a thing for you to see. I'm sorry.'

'What will happen to him?' I was thinking of Ettore, Ettore and his claims to be 'doing something'. I was sure it was Pietro who'd drawn him in – him and his journalist friends. What if they were discovered? What if that had been Ettore, pounded and kicked in the street?

'I don't know,' Dante said.

We sat in silence, listening to the distant roar of the parade, the tinkling of a nearby fountain.

'What were you planning to do, Eva, running over to him like that?'

81

I shook my head. 'Nothing, really. I just wanted them to stop. I couldn't bear it.' I swallowed. 'You must think me a fool.'

'No, I think you a gentle and empathetic young woman who always wants to help, just as you've helped Chiara, helped me.' He sat back. 'But you must be careful all the same. These are dangerous times. I wouldn't want you to come to any harm.'

'What is happening to Italy?' I said very quietly. 'What are we becoming?'

Dante turned to look at me. 'Eva, we have to keep our heads.'

'But why is what counts as an Italian, as a citizen, being narrowed into a weapon? Why must there be such violence against anyone deemed other?'

'Il Duce must know what he's doing.'

'Must he?'

'Look, he's doing what he needs to do in order to get an alliance with Germany that will protect us; that will mean that Italy gets the fuel and food it needs.'

'But at what cost?' I said quietly.

I considered telling Dante of my own background, my own experiences. I even tried the words out in my own head: *I should tell you, by the way, that I think you misunderstood me when I'd said I'd grown up in Trieste.* But I couldn't bring myself to say the words, because it would mean admitting that I'd misled him, and what if it angered him? What if this man who'd finally begun to allow me into his life decided to push me away? I couldn't face it, not then. Everything seemed too precarious, as though balanced on the edge of a shelf waiting to smash to the ground.

All at once, I remembered what Greta had told me. 'You know, Greta told me last week that things had been moving themselves in the house. That plates had been jumping off the dresser.'

I thought Dante might be annoyed or perturbed, but instead he began to laugh. 'Greta, much as we adore her, is full of nonsense and superstition. She is getting old and forgetful and she's dropping things. She doesn't, of course, want to admit that: it's easier to blame the plates.'

'I see.' But I wasn't entirely convinced.

'I should replace her, really – pay her a retirement sum and hire someone who can manage the place. But then again, she is so very loyal. I've known her all my life, you see. She worked for my mother and came to us after she died.'

'When was that?'

'Oh, five years ago? And anyone who could put up with my mother deserved some kind of reward!'

'What do you mean?'

He hesitated. 'I mean she was not a warm person, my mother. Not an easy person. Greta was far kinder to me when I was young than she was – than either of my parents were, really.' He stood up. 'But that's all a long time ago now and you don't need to hear about my rather glum childhood, not after what you've seen today. You're shaken.'

'You've been very kind, thank you. I feel much better,' I lied.

He smiled and I was sure he'd seen straight through me. 'Well, I'd best try to find Alessandro. Which way are you walking?'

'Back to Trastevere. I'll get the tram.'

'Let me at least walk with you to your stop.'

We strolled out of the park and along the Viale Gabriele D'Annunzio, past walls plastered with film posters: glamorous actors gazing down at us.

'Have you seen *Stasera alle Undici*?' Dante asked.

'The film? No, I confess I rarely go to the picture house.'

'Ah, well you must see it. It was shot at the Cinecittà Studios

83

here in Rome and it's quite marvellous. In fact, let's go. At the weekend. I'd been meaning to see it again and I'm a member of a fine little cinema near the house.'

My heart jumped. He'd said it so smoothly, as though it were just a small thing, but, of course, it wasn't — at least it wasn't to me. 'Well, that would be lovely, but I wouldn't want you to put yourself out if you already had plans.'

'No, no, I insist. Let's say Sunday afternoon, shall we? It's a nice place in Piazza Farnese. I believe it's showing at three o'clock so I can meet you there just before. In the bar.'

It was all done so casually, and so apparently spontaneously, that I scolded myself for the fluttering sensation in my chest.

As I walked back to our apartment, the excitement merged with anxiety, as I thought again of the man in green and what must be happening to him now. When I pictured his face, I saw instead Ettore's: pale, covered in blood.

8

The Imperiale was nothing like the cinemas I was used to, where vendors sold salted pumpkin seeds wrapped in newspaper to groups of laughing teenagers and where the carpeted floors were littered with peanut shells. In the Imperiale, there was a fine-looking bar, all steel columns and glass, where elegant men and women sat sipping coffee or drinking cognac from glasses and cut-glass tumblers. I felt terribly self-conscious entering the place. Everyone was dressed far better than I was, the men in perfectly tailored suits, the women in silk blouses and stylish little hats, smoking from long cigarette holders in a way women of my class would never dare do in public.

After a moment, I caught sight of Dante, but he hadn't yet seen me. He was standing at the bar talking to a woman in a silver fur with a little black bowler hat perched on her head, and he was laughing at something she was saying. He was so handsome, I thought. Far too handsome for me. I couldn't understand how I hadn't thought that when I first met him. I stood very still watching, wondering whether I should just turn around and walk back down the steps to the street. I didn't belong there. I wasn't quick enough, however, for Dante looked up and saw me. 'Eva! There you are!'

The woman turned to look at me and I saw that she was attractive, perhaps in her late thirties, with red lipstick and highly shined hair. She gave me an inquisitive smile, but Dante did not introduce us. Instead, he came over to where I was standing and said, 'Eva. How lovely you're looking. Let me take your coat.'

He ushered me to the cloakroom, where he gave my coat to a boy in blue livery and then insisted on ordering me a drink. By the time we'd returned to the bar, the woman in the silver fur was sitting down on a high stool with a group of friends.

I accepted a vermouth with ice, which I sipped while Dante told me about the movie we were about to see and the others the director had filmed. He knew everyone, it seemed, from the man serving drinks to the various men and women who entered the bar, slapping the men on the shoulder, kissing women's hands. Then he would turn back to me and continue his rhapsody on the director, Oreste Biancoli, and the whole of Cinecittà, the enormous studios founded by Il Duce. We didn't speak about Chiara, or Alessandro, or Massimo, or anything that had happened in the house, only of the glamorous world of film.

After a few minutes, a bell rang, signalling we were to take our seats. We entered the auditorium, which was far finer than the screening rooms I'd visited before. An usher showed us to luxurious seats of red and green velvet, each with their own little table for drinks. Not long after we'd settled, the Luce newsreel started up, and there was Il Duce himself, represented in jerky black and white, speaking of the conquests of the regime. At his appearance, everyone in the audience stood up and began to clap and some to cheer, gradually quietening down to listen what he was saying, which was something about cinema as a weapon. Then there was a clip in which Mussolini was talking to the directors of the film, suggesting that they make certain cuts to strengthen it.

Had he really had a hand in the film, I wondered, or was this, too, simply propaganda? Il Duce once again as the super-man who could do it all: lead the army, reap the fields, rebuild the Roman Empire. I glanced at Dante, wondering what he thought. The light from the film flickered over the contours of his face. He was staring at the screen, his face unreadable, his eyes bright.

There was a short pause while the projectionist put in the film reel and then the titles started up, the names of the actors appearing in huge letters on the screen: John Lodge, Francesca Braggiotti, Ivana Claar.

For a time, I became lost in the world of the film and its characters – the beautiful society lady, the gangsters with whom she becomes embroiled, the man with whom she falls in love. Every now and again, however, I'd become aware of Dante's presence so close beside me, the smell of his cologne, his arm resting on the seat. Occasionally, he would lean closer to me to murmur some explanation about what a certain character meant, or where something had been filmed, and I couldn't quite believe I was here with him; that he had wanted to invite me.

The whole afternoon had a sort of strange, enchanted qual-ity about it. I was carried away to another world of beauty and possibility and felt myself to be a different, braver person. For an hour or so, I forgot about the strain and worry of the world outside and existed only there, in the company of the characters in the film and the intelligent man just a few inches to my left who, for some reason, wanted to spend his Sunday afternoon with me. I thought nothing of my own failures and shortcomings, nor of the approaching storm. The credits rolled, the lights came up, but some of the magic had lodged within me, or maybe I'd drunk too much vermouth.

I stayed with Dante for a further drink at the bar, though I sipped this one more slowly to make it last, and we talked of what we'd seen and what it meant and how much we'd enjoyed it. 'I knew, you see,' he told me. 'I knew you'd enjoy it, that you'd understand it.'

I was still thinking about that as I walked home, and the night no longer seemed so cold.

I went on for some weeks like that. Even the queues for the food shops and the news of an ambassador shot dead in Austria didn't bring me back to earth. It all seemed to happen in a different world that wasn't part of mine. The images of the women on screen continued to flit through my head – their perfect bow lips and their bias-cut satin gowns. Though I should have been saving my money, I decided to permit myself a little luxury. I walked about the counters of a perfumier's shop and allowed myself to be flattered and cajoled by an immaculately made-up shop girl who complimented me on my high cheekbones and clear skin and showed me an array of different lipsticks in golden cases. At last, I chose one in a beautiful pink colour: Diva, it was called. It seemed part of the magic. When I got back to the apartment, I locked myself in the bathroom and practised putting it on, blotting my lips with tissue.

My mother, I remembered, had had only one lipstick, in a dull red colour, mostly dried up for she rarely used it, though if there was a special occasion, such as a christening or wedding, she'd use a little to redden her cheeks. Mostly, though, it stayed at the back of her drawer, unused. The foundation she brought out often enough, though – heavy, ugly stuff, thick enough to cover up the bruises. I would not think of that, though, but of now.

★

On the afternoon I was due to visit the house to give Chiara her piano lesson, I took my time curling my hair and applying some of the pink lipstick, rubbing a little on my cheeks. I inspected my reflection in the stained bathroom mirror. I was hardly Greta Garbo, but I was pleased with my appearance – the kohl made my eyes look larger, and the lipstick defined my lips in a way that made me look bolder.

I'd hoped to make it out of the apartment without a fuss, but Mirella missed nothing. She took my chin in her hand and turned my face from one side to the other. 'Are you sure you know what you're doing, Eva?' she asked.

I shook her off. 'I'm not doing anything. I just wanted to look nice, that's not unreasonable, is it? A girl is entitled to make something of herself.'

'He's much older than you, isn't he?'

'So? Maybe I'm bored of boys our age.'

Mirella folded her arms and leant back against the wall. 'You, with all your experience.'

'Mirella! Stop bullying me!' She was right, though, that I'd had few relationships; barely any real ones in fact. 'I've just never really met anyone I liked before.' Or at least I'd never met anyone I liked so much that I could dare contemplate getting close to them. And Dante had somehow made it seem so easy, as though it was the most natural thing in the world.

'Darling, you've never given anyone a chance.' She paused. 'Why do you like him?'

'Well, he's been very kind to me. He seems, I don't know, confident, reassuring.'

'With a nice house.'

'Yes, all right, with a nice house!' I glared at her.

'And a ready-made family.'

I didn't reply to that. She didn't know how it felt never to have had a proper family who loved one another, nor quite how alone I felt.

'You know he'll expect you to look after his children, don't you? And provide him with lots of lovely chubby babies into the bargain.'

My cheeks were now crimson. 'Mirella, please stop trying to embarrass me.'

'I'm not trying to embarrass you, *cara mia*; I'm trying to make you think about whether this is what you want; that you know what you're signing up for.'

'I like him, all right? I think he likes me. It's nothing more than that at the moment.' But I hoped it would be. It was, I suppose, what I'd always wanted: to be part of a family that needed me, that was so different from my own. To feel protected, wanted, loved.

'But do you really want to form an attachment to someone here? In Italy? Do you really want to make your bed in a country that's throwing out people it decides are racially inferior? How well do you even know this man?'

'I don't see why you're making such a fuss about this. Nothing has happened between us and maybe nothing will. Can't you just let me have a little happiness?'

'I want you to have happiness, trust me I do, Eva, but sometimes you don't think things through.'

I looked away from her. 'Because you think I'm stupid, just like Bruno does.'

She spoke more quietly. 'No. Because I think I won't be here for much longer, and I need to make sure this man is going to look after you.'

I looked back at Mirella and saw that her eyes were full of tears. I'd been helping her look for work opportunities abroad, in the papers and through friends. I didn't accept, though, that she would leave. That she would really have to.

All of my annoyance evaporated and I hugged Mirella, my face pressed against her cheek. 'I think he's a good man, Mirella. And you have enough to worry about, enough to do. You mustn't worry about me.'

'I'm going to tell Bruno to keep a check on this fellow, and peck out his eyes if he needs to.'

As I shut the door behind me, I began to cry, knowing that I was ruining my make-up.

By the time I reached the Cavallera house, my tears had dried, but I was still distracted, so that when I entered the house I wasn't at first aware that anything was wrong. The sensation only came upon me later. I stood in the hallway staring again at the photograph of Adelina, and then at my own face in the hallway mirror. I cursed myself for my silly lipstick. I looked, I thought, like a child who'd been trying on her mother's make-up. I took out my handkerchief and rubbed the lipstick off. Just as I did so, Dante appeared in the hallway and smiled at me.

'Checking you look pretty? Well, good news: you do.'

'Not like her, though.' The words rushed out without my meaning them to. 'Your wife, I mean. She was very beautiful.' I nodded towards the photograph.

The smile stayed on Dante's mouth but left his eyes. 'Yes, she was,' he said. 'Everybody said so. But yours is a different kind of beauty. A simpler kind. And you don't need that lipstick.'

He'd seen me, then. I blushed.

'Come. I have something to show you.' He walked through to the living room where the wasps had attacked, though there was no trace of them now. In place of the old-fashioned chandelier was a new one, dripping crystal, sharp and bright and modern.

'What do you think? Magnificent, isn't it? The old one was

91

damaged, as you know, and I thought I needed a change.'

I stared up at the chandelier. It was far larger than the original light and, I thought, grotesque.

'Goodness, it's quite something.'

'Isn't it? It's the same style as Ciano has at their villa.' Count Galeazzo Ciano, Foreign Minister, Il Duce's son-in-law, the setter of the latest fashions. 'A little extravagant, perhaps, but I'm celebrating.'

'Oh, yes?'

'Yes. I've received something of a promotion, to a new post.'

'Well, that's wonderful, Dante. Congratulations.'

'Thank you, Eva. I confess, it's a relief. I'd worried that my being a bachelor would destroy my job prospects, but clearly they've decided to give me a chance. I am trying to make a new beginning of things. A new chapter. A better one.' He met my eye and suddenly looked down, a little shy.

My heart skipped.

'I'm hoping too that things will start to look a little rosier for Chiara,' he said quietly. 'I've spoken to the school and told them they need to up their game, bring those girls to book. I'm very glad to you for bringing that to my attention.'

I nodded, but my stomach curdled at the thought that this would have got back to Chiara. 'You didn't tell her, though? That I'd said anything?'

'No, no. I've not mentioned it to Chiara at all. Best not to worry her. I'm grateful to you for trusting me, however. Not all women are like that. They'll assume the worst of men.' He smiled and it was, I thought, an unhappy smile.

I thought again of Adelina and wanted at once to know everything about her – about her friendships and her desires, what she'd thought, what she'd feared. It was a sudden and powerful feeling that grabbed me from nowhere. I looked again at the chandelier, the fall of crystal, and had a clear picture of

Adelina in a black dress walking down the steps. Where had that come from?

At that moment, Chiara appeared where my imaginary Adelina had been, her hands behind her back.

'There she is: my lovely girl. I'll leave you two to your lesson.' Dante gave a humorous little bow and exited the room.

Without saying anything to me, Chiara took her seat at the piano and began playing Grieg. It was while Chiara was playing that I noticed it – a sense of the air being heavy, full not of insects this time, but of something else, some energy. I had a strong sense of being watched, of whispers that I couldn't quite hear. And yet there was no one there, no one but Il Duce and the King staring out from their picture frames and I began to fear that it was my old illness, rising again to haunt me.

Abruptly, Chiara stopped playing. She was looking at me.

'Is something wrong, Chiara?'

'I don't know. Do you think there is?'

Had she felt it too? That strange sensation in the air? Or did she know I'd told Dante about the bullying and feel that I'd betrayed her. 'I'm not sure I know what you mean, Chiara.'

She began playing again, faster this time, faster and faster until she lost control of the piece and the notes scattered into discord. Then she sat very still.

'You're angry with me,' I said.

She remained motionless, her gaze still on the piano keys. 'You don't want to be part of this family. I don't need another mother.'

My chest tightened. What had she overheard, or intuited? Was it the cinema visit? 'I don't think anyone is suggesting ...' I floundered. 'I don't know why you would say that.'

She finally looked at me and I realised she was crying, tears spilling and rolling down her cheeks.

'Oh, Chiara. I only want you to be happy. I'm not trying to

take anything from you or replace your mother. I know how much you loved her.'

'You don't know anything at all!' With a thud, she shut the lid of the piano and ran from the room.

Watching her, my heart began to fall. I had somehow ruined the fragile friendship that had begun to grow between us.

For a minute or so, I sat still in the silence. I did not feel, though, as if I'd been left alone. A tendril of fear crept down my back. Something else was watching.

The following morning was bright but cold. I dressed in my muffler and gloves and walked quickly over the Ponte Garibaldi and the grey-green Tiber towards the school, keeping my face down against the wind, thinking again of Chiara's sudden turn against me and how I might set it all right.

On the other side of the bridge, I stopped at my usual cafe to collect a pastry. Inside, the air was a warm rush of cigarette smoke and toasted coffee and chicory. Ettore was there in the corner, as he sometimes was, a newspaper spread before him, a cigarette in his mouth. His face, however, was grey and when I approached him, he did not smile. 'Have you seen this?' He pointed at the paper – it was *L'Osservatore Romano*, the daily newspaper of Vatican City State, which retained some independence.

I glanced about me, in case anyone was watching or listening. Two men were at the bar drinking espresso, paying us little attention. Above them, the standard sign: '*Qui non si parla di politica*'.

'Well? Have you seen what's happening, Eva, or do you still have your head in the sand?'

'Ettore,' I cautioned, but he wasn't listening.

He stabbed his finger at the headline. *JEWISH HOMES SET ON FIRE*. 'Homes, shops, businesses, synagogues,' he whispered. 'All across Germany, on Wednesday night.'

I took the seat next to him and stared at the picture below the article — a grainy photograph of a row of shops, their windows shattered, as couples walked unconcernedly past. I felt a jolt of fear. 'Who did this?'

'Who do you think?' he said. 'Goebbels is claiming they were spontaneous outbursts of anger at that young Jew who shot the German diplomat. But this' — he thrust his finger at the newspaper — 'there's nothing spontaneous about this. All different cities, all the same night. Scores of people killed.'

A cough. The proprietor was drying glasses, but I could see he was looking over at us with concern.

I took Ettore by the arm. 'Let's talk outside.'

Ettore glanced about. 'Yes, yes, all right.'

He pocketed his cigarettes, stuffed his paper into his coat and followed me. We stood outside in the shelter of the cafe awning and he struck up another cigarette. He looked older, somehow; worn out. I thought again of the man in green.

'You really think they condoned it? The Nazis?'

Ettore blew out a stream of smoke and shook his head at me. 'They didn't just condone it, Eva, they ordered it.'

It wasn't easy to take that in: the idea that a government would order the whole-scale destruction and murder of its own citizens. 'This is madness.'

'Yes. Madness, bigotry, nationalism gone feral. Same as is happening in Italy.'

'Il Duce needs to condemn this.'

'Condemn it! No way will he condemn it. Eva, wake up. Haven't you noticed how everything is Germany, Germany these days? Haven't you noticed the rest of the world has abandoned us?'

'Well, of course I have. But isn't that precisely why Il Duce hasn't spoken out against Hitler, or at least he hasn't until now?'

'That's what your new boyfriend tells you, is it?'

95

I leant back against the glass. 'He's not my boyfriend.'

'No?'

'No. But yes, all right, that is what he says. It's what lots of people say.'

'People who aren't paying proper attention. People who still can't see what's in front of them because it's inconvenient and they don't want to believe they've been misled. People who are unwilling to stand up, take risks.'

I glanced at his face, his hazel eyes, his pallid skin. We still hadn't spoken of what risks he and Pietro were taking, what exactly they were doing, but I was quite certain they were involved with the anti-fascists in some way, and I knew what danger that implied.

'I don't want you to get hurt, Ettore.'

'Better to live one day as a lion rather than spend your life as a sheep – isn't that what your beloved Duce says?'

'He isn't… I don't think that anymore,' I said quietly. 'But nor can I quite believe that things will get as bad as they are in Germany. I don't think he'd allow that to happen.'

Ettore shook his head. 'I wish I believed you, *mia principessa*. But you're wrong. Yesterday, you know what the Grand Council of Ministers voted through? The law for the Defence of the Race.'

I felt the familiar sensation of fear and dismay. 'And what does this say, this law?'

'That all Jews must be dismissed from the army and public services, and from banks and insurance companies. That they may not own their businesses, own their own land. That Italians cannot marry people from non-Aryan races.' He leant back against the glass next to me and blew a thick line of cigarette smoke into the cold air. 'And they voted this through the day after the attacks on the Jews of Germany, when they could see the way it was going, and when they knew exactly what it meant. So you see, Eva, it could get much, much worse in Italy. You just don't want to accept it.'

Maybe it was only because of what I'd just learnt, but Rome itself seemed more hostile that morning as I made my way up Via Arenula towards the school, the shop owners rolling up their black iron shutters, the tram cars screaming past. My mind ran from the images of the burning German shopfronts back to the time I'd seen the books burning. It must have been when I was nine or ten. The *squadristi* had collected all the Slovenian books from the library and heaped them up outside in the square. People had gathered around to watch, not really understanding what was happening. The librarian was there, a small, white-haired man, wringing his hands. It was not right, he said, to burn books, books of any language, for books were precious things. Yet the men had made him go to the storage room and bring them all the Slovene books from there too. 'What could I do?' he kept asking us. 'What could I do?' And none of us knew.

The men had seized books from people's homes too – not from ours as my father had already got rid of everything – but from the libraries of the richer Slovene families: beautiful, gilt-edged books and manuscripts that they slung onto the enormous pile. They poured petrol from a can over the books and one of the group – a man with a broad red face like a cured ham – shouted about how Italian was the only language now in Trieste and that Italian was to be pure and cleansed and free from foreign influence. A match was thrown and the first flames sparked up, moving from the edges of the pile to the centre, where they grew into a great golden pyre, occasional bursts of flame shrieking up into the sky.

The men kept throwing books onto the blaze and we all stood there, silent, watching the titles of the books being burnt

97

away, not just textbooks and novels and manuals, but children's books. I didn't understand why it was necessary to burn books. Books never hurt anybody, did they? I didn't learn until much later that my mother had kept some of our books. She had buried them to save them. She'd hidden them even from my father. 'We must hide things if they are to survive.'

Though I knew I was deceiving myself, I had hoped, some-how, that it was all a terrible mistake. But on 17 November, the King signed the new Race Laws and they came into effect. I felt sickened by what was happening, ashamed, fearing it was something I'd helped to create simply by my silence. Mirella wept openly when she saw the papers and I held her, tense and afraid. I had no idea what to say, other than that I was sorry and horrified and shocked, but that was wrong because I shouldn't have been shocked. Hadn't the newspapers been spilling bile about the Jews for years? Hadn't there always been an anti-Semitic element within the Fascist party?

'It's always been there,' she said, 'lurking in the background. We were stupid to think we were safe. Well, now my parents will have to give up their foolish notion that they should stay in Italy. They'll have to accept we're not wanted.'

By the evening, I was eager to see Dante, wanting to discuss it all with him, wanting him to tell me how any of it made sense.

But when I arrived at the house, I found them occupied with something else entirely.

'It's the most absurd thing,' Alessandro told me excitedly as I entered the hallway. 'Water. From nowhere!'

I followed him into the living room, where Greta was at work with a mop and bucket. Her face was without a trace of a smile.

'You see?' she whispered to me. 'This house. It's not just in my old mind, though I know that's what he thinks. Something, something is here.'

I felt a pinprick of fear. 'What's happened?'

She pointed upwards, at the ceiling. 'Water dripping from above, just now, but there's no reason for it. No source.'

'Surely there must be.'

She shook her head determinedly. 'No.'

'Is Dante in?'

Again, the shake of the head. I felt a rush of disappointment.

I walked upstairs, convinced the dripping must be falling from the bathroom, which was directly above the living room.

Chiara was in the hallway upstairs. She looked very pale. 'It's not coming from there.'

'It must be.'

'I don't think so. We haven't even been using the water.'

She followed me as I went into the large, tiled room and looked about. There was no water in the bath or the sink, and none on the floor. I felt a coldness seep up my body.

'Perhaps one of the pipes has burst.'

Chiara didn't respond to this suggestion. It was the first time I'd seen her since she told me I didn't understand anything, and I'd thought she might apologise, but she didn't.

I knelt down and saw that there was a small circle on the floor, like a shadow. But no water. 'Has it happened before?'

'No, never.'

I walked back downstairs to where Greta was drying the floor and I stared again at the ceiling, still that feeling of coldness creeping through me.

Alessandro grinned at me. 'You see? *Pazzo*, isn't it?'

'It is odd, I admit, but it must just be something wrong with the pipes. Your father will need to call someone in, that's all.'

I didn't understand why Chiara and Greta were so silent while Alessandro appeared so cheerful. Was he masking his fear

99

in order to seem manly, or was he playing some peculiar game?

Greta took her bucket and mop and left the room and Alessandro disappeared upstairs, whistling. I watched him go, increasingly perturbed. When I turned back, Chiara was staring at me.

'What is it, Chiara?'

She gave a little shrug. 'It's odd, that's all. The wasps, the water. These things seem to happen when you're here.'

I smiled at her. 'But Chiara, I've only just arrived.' Was she saying it was all somehow my fault, or that the house – and they – didn't want me there?

Though I tried to make conversation, tried to regain our former intimacy, Chiara's demeanour throughout the lesson remained distant, as though our closeness and conversations had never happened, and I couldn't help but feel unhappy and uneasy.

For the whole of the lesson, I was listening for the door, listening for footsteps, hoping that Dante would return and, reassuring as ever, somehow smooth everything over. But he didn't come home, and by the time I saw him again, everything had changed.

It all happened far quicker than I'd anticipated, and it was through a woman I myself had contacted.

Mirella told me the following week as she brought me my morning coffee. She was leaving. She was heading for France, where she'd secured a role as a violin tutor, and she was leaving in a matter of weeks.

'It's all organised, Eva, through that woman you put me in touch with. Don't try to talk me out of it.'

'So soon? I know it's what we've been working towards, but does it really have to be so soon?'

'You know it does. I've finally been offered this opportunity, so I must leave.' Her voice was sharp with distress. 'Oh God, please don't cry, Eva, this is not helping me. It's already bad enough that I'm going without my family.'

I tried to stop the tears coming, but I felt as though my heart would break, for Mirella was my family. 'I'm sorry, Mirella. I know it's what we've been trying to find, but I will miss you so terribly, and I just can't accept that any of this is happening. I don't understand how it's all changed so quickly – oh, I know, I know, there were undercurrents of this before, but it's all suddenly risen to the surface like... I don't know what like. I'm sorry, Mirella. It's wrong and it's awful.'

'You think I understand? You think I understand how one day I have a job and a position and friends, and the next day I'm not even allowed to be a cleaner in an Aryan man's house? You think I understand how my father, who, until a few months ago, was a respected academic wanted for speaking opportunities all over the country, now can't get a job in the whole of Italy? I only know that it's a hatred that has long existed and is rising up now, because of Hitler, because of this war they think is going to happen, because Mussolini himself is so obsessed with the Italians being warlike and strong. And, for some reason, that now means the Italians must be purebred like horses, or dogs.' She laughed, but she wiped her face and I saw that she was crying too.

I took hold of her hand. 'You heard what the Pope said on the radio: that there was only one single human race. That all the Nazis' claims of racial superiority are wrong and evil. How can Il Duce continue with his policies in the face of that? And there are still German people coming here, aren't there, thinking it's safer than their homeland? Couldn't you stay a little longer and see what happens? You could get discriminated status, you know, to make sure you weren't penalised in any way. I could speak to Dante. He seems to have contacts everywhere. He has a friend who works for the Party.'

She shook her head. 'Jewish people are coming here because they can't get into other countries, or because they don't understand what Italy's becoming. And the people like my parents who say this is just an interval are refusing to see the truth. This will only go one way, no matter what the Pope says, no matter what anyone says, and this might well be my last chance to get out. You know they're turning back German Jews from America? If I leave it any longer, that might be me.'

I knew deep down that she was right. 'Do you know anyone in France, though? What will you do when you arrive? How will you manage?'

'There are a few of us going together. It's been arranged by some sympathetic families. I'll be all right.'

I chivvied myself. 'I'll help you get everything together that you need. I've saved a little money. You'll need warmer clothes for a start.'

She sat on the side of my bed. 'You could come with me, Eva. I could see if they would take you too.'

I stared at her, my brow creasing.

'It's Jews now, Eva, who are the main target. But tomorrow? Will anyone who isn't Italian be safe? You've told me snippets of what happened in Trieste when you were younger. I know you don't want to talk about it or think about it, I know you want to burrow down and make it all go away, but there's still anti-Slavic sentiment in Italy, you know there is. It's even stronger in Germany.'

I thought of what Mussolini had called the Slavs years before: 'inferior and barbarian'. But I'd shed that identity almost entirely. Now I was something else.

'And even if they don't come for you, Eva, do you really want to stay here while things get worse? Because they will only get worse. You know that, don't you?'

I took my hand away from hers. 'I'm not as brave as you, Mirella. I can't just start again. It's taken me years to establish myself here as one of them. This is my home. I'm Italian now.'

'Not in the eyes of—'

'I'm Italian,' I said again, more firmly.

'And you think that I'm not?'

'No. God, no, I don't think that at all. I think you're the best of us.'

Mirella paused. 'Consider it properly, Eva: what you're doing, why you're staying. This man: does he love you? Will he protect you?'

I looked down at my hands. 'I think he will, Mirella.'

'You must tell him you are Slovene, Eva. You must tell him that now.'

'I'm Italian,' I said quietly.

She shook her head at me. 'You think this will make you safe. It won't.' She stood up. 'I'm going to do some marking. Drink your horrible coffee before it goes cold.'

After she'd left, I burrowed down beneath my covers, praying it would all go away, that I myself could cease to exist. Though the day was just beginning, I wanted it to end so that I could sleep and sleep and sleep.

9

It was the coldest December I'd experienced in Rome, a bora wind whipping through the city, and temperatures falling at points to below freezing. It became increasingly difficult to get hold of coal, so that our little apartment was often very cold, and we wore all our clothes at the same time, on top of each other. At night, I prepared the little terracotta *scaldino* and put it in our bed to heat the sheets. Often, Mirella and I would sleep in the same bed for warmth and comfort, but really it was no comfort all because I knew that she'd soon be gone, and I could feel her pain in her too-thin body. Her parents were still refusing to leave Italy: it was their home, they insisted, and things would settle down; they were not running from the place to which they'd devoted their lives. Mirella, however, saw what was to come. She saw that they were drowning.

Occasionally, she would suggest again that I should leave too and my heart was torn, because I wanted to be with her, and I wanted not to see or be part of the terrible things that were happening in Italy, but at the same time I was afraid to go. Also, something was happening to me: I was, I thought, falling in love.

Dante worked out from my chilblained fingers and chapped lips that I was too cold at home. He bought me some good leather gloves and a woollen hat as gifts, not allowing me to refuse them, and he insisted that I stay longer at the house in the evenings, where they had a good fire and where it was always warm. He seemed like an anchor, a safe place, at a time everything else was falling apart. Our conversations became more intimate. He told me more about his childhood: about his beautiful society mother who'd had little time for her son. I couldn't help but hate her. He spoke too about his father, a weak man, Dante said, who'd managed to buy his way out of service in the war. When the small boy's attempts to gain his parents' attention through hard work had failed, he had re-sorted to disruptive behaviour. 'Maybe that's where Alessandro gets it from. I don't know. I set a fire in my father's study, you know! Sent all his papers up in a blaze. But even then they didn't engage with me – just dispatched me to a military academy to have them beat some sense into me. Well, it did that, I suppose.'

'I'm so sorry, Dante.'

'Oh, don't be. It was good for me, as it turned out. Gave me a sense of belonging, a sense that I was part of a nation that was far greater than my parents, the son not just of a limp-wristed banker but of Rome, of the empire. I suppose that's why the Party seemed so appealing to me as a young man: that sense of nationhood and order and belonging.'

I understood that in a way. I myself had wanted so badly to find an acceptable identity. But Italy's focus on nationhood had now become frantic: no longer a source of warmth and comfort, but a fire burning everything in its path; a means not of including people but destroying them.

'Do you not sometimes think, though, Dante, that this busi-ness of Rome, this idea of *romanità*, can be taken too far? Or in the wrong direction?' It had become a sort of cult: the idea that ancient Rome would rise again were we just to become sufficiently warlike.

'What d'you mean?'

'I mean...' I licked my lips. 'The new laws.' Making myself press on, I told Dante about Mirella and her decision to leave the country. 'Mirella and her family: what harm can they do Italy? They've only ever helped this nation. They're more patriotic than almost anyone I know. Why turn them into the enemy?'

Dante nodded. 'She'll be safer now, though. You'll be safer too. And you, you will miss her, of course, but you'll find other people to care for, perhaps.' He looked at me and I knew he was talking about himself. He was asking me if I cared for him.

'I'm sure I will. But it isn't right, Dante, it can't be.'

He frowned. 'All I can tell you is that Il Duce must know what's right for us and what's right for Italy. If we're heading for war, and many think we are, then we must be the strongest we can be, as a nation and as individuals.' He took my hand. 'You mustn't think like this, Eva. I don't want you to be unhappy. You've brought such joy and light to a house that had very little of those things.'

'Oh, I don't know about that. Chiara doesn't seem to be very pleased with me at the moment.' There had been no further outbursts, but she'd remained distant, despite my attempts to draw her into conversation, despite my efforts to find out what was wrong. It wasn't just Chiara, either. Though I told myself it was only my own paranoia, I had the occasional sense that the house itself didn't want me there; that something was watching me, hostile. I'd sometimes feel an icy wash of fear, just as I had that day in the piano room.

'Chiara is very fond of you. She's talked more to you than she has to anyone for a long time.' Dante paused. 'But I suppose it's difficult for her to get used to the idea that there should be someone else in my life. She will come round, I'm sure.'

The blood rushed to my face. Things seemed to be moving so quickly. I thought again of telling him: My parents were Slovene. I should have told you before. But I could not. Because I wanted him to desire and need me. I wanted him to make love to me and I wanted to feel his body against mine, I wanted to become part of a family that was truly Italian and I feared that if I said anything to ruin what was growing between us, that would be the end of the one piece of happiness in my life, the one thing that appeared to be going right.

So I smiled at Dante and I decided that I would stay in Italy, at least, I thought, for now.

Ettore and I went to see Mirella off, even though she'd instructed us not to. 'It's hardly a bloody leaving party. Stay at home in bed.'

It was a raw, freezing morning, the sky gunmetal grey, gulls wheeling and crying above us as we helped Mirella carry her cases up into the ship. I'd never seen, never mind been aboard, an ocean liner and it seemed to me an enormous and terrifying beast, its bulbous bow rising out of the dark water, its vast deck creaking and juddering, its great funnels belching black smoke. Dozens of Jewish people, some in pairs, some with their families, were loading their possessions and saying good-bye to relatives and supporters and friends. It will stay with me forever, that morning. The stench of diesel, the deafening blast of the ship's sirens, the pale, strained faces, the bewildered children staring into the grey drizzle, uprooted from the place they called home. Most of the passengers were well-off people in decent clothing and with leather cases, but some were poor families from the ghetto carrying their few possessions in card-board suitcases bound with string, staring about the ship with a dazed sort of fear. They had, I guessed, sold almost everything to pay for the passage to France.

'You must write to me,' Mirella instructed us, as the siren sounded again, a deep and mournful sound. 'Every week. You must tell me what's happening. You must keep playing. Find a new violinist. And you must look after each other, you hear me? And Bruno, of course. You promise? You must teach him some more bad words.' He had always been her bird, really, and the trio had been hers too. I felt a gnawing, penetrating sadness that it was all falling apart.

'We promise, Mirella.' I hugged her, feeling her skeletal frame beneath her clothes, feeling her body shaking. It'd been weeks since she'd eaten properly, though I'd brought her biscuits and chocolates and sweets. She couldn't, she said, because she felt as if she and the world were suffocating.

'You're sure I can't convince you to come?' she asked.

'Not yet,' I said, hugging her even harder. 'But I'll keep thinking about it, every day. See how things progress.'

She shook her head. 'Not yet, not yet. It's what my parents say, though I tell them it'll soon be too late.'

It wasn't just her parents. There were many Jews who still clung to the hope that the measures would be reversed; that Italy – supposedly such a benevolent country – would somehow come to its senses. Although I didn't believe that by that stage, still I fooled myself that my situation was different, that staying was still my best option.

'I'll keep thinking, Mirella. I promise you,' I shouted above the siren.

Ettore came forward and hugged Mirella. I could tell he was trying not to cry.

'Bully her for me, will you?' she told him, and then Mirella herself was crying – we all were – and the gulls were still shrieking in the sky.

108

When I look back on my old self now, I want to grab hold of her shoulders and scream at her to listen: to stay with Mirella on that boat.

I don't like to think much of the days that followed, for I felt more lonely than I had since my teenage years, living in that cold apartment with only Bruno for company. And though my feelings for Dante continued to grow, they were shot through with sadness for the loss not only of Mirella, but of the Italy I'd thought I knew. I couldn't decide whether to follow her. I wasn't sure if I could.

On the last day of December, Dante insisted that I join a small gathering at the house of one of his colleagues. It wasn't supposed to be the end of year; the Fascist New Year ran from 29 October, the day Il Duce had become our leader. There were certain things, however, that Italians wouldn't give up. At around half past eleven, we left the house for the Piazza Navona to see some of the celebrations. As we walked, there began all around us the sounds of crockery shattering and children screaming with laughter as people tossed cracked glasses, old bottles, threadbare curtains and three-legged chairs out of the windows of their apartments, down onto the streets below. Out with the old, the unwanted, the moth-eaten, the dusty, in with the bright new year: 1939.

It was below freezing and had been for days, but the mood in Rome was more cheerful than it had been for some months. There was a sense of new beginnings, of hope, the same sense that comes with every new year, where people feel that there's a chance to lay aside the mistakes and failures of the previous year and start again afresh. Only this time, it seemed more important because the mistakes had been so much bigger, the closeness to catastrophe so acute. This year we would get it right. That was what I myself felt, at least – that I would be a better person in the new year. I would be braver, stronger, less afraid.

From the Piazza Navona, we could already hear the whizz and bang of fireworks and the roar of the growing crowd. Above us, the occasional sparkle of colour. And then, as we rounded a corner, a great shower of objects rained down from the balconies – glasses and bottles, light bulbs and broken boxes, the inhabitants of the apartments above whooping and shouting as they threw their pasts out onto the road.

'Quickly – in here.' Dante grabbed my hand and pulled me into the shelter of a doorway as the broken objects continued to pour down. 'These people! They're insane!' He was laughing, which made me laugh, and I suppose we'd both drunk too much, but I felt ridiculously happy and nervous at the same time.

He didn't let go of my hand but rather took hold of my other one and he was very close to me, his breath warming the cold air. And then he was kissing me and his hands were on my waist, my face, and it was everything I'd wished for – to know that he desired me and wanted me as much as I wanted him. His mouth was sour with brandy and cigarette smoke, but somehow that was wonderful too.

After a while, he broke off and held me by the shoulders and then we both laughed again, a sort of release.

Dante's expression grew serious. 'Marry me, Eva.'

Time froze. I hadn't expected that. Not that I hadn't expected it ever, but not so quickly, not then, not while things felt so precarious, not while I was still wondering whether to join Mirella. I felt all the heat leave my body and I felt that I was just a skeleton standing there with Dante's hands holding me up.

'Forgive me. I've frightened you.'

'No, no! I just – I hadn't thought ...'

He removed his hands. 'It was too much for me to expect. You are young, so very beautiful. What would you want with an old widower like me?' I could see the hurt in his eyes.

'No, you misunderstand me!' My reticence was more to do with Italy than Dante, though I felt I couldn't tell him that.

He gave an uncertain sort of smile. 'So, it is not a no?'

'No, it is not a no!' I smiled back at him, but some part of me was afraid, even though here it was: my chance to be part of a proper family, to be properly Italian, to be accepted.

'And could it possibly instead be a yes?'

I put my hands to my face. 'Yes. Yes, I suppose it could be!'

He laughed and kissed me again and again. 'Then the year has started exactly as it should. The most gorgeous girl in Italy is mine!'

At that moment came another shower of crockery, then another burst of fireworks. We screamed, we laughed, and Dante picked me clean off the ground and twirled me around and around until the sparkling sky above us was spinning.

Part Two

10

Rome, 1939

As the year began, it seemed to me that the air itself crackled with energy. For those first few days, I felt as though I was suspended, floating. Dante bought me a ring – a beautiful, glittering gold band such as I never imagined I'd own with a diamond in the centre and, either side of it, two red rubies like tiny drops of blood. Wearing it, my hands seemed more refined and elegant, and I couldn't stop myself from staring at them. I imagined what my mother might have thought had she still been here to learn that her daughter was engaged to someone so respectable, so stable, so handsome. She would have wanted, I thought, to know he was kind as well and would protect me. I would have told her that yes, yes, he was and yes he would; that he would never treat me as my father had treated her, had treated me. Because he was not, I thought, anything like my father, my father with his big rough hands and his sense of wounded pride and embitterment towards the allied powers and all those he thought had done him down. I didn't concur with everything Dante said, but then which couple were entirely in agreement? Compared to what I'd seen of my parents' relationship, ours seemed a near-perfect union.

Carmela and Serafina were delighted when I told them, I suppose because it was a happy thing, something to celebrate, at a time when everything had for so long seemed so gloomy. They had a myriad of plans for the wedding and all sorts of advice to give me, about men and marriage, that they seemed to have gathered from magazines. I must not go to bed in my hair curlers, and I must never have crooked seams on my stockings. I must let him sleep late on Sundays and I would have to pray that he didn't snore. I must let him drink his coffee before I drank mine and I must ask his opinions on everything. 'Not that you'll always agree,' Carmela said, 'but at least you'll know then what you have to conceal, and the things on which you'll need to persuade him.'

When I met with Ettore at our usual cafe, Caffè Panella, he didn't at first notice anything different about me. He was too anxious to tell me of what he'd heard from Spain, where people he knew were still fighting.

'New Year's Eve itself,' he said. 'Can you believe it? The most brutal air raids yet, and it was our bombers – ours and the Germans' – sent in to help our good friend Franco. Over forty killed in Barcelona; Madrid shelled to bits. Some way to ring in the new year.'

I'd heard of the shelling on the radio, but there'd been so much shelling, so much bombing now for years.

'And they're still going,' Ettore continued, agitated. 'Italian forces – volunteers, they claim, but we all know Mussolini sent them – bombing passenger trains, for Christ's sake.' He stared at me. 'This doesn't bother you?'

'Of course it bothers me, Ettore.' I spoke very quietly. 'More than that, it distresses me. That's why sometimes I almost don't want to think about it. Sometimes I just want to be able to live my life, the same as everybody else does, and focus on things I can control.'

'But that's how everybody thinks. And it's why fascism will destroy the whole of Europe.'

'Ettore—'

'Because that's what it does – it's a destroying force that sweeps away everything before it. You see that, don't you? It wants to destroy the established order – its businesses, its communities, everything – and start from scratch. That's what it's done in Germany and it's what it's now doing in Italy and Spain. It's like a fire scorching everything in its path.'

'Like Nero,' I said quietly. 'Burning it all down to build from the ashes.'

'Exactly.'

As I picked up my cup, Ettore's eyes focused on my hand.

'That sly old devil. He moved very quickly.'

'Ettore!'

'Well, it's true.' He gave a short laugh. 'You've known him for what, three months? When did he ask you?'

'New Year's Eve.'

'Did he, now?' He folded his arms, scrutinising my face. 'Is it what you want?'

'Yes, it is.' And it was, I thought, though part of me was still fearful: of how the children would react; of what would happen in Italy; of the presence I sometimes sensed in the house.

I thought Ettore might question me further, argue with me, but he said only, 'Well then: to you,' and raised his coffee cup to chink it with mine.

He was, I understood, stifling his opinions so as not to ruin my happiness, and the whole thing suddenly felt tarnished, vacuous. I felt the burn of tears behind my eyes. 'I wish Mirella was still here.' It had been my main sadness during that time. That she was not there to share my news; that she might be disappointed when she found out.

'Have you heard anything further from her?'

'Not for a week or so.' She'd written of how difficult the voyage was, everyone cold and anxious holed up in the stinking bowels of the ship, the children fretting and vomiting, but how they'd at last reached France and been allowed into the country, and how now I too must leave. 'And you?' I said to Ettore. 'You've been... busy?'

He nodded. 'There's much to do, though sometimes it seems too big, too hopeless.'

It *was* hopeless, wasn't it? Lined up against the Fascists and the Nazis with their wealth and power, what could any of us really do? I didn't see then that wasn't the point of the Resistance. They never expected to win. What mattered was that they tried, that hope was not allowed to die.

At that very moment, a group of Blackshirts entered the cafe, brash and loud in their heavy boots and dark uniforms. Immediately, the mood of the place changed: backs stiffening, conversations ceasing. The men took a table not far from us and called over to the waiter for drinks. I prayed that they would take no notice of us. I could see them, though, running their eyes over me, then Ettore, trying to work out what we were about. That's how it was, then. They were always on the lookout for anyone out of line, anyone slightly different.

I put my hand on Ettore's, hoping they'd assume we were a happy couple, a normal Aryan pair. 'I worry about you,' I said to him very softly.

'Don't worry about me, Eva. Worry about this country. Worry about what's coming next.'

I tried not to let myself think too much about what Ettore was doing, what might happen to him, or what was happening all around us. It was too much for me to take in and it would have involved acknowledging my past and the risks that I still faced. Instead, I busied myself with wedding preparations, assisted by

Carmela and Serafina. They had consulted their magazines and their friends and I was to buy fabric from Bassetti's, flowers from Rosario's and marrons glacés from Rosati's in the Via Veneto. It would be the most wonderful wedding there had ever been. Even Signora Gioiosa, our joyless landlady, was interested, putting on her spectacles to stare at my ring. 'He's a rich man then, is he? When will you be married? Because I need to know about letting the apartment.'

I was nervous that Dante hadn't yet told the children. I recalled Chiara's words that the house didn't need another mother. I thought of Alessandro's peculiar watchfulness. 'I don't want them to feel I'm trying to take Adelina's place,' I told Dante. 'I don't want them to feel I'm an interloper.'

'They won't think that, my darling. They'll be delighted. They like you very much. And they're my children: they won't question my decisions. It will all be fine, don't worry.'

He insisted that we should tell them together. We would all go out on the night of Epiphany to see the celebrations and this would be the perfect time to break the news. I wasn't so sure about this. I thought it would be better if Dante spoke to them in advance, without me there, but he brushed aside my objections.

'*Mia carissima*, you are worrying too much about their reaction. They will accept what their father tells them. And how could they not want me to marry a woman as gentle and beautiful as you?'

He often called me beautiful now. He would take my face in his hands and turn it up to his so that I began to believe that I truly was beautiful. When I looked in the mirror, I could acknowledge that maybe my large, hazel eyes were not odd and childlike as I'd once thought, but 'movie-star eyes', as he called them. That maybe my mouth, that I'd always thought too wide, was, as Dante said, 'sensuous'. Men had called me beautiful before, but men in Italy always said things like that to any girl walking down the street. Dante seemed to mean it, and for the first time in my life I felt truly wanted.

Already he'd given me money to have some new dresses made and I ordered one for Epiphany: a frock of blue velvet and lace that made me feel like a new, glamorous person, not the awkward Eva of old.

On the evening of 6 January, I dressed myself in my new outfit and shawl and I applied a little make-up – not too much, as Dante liked me to look natural, but in the winter cold, my skin had dulled and it was only right I corrected it. I felt self-conscious walking to the Piazza Navona, worried that I'd skid on the icy pavements in my high-heeled shoes; nervous that Chiara and Alessandro would have already guessed what their father planned to tell them this evening and that they were none too happy about it.

The piazza was decked out with lights, small fairy lights glistening in the trees, lanterns hanging from the shop canopies. Several large Christmas trees had been placed in the centre of the square and hung with decorations so that the place looked like an enchanted forest. A small choir was singing 'Astro del Ciel'. Around the sides of the piazza, people had set up shooting galleries and toy shops, and cabins selling mulled wine, torrone, gingerbread and cups of hot chocolate with cream.

'Eva!' Dante was already at one of these stalls buying cups of wine. 'Some for you?'

Chiara was wearing a fur about her neck. I wondered if it had been her mother's. Alessandro wore a black coat and gloves like a young member of the SS. He was taller, I noticed – he seemed to have shot up a few inches.

'You look nice, Signorina Valenti.'

'Thank you, Alessandro.'

'You wouldn't believe how much trouble I had getting this one out of the house,' Dante told me jokingly, taking Chiara's arm. 'I think my daughter thinks *la Befana* is going to get her!'

She looked at the cobbled ground.

'I'm sure *la Befana* would have no reason to come for our Chiara,' I said, trying to catch her eye. 'She's always a very good girl.'

La Befana was the Christmas witch who was supposed to come for naughty children at Epiphany. But Chiara was not really a child. I was doubly worried now, that Chiara had guessed at what was going on and hated me for it.

'It's only that it's so cold, that's all,' she said.

'Come on, then,' Dante said. 'Let's go and warm ourselves at the fire.'

'Look! There she is!' Alessandro shouted. He was pointing towards the other side of the square at a woman in a black dress and hat, complete with broomstick. She was surrounded by a group of children, but as we stared at her, she turned and pointed a long fake finger directly at us. '*Cribbio!*' Alessandro laughed. 'Maybe Chiara was right to be scared. I think she must know things about Chiara we don't!'

'In fact,' Dante said, 'Eva and I have some news for you, children.'

Chiara grew very still. She knew. Alessandro, though, was not really listening, but watching the witch, the crowd.

'I'm delighted to tell you that she and I are to be married. Isn't that marvellous news?'

Silence.

'Well, don't you have anything to say?'

'Congratulations,' Chiara said quickly.

'Yes, congratulations,' Alessandro added. 'What marvellous news.' His voice, though, was a dull echo of his father's.

'I certainly think so,' Dante said, smiling broadly at me and his confidence boosted mine a little. Of course it was a shock for them, so soon after their mother's death. It would take them time to get used to the idea and I would have to do my best to help them.

'When will you be married?' Chiara asked.

'Quite soon, I should think,' Dante answered her. 'Then Eva can come and live with us. Won't that be nice?'

Chiara nodded. 'Yes. Very.'

I saw something in her expression that I couldn't quite read. Fear? But what could she be frightened of? I was hardly an ogre.

At that moment came a piercing cackle of laughter and *la Befana* was upon us, or rather a tall woman – or was it a man? – dressed in a black dress and a grotesque mask with a twisted nose. It was not Chiara the witch lunged at, however, but me.

'A dance, my pretty one?'

The witch swung me away and I looked back at Dante, hoping he would help me, but he was laughing, as was Alessandro, as it seemed was everyone. The whole piazza was ringing with it and with the music from the band. I tried to wriggle free of the witch, who I was sure now was a man, as his hands were gripped tightly around my waist and from his body emanated a powerful smell of stale wine. I couldn't escape from him, however, and was too embarrassed to make more of a fuss, so let myself be twirled about the square, a leaf powerless in the wind, as the music blared. The wine and the music and the smell combined to make me feel light-headed and sick and when he whispered to me, 'You can't get away now,' I thought perhaps I was imagining it.

When he finally let go of me, I almost fell over on the cobblestones. The witch bowed before me and I saw that he had long, greasy hair tied back in a ponytail. I wanted to vomit, but I stretched my mouth into a smile and hurried back across the piazza to Dante.

We decided that we would have a small wedding and soon, as Dante was keen for me to move in as quickly as possible ('away from that horrible, damp apartment of yours'). This made sense, as I was lonely living there without Mirella and, though I was nervous, I confess the thought of being in Dante's bed thrilled me.

'You don't mind, do you?' he asked. 'It not being a more formal sort of wedding? It just doesn't seem the time for a grand ceremony. And besides, I want you all to myself.'

'Oh, I don't mind at all. I wouldn't have liked a big wedding in any event. It would have made me too anxious. I've never much liked events that focused the attention on me.' And Dante was right that a grand ceremony would hardly have suited the still relatively sombre mood that pervaded Rome.

'I was thinking February,' Dante said. 'I know that's soon, but there isn't much you need to get ready, is there? I should think you could have a lovely simple dress made up quite quickly. I'll speak to the church. Get it all sorted out. There's really no reason why we should wait. You should invite your relatives, of course. That uncle you mentioned, for example.'

I licked my lips. 'I don't think I will. I've had little contact with them now for years. And they're poor; I couldn't expect them to travel.'

All that was true. But of course it was not the real reason I was not inviting them.

'Well, you must have a friend or two there, though, at least,' Dante said. What about those sisters I met?'

'Yes, I'm sure they'd love to come. And my friend Ettore from the trio, I must invite him. He's been wanting to meet you for ages.'

★

But Ettore, it turned out, had bigger issues than my wedding. When I arrived at his apartment to ask him, he immediately told me the news: Pietro had been detained. He was being sent into *confino*. Nothing to do with their mysterious political activities; simply because he'd been denounced as what they termed a 'pederast'. Someone had informed he was a homosexual.

I put my hands to my face. 'Ettore. No.' It was what I'd feared for so long, but never quite admitted to myself. 'Where are they sending him?'

'Some wretched village in the south – in Lucania – where he knows no one and will have nothing to do for months on end. He'll go mad there, I know it.' He was pacing about the kitchen, smoking.

'What will you do?'

'I'll go with him. I've already started packing.'

My heart began to race. 'You can't though, can you?'

'Not exactly, no. But I can move to Bari, which is only a few miles away.'

'Will you be able to see him, though? I thought they kept them all closeted away?'

'Maybe. I don't really know. I have to at least try, haven't I?'

I could feel my palms growing clammy, my stomach souring. 'But, Ettore, what if they realise you've followed him? Won't that be worse? For him? For you? They haven't come for you yet, but—'

'I can't just stay here, Eva!' he shouted at me. 'I can't just leave him on his own!' He crushed out his cigarette in a saucer, then continued his pacing. 'You know what Pietro's like. How morose he gets, how intense. I can get work in Bari. And there are people there who understand us.' He must mean another group of anti-fascists, but I didn't want to ask. I wanted desperately to do something – to stop him, to save him – but I didn't know what that would be.

I pulled at my lip. After a moment, I said, 'What will you tell the school?'

'I haven't decided that yet.' He opened his lighter and lit another cigarette. 'You mustn't say anything, all right?'

'Of course I won't. Is there anything I can do, Ettore? Anything I can do to help?'

He finally sat down at the table. 'Many things, Eva. There's a movement growing. You could be part of it.'

Instinctively, I shook my head, thinking of the priest, shot dead, the men strapped to trees, the fear in my mother's eyes. 'Ettore, I want to live. I want to exist. I want to have a family. I'm not as brave as you.'

He snorted. 'You think you can live in what this country is becoming? You want to raise children in this place?'

He sounded so angry that my eyes filled with tears and I had to blink them back.

Ettore breathed out. 'I'm sorry, Eva. I'm not being fair. It's too much to ask of most, I know, but it feels like we're right on the brink, staring over the abyss.' He was looking at his hands, as though they might hold the answer. 'What did you come to see to me about anyway?'

'Oh, nothing really.' I fiddled with my engagement ring.

'You'll be all right without me, won't you?' Ettore glanced at me, then away. 'We can speak on the telephone, though we must be careful what we say. There are always people listening in.'

'Yes, I'll be fine. You mustn't worry about me.' I felt, though, bereft and inadequate, because part of me knew he was right, and that I should do something to fight back. It seemed, though, too big, too hopeless, too vague. Who would I even be helping? And what on earth could I do?

'We'll have to talk in code,' Ettore said. 'I'll work something out before I go.'

Over the next few days, I felt a growing dismay at the idea that Ettore too was leaving Rome, that the trio was to be no more. I had, I realised, grown very reliant on Mirella and Ettore. They'd become my family in Rome in a way my real family had never been, and I feared that without them, I myself was hollow. I worried too that I was letting them down; that by choosing a safe life over sacrifice and resistance, I was failing both them and myself. It didn't seem, however, as though I really had a choice. I'd committed to marrying Dante and everything was already in train: the church was booked, the invitations sent, everyone I knew had been told. Carmela and Serafina were delighted to be invited and to have a project. They insisted that we went shopping together to find a suitable dress and shoes.

'And you will need white lace gloves and stockings. Typical man thinking that there isn't much a woman needs to do to get ready for her wedding! Oh, I know he's a dreamboat, but it seems he's as hopeless on that front as the rest of them. We'll need to make a start this week.'

They were very much against the idea of a simple dress, such as Dante had described, and brought into work pictures of frills and beautiful lacework. This made me nervous, however, as I wasn't at all sure what Dante would like, and I couldn't ask him because, of course, it was all supposed to be a surprise. At a loss, I found myself asking Greta, for she had at least known him for many years. 'You know his tastes.' I thought of the horrendous chandelier. Hardly simple. 'I just wondered if you had any thoughts. I wouldn't want, you see, to get it completely wrong.'

Greta looked at me steadily, put down her mop and said, 'Come.'

She led me into the living room and to a cabinet on which three leather-bound volumes were stacked. She took the middle volume, then sat on the sofa to leaf through it.

'Sit down,' she commanded. 'Here.'

She passed me the volume open on two pages of wedding photographs and I realised with a lurch that it was Adelina, stunningly beautiful, wearing a long white dress; Dante next to her, younger and even more handsome, smiling.

I felt a shiver run through me as I stared at the photos. I felt very much like a voyeur, an intruder into Adelina and Dante's past. I was sure he wouldn't have wanted me to see these photos and I kept glancing at the door, worried that at any moment he'd arrive home. I couldn't stop myself from looking, though: Adelina and Dante at the door of the church, staring not at one another, but the camera. Adelina holding a huge bouquet, a group of small girls around her.

There were photographs, too, of a large number of other people in different groupings and poses: small children strapped into tiny suits, with huge bows in their hair, old women cloaked in black linen. It had evidently been a large affair. Perhaps that was part of the reason Dante wanted our ceremony to be smaller, different.

I looked carefully at the photos of Adelina – her dress did not seem at all simple. It was a gorgeous affair of lace and silk, which hugged her slender figure.

'You think this is what he likes, then?' I asked Greta. 'This is the sort of thing he would want me to wear?'

'No,' she said firmly. 'She wouldn't like you to wear what she did.' Greta got up and left the room, leaving me holding the album.

Had I misheard, or had she misspoken? Surely she must have meant '*he* wouldn't like you to wear what she did.' Yes, that was what she had meant.

I took one last look at Adelina in her beautiful dress and closed the photograph album.

★

I wished I had someone to discuss it all with, who would know how to advise me, but there was no one. I didn't feel that I could tell Carmela and Serafina or the other girls at school. I certainly couldn't tell them about my conversations with Ettore. Nor could I bring myself to admit to them that I didn't fully know the man I was about to marry, though perhaps few women did. Surely my mother couldn't have known what my father was like, or she would never have married him. I couldn't ask Chiara either – it seemed far too intrusive and embarrassing a question and she'd continued with her distant and formal manner, which caused me an aching sadness.

I'd received a longer letter from Mirella, which I read over and over, but I could hardly have opened up to her in my reply. Her life was so much more serious and complex than mine. She lived in a boarding house with several other new arrivals and she wasn't only teaching but had become part of the movement helping others get into and settle in the country. There were so many people, she told me, who were still trying to get into France; so many who were being turned back. There were stories of people drowning themselves and their children in the harbour rather than face what awaited them in Germany. Some of the people she'd met had been trying to flee for months and by the time they arrived, they were haggard, penniless, destroyed. They spoke of terrifying things happening in Germany – of camps where Jewish people and others were worked to the bone, not just men but women and children. I almost couldn't bear to think of it. Did Il Duce know this was happening? 'We have aligned ourselves with a monster,' Mirella wrote. 'And, Eva, maybe that's just as bad as being the monster ourselves.'

How, then, could I write back to her with my worries about what kind of wedding dress to wear? Ridiculous. I felt again that I was letting her down, letting Ettore down. I felt too an awful sadness, a selfish and stupid sadness, that Mirella was not with me – could not advise me on what to do and help me prepare for my wedding in the way that I'd always imagined she would. I felt terribly alone, even though I knew I should feel grateful that I was wanted and desired by a man who could offer me not only love, but protection in a world that was increasingly frightening.

We were on the precipice of something dreadful – everybody sensed it – though, of course, that was not what our papers claimed, nor what most people said aloud. We didn't so much read the news as interpret it, as one might a code. Anyone could see that the storm clouds were once again gathering and that the attempts to appease Hitler had failed. On 11 January, Neville Chamberlain, the British prime minister, arrived in Rome for discussions with Il Duce. I thought at first this might be hopeful, but Dante told me the visit was meaningless.

'His visit will achieve nothing, I'm afraid. He thinks he can smooth everything over with words. Il Duce will be civil, of course – he's a statesman – but he won't give ground on what is rightfully ours. He'll restate our territorial rights and that silly little man will get back on his train to England.'

Dante was talking about Tunis and Dalmatia – the lands that had been taken from Italy after the war and which had poisoned the minds of many Italians against the British and the French, seen as the smug and calculating victors. Their countries, we were told again and again, had not the poverty Italy had, the starvation and squalor of the south, the paucity of resources that made Italy the poor cousin of Europe even before the international sanctions were imposed. I'd seen that terrible poverty myself – the children without shoes, without proper clothing, unable to go to school – and it made me angry to think that these countries were worsening their suffering simply to make a political point about a country far away. It was only later that I saw it differently, only after I understood what Il Duce had really done in Abyssinia: when we learnt of the chemical warfare waged against a largely unarmed people.

Despite Dante's pronouncements, Chamberlain seemed to be accepted warmly by the crowds who waved and clapped him as he was driven about the streets of Rome. I saw him myself, a grey-haired man with glasses smiling from the back of a black Rolls-Royce. He looked, I thought, like an amiable professor, come on a city tour. Perhaps that was why people liked him. He was the antithesis of our military Duce and the furious Führer. He was clearly a man who did not want war, and by that stage, I think there were many who, though they might not say it out loud, were terrified of what was to come.

Not so Dante. If anything, he became more pro-war as the weeks went on, and I struggled to understand him. There was, he said, no other way to resolve the situation. Was Italy to be restricted, stuck in its box, not taken seriously by the other European nations for its entire history? We had a strong leader now who commanded respect from other heads of state and who was forming an alliance with the man who told them all how it was to be. This was no moment to retreat. It was time to rebuild Italy and take back what the supposed victors had stolen. Time to restore our prestige. We must remain firm and if Britain and France would not accede to our just requests, then so be it. That was on them.

Alessandro warmly agreed with his father and spoke of Italy returning to its rightful place in the world, how Italy itself *was* war, how he would fight. But he was only a boy. He had no memory of the Great War, no experience of what it was actually like to be constantly afraid, constantly in survival mode.

I'd been a small child during the war and I'd grown up in its aftermath. I'd seen my mother's fear when she spoke of those times: of the terror of aerial bombardment, of how Trieste had come to a standstill, leaving people facing hardship and suffering and hunger. I'd seen how war damaged my father, both in body and in mind, and he was only one of millions. There couldn't be another war, could there? As January progressed it felt increasingly as though the answer was 'yes'.

On 26 January, Franco's Nationalists captured Barcelona. Dante said we should go to Palazzo Venezia that evening: members of the Fascist party had been told to take their uniforms to work and to change into them afterwards and report in front of the Palazzo. It was certain that Il Duce would speak.

By seven o'clock, the square and all the streets surrounding it were packed with thousands upon thousands of people, and though Dante kept his arm linked with mine, I felt brittle and nervous. The mood of the crowds seemed edgy, overexcited, emanating a dangerous energy. All the surrounding buildings were floodlit and, as we waited, searchlights played over the white columns and figures of the Vittore Emanuele monument. In my stomach, I felt growing fear. And then, out onto the balcony of the Palazzo Venezia, strode the man himself, and the noise around me grew to a roar. 'DU-CE, DU-CE, DU-CE, DU-CE.'

Mussolini stood, basking in the glory of the crowds, his chin upturned. Then he motioned them to silence. He told us that Barcelona had fallen, then paused to listen to the responding cheers. 'Your shout of exultation blends with that rising from all the Spanish cities liberated from the Reds. Franco's magnificent troops and our fearless legionaries have not only beaten Negrín's government, but many others of our enemies are now biting the dust.' At this point, his voice was almost drowned out by the applause.

131

He went on: 'Their motto was "*No pasarán*", but we did pass, and I tell you we will continue to do so.'

There were cries from the crowd of 'We want Corsica!', 'We want Tunisia!' and 'Down with France!' Though I was trapped within an enormous crowd, I'd never felt so much like an outsider. I couldn't understand why all these people were cheering and shouting. Why did they not stop to think?

Later that night, Dante kissed me and he was as fervent as he'd ever been, as though the speech, the whole evening, had excited him. My body responded but my mind was still on the blinkered crowds; how I had once been part of them, how my husband-to-be still was. How could I make him understand without risking losing everything?

II

The date was set for Friday 17 February. Valentine's week. 'For true lovers,' Dante said.

I had the wedding dress made up by a local dressmaker, plain white silk with a cinched waist, and I went shopping with Carmela and Serafina to buy white gloves and high-heeled shoes and perfume with the money Dante had given me. Their excitement was infectious and it helped buoy me over the coming weeks, despite the dark clouds that grew over Europe, my fears about Ettore; despite my concerns about Dante's views, Alessandro's strangeness, Chiara's continuing coolness towards me. I'd hoped that as the wedding date neared, Chiara would thaw, but our lessons now were stilted, and we spoke only of the music and her technique, never of her nightmares, or her wishes, or the fact that in a matter of weeks I was to be living there as her stepmother.

I summoned the courage to ask her what she intended to wear, and if she wanted me to speak to her father about money for a new frock. Though I didn't say it, I couldn't bear for her to wear one of the many dresses her talented mother had made her.

She turned to me and her eyes were strangely glassy and blank, like a doll. 'Thank you, but I don't really need a new dress. I have plenty already.'

I swallowed, preparing my words. 'Chiara, I know it's all happened very quickly, and that must be difficult for you, but I love your father. I think he loves me. I'll do my best to be a good wife to him and to look after you and your brother.'

Something crossed her face – a shadow of anxiety. 'I'm sure you will.' A pause. 'You must forgive me, Eva. I feel numb, sometimes, as though I'm watching my life from the outside. I have a strange feeling in me sometimes, as though I've been through all this before; that nothing is new.'

Grief, I thought. It was grief resurging as her mother's place was being usurped and I felt a terrible guilt. 'I'm not trying to replace her,' I said. 'Or erase her. I don't want you to think that I am.'

'You won't erase her,' Chiara said quietly. 'That isn't what I think at all.'

I noticed, however, as I left the house, that the photograph of Adelina had been turned around so that she faced towards the wall. Had Dante done that? I wasn't sure, but it made me feel uneasy.

January became February and in the Borghese gardens, the almond and judas trees turned to mauve and pink. I continued with the wedding preparations – the flowers and the confits and the clothes. I bought a beautiful nightgown of cream satin to wear on our wedding night and a shiver of excitement passed over me as I touched the fabric, imagined Dante running his hands over me. I was anxious, however, about how it would be, our first night together. Would I bleed? Would he expect me to? I had no idea and there was no one I could ask. Again, I longed to talk to Mirella. And though I could never have asked my mother such things, I still wished very much that she was there. I remembered when she'd mended my dresses for me, then stood to survey how I looked. 'My little girl, getting so grown up.' What would she think of me now?

All the while, the noise from outside, the growing belligerence, was rising to a roar, and the louder the noise, the more anxious I felt, worrying that I would be found out for what I was and deemed a liar and a traitor. Was concealing your origins a crime now? Would I be viewed as an enemy of the state? What if some distant relative turned up in Rome and outed me as the Slav that I was? What if one of the teachers at school who knew I was Slovene discussed it with someone that Dante knew? Though I knew, rationally, that this was unlikely, the thought still woke me in the night and intruded on my thoughts by day.

At the very end of the month, the Führer had made a speech to the Reichstag in which he talked of further expansion to secure supplies for Germany. He claimed that Europe could 'not become pacified before the Jewish question has been settled'. Settled. Cleared up. Even when diluted by our media, the story was deeply ominous. I thought of all the people Mirella had written of, desperate to find a haven in America or Palestine or anywhere. Other countries would have to accept those people now, wouldn't they? Because they must understand what Hitler was going to do.

'Surely Il Duce should stand up to him now,' I said to Dante one evening. 'Why must we go along with this? It's not what Italian people believe, is it?'

He smiled at me indulgently. 'It's not as simple as you're seeing it, Eva. It's a complicated political matter. In that very same speech you're talking about, Hitler praised Il Duce and talked warmly of his links with Italy. He can't throw that all to the wind at this crucial moment simply because Hitler is getting a little cranky. And it is, after all, just talk.'

I pressed my lips together and allowed him to kiss me on the neck. No doubt it was more complex than I understood, but it couldn't be right for Italy to stand by, or – worse – to stand beside, as people whose only crime was being of a different origin were hounded from their homes. I couldn't risk saying any of that, though, lest Dante grew irritated with me and began to question why I wanted to protect outsiders, lest he somehow detected that I was myself not as Italian as I had made out. I wanted desperately to talk properly about it to Ettore, but though we'd spoken several times on the telephone, he was always wary, fearful that the OVRA were listening. He had decreed that we must refer to Pietro as 'the horse' – he had gone there to see how his 'horse' was doing. So all of our conversations were slightly ludicrous dialogues about whether he had been able to see 'the horse', and how 'the horse' was kept in its stable most of the time, and how he was worried it was being inadequately fed. How on earth could I tell him about my fears when someone might be listening in?

In February came the news that the Pope had finally expired, his last words said to have been, 'Peace, peace.' It was difficult not to feel that all hope of avoiding war had died with him, for the very same day in Spain, Catalonia surrendered to the Nationalist forces, making it likely Franco would win. If I allowed myself to think too much about it – about how the nationalists were taking over Europe, the nationalists who hated the Slavs, the Jews, my friends – I became panicked. I tried to think instead of the man I loved and our future and the significance of what I was about to do – binding my mind and body to Dante's, devoting myself to him for life.

Dante did everything to make me feel comfortable, leaving me little presents and complimenting me every day. It was almost, though, as if the house detected my agitation or that of the world outside as, at times, I felt that strange thickening of the atmosphere that I'd first sensed the day Dante showed me the new chandelier. It was, I told myself, only my slightly warped mind, working its strange way through my current and past stresses, but occasionally it was so strong as to seem a real, unavoidable thing, like a hailstorm or a rumble of thunder. On one afternoon I could have sworn that the cupboard door in the hallway closed by itself, not slammed shut by a gust of wind but closed quietly as if by a hand, tidying the place for visitors. It must, I thought, be the weight of the door closing itself, but I was left with a feeling of distinct unease to add to my other worries.

Then came the day itself. My wedding. The morning began cold but bright and when I opened the window into the court-yard, two pigeons rose into the air, their wings a blur of grey and white. I was seized at that moment with a sudden urge to fly away myself: to pack my bags and leave the apartment and try to follow Mirella to France, or to find Ettore in Bari. *Don't be so utterly ridiculous, Eva.* Why should I run on the happiest day of my life? Why must I sabotage my own hope of joy – ruin everything good?

My stomach was tight like a clenched fist and no food would go down. Better, I thought, that I should stay empty and light. I wished again that my mother was there, or Mirella or Ettore, or that I had a sister who could tell me what to do. There was only Bruno, though, with his beady eye and his cackling laughter. 'Stupid, stupid,' he squawked, and I told him to shut up and eat his pumpkin seeds. 'No one gets to be mean to me today.'

At nine o'clock, Carmela and Serafina arrived to help me get ready, though really there was not very much to do. I'd decided to leave my hair down, with a small plait at the front, as Dante said he liked it that way, and to pin some white roses into it. My hands were shaking so much that I struggled to pull up the silk stockings and Serafina laughed at me and said she wasn't surprised – that it was a big day and she would be as jittery as a bug when the day came for her to get married. The girls both helped me with the dress as there were tiny pearl buttons all the way up the back. 'He'll have to help you with these later,' Carmela said, eyebrow raised. 'If he has the patience!'

She drew kohl liner around my eyes, but I wiped most of it away as I knew he wouldn't like that and wasn't sure I much liked it myself – it made me look too old, too knowing. I put on my lipstick, though, and as I did so, I thought of my mother. I wondered what she'd felt on her wedding day. Had she believed, then, that my father would love her and care for her, or did she already know what he was, but had no choice but to go along with it? I remembered her saying that her parents had thought my father was a good match: a sturdy, healthy-looking man with a secure job come to take their daughter off their hands. Well, he had done that.

All my doubts dissipated when we reached the church. Dante was already standing there, waiting, with Massimo and the children, and my heart leapt to see him, confident and resplendent in his midnight-blue suit, his face clean-shaven and his hair gleaming with brilliantine. I could barely believe I was marrying this man – that someone so handsome and capable should want me. And he *did* want me: I could see it in his smile when he saw me, and in his eyes, shining dark.

'You look beautiful,' he whispered, taking my arm. We walked down the aisle and he had none of my nervousness – he was steady and confident and his confidence spread to me so that by the time we were standing before the priest, I no longer felt queasy, only slightly light-headed. There was a powerful smell of incense and of the lilies which were placed at the front of the church. The priest's voice seemed overly loud, echoing off the walls, as he talked of how marriage was instituted for the procreation of children, as a remedy against sin and to avoid fornication,

'To have and to hold, from this day forward, for better, for worse, for richer, for poorer, in sickness and in health, until death do us part.'

I was only vaguely aware by then of the vows to which I was agreeing, as the beat of the blood in my ears drowned out everything that was being said and I could think only of Dante's dark eyes on mine and of the fact that I was finally accepted and loved and safe.

The rest of the day passed in a sort of blur: the rice confetti outside the church as we emerged; Chiara in her plum-coloured dress, doing her best to smile, gauche at the sisters' questions; Alessandro pink-cheeked with wine and strangely nervous; Massimo with his hideous ginger moustache staring at me and telling Dante he was a very lucky man. We went to kiss the foot of the statue of Saint Peter as all brides and bridegrooms did at that time and I was embarrassed at all the people staring and smiling. We posed for pictures and I tried not to think of Adelina in her beautiful dress. We drank champagne from elegant glass flutes and I immediately grew confused and then sleepy as I'd eaten nothing that morning or even the night before. Dante whispered to me that I looked perfect and that I'd done very well and I clung to his arm, wishing it could just be the two of us on our own now. I would look at him over the table unable to quite believe that he was my husband. I knew that Carmela and Serafina were jealous as they kept telling me how good-looking and charming Dante was, and he flirted with them mercilessly, occasionally smiling at me to show me that it was all right – he was merely teasing; he was merely being polite.

Then, at last, we were alone in the darkened room that I assumed had been the room he'd shared with Adelina – a grand double bed, twin mirrors, dark-wood cupboards – and I was frightened. It was my wedding night and I was still not sure whether I would be what Dante expected; whether my body, until now sheathed in silk and lace, would be what he'd anticipated or wanted. I was acutely conscious that he would be measuring me up against his first wife in the bed that had once been hers and I feared I would fall short.

Having felt sleepy all afternoon, I was suddenly very awake and feeling slightly sick. I worried that my breath would be sour and I was about to go into the bathroom to wash and prepare myself when Dante came into the bedroom, his jacket and tie already removed. He began, without saying anything at all, to unbutton his shirt, then his trousers and I simply stood there, frozen, wondering what he expected me to do, whether I should be removing the dress, or whether he would think that forward and unbecoming. Then he crossed the room and his lips were on mine, his breath full of cigarette smoke and brandy, and he was on top of me, pulling up my dress, pushing my underwear aside, and was suddenly and roughly inside me, so that though I'd craved this man for months, in the moment I was unprepared. Although I'd heard it would be painful, I hadn't expected this searing, burning sensation, this feeling of being split in two. I did not cry out, but remained entirely silent, still frozen, as Dante moved on top of me. When he was done, he withdrew from me and lay on his back beside me.

After a minute, he lit a cigarette. 'I knew you'd be a virgin,' he said, and kissed me once more on the lips. 'I will leave you to get your beauty sleep. Rest well, my little wife.' Then he got up and left the room.

For several minutes, I stayed there on the bed, numb. After a while, I became aware that I was cold and I dragged myself up and to the bathroom. There was blood, a decent amount of it, not only on my thighs but on the wedding dress which I still wore.

It took me a long time, but I managed to remove the dress, undoing the small buttons all the way down the back and then laying it in the tin bath so that it looked like the body of a dead woman. My beautiful silk stockings were laddered and I peeled them off and laid them too over the tin bath. I would've liked to have washed myself properly, but I didn't dare. Dante might hear me and come back. I would have to rinse myself as best I could in the sink. I sat on the toilet, burning with pain, then turned on the water tap.

Blood. Blood came from the tap – a stream of crimson liquid. I let out a gasp, then clasped my hand over my mouth and backed away towards the bathroom door. I heard footsteps on the stairs and turned with dread, thinking maybe Dante had heard me and was coming to see what had happened. When I looked back at the tap, I dropped my hand from my mouth. The water was running clear. I walked towards it slowly. There was no blood in the sink. No blood anywhere but on me and my wedding dress. I put my hand under the tap and the water ran over my hand, transparent. I looked at my face in the cabinet mirror and I saw that my lipstick had smudged across my cheeks, my eyes seemed sunken and my hair was standing on end. I looked what perhaps I was: a madwoman.

12

It was already light when I woke, the morning slanting through the slits of the shutters. I'd slept late. Beside me, a cup of coffee cooling, the milk already formed into a skin. Had Dante brought this to me? Or Greta?

I opened the shutters so that I could look down onto the square outside where a black cat was tormenting the pigeons. I felt different this morning – older, clearer.

We were not to go on honeymoon at once, but in the summer when the weather was finer and Dante's work less frantic. Dante had decided this some time ago and I was glad of it now because I was slightly afraid to be alone with him, though I could barely admit it to myself, having desired him for so long.

I cast my eye over the hangings, the pictures. Was this, then, to be my room, my room alone? It appeared to contain nothing of Dante's – no cigarettes or books or razors or any of the things I imagined a man might keep in his bedroom. It was very much Adelina's room. The decorations, the furnishings, the ornaments – they were of a very distinct taste. They all had that slightly old-fashioned elegance that I associated with her, whereas Dante's tastes seemed brasher, more modern, more fashionable. Did couples in Rome generally have separate rooms? Perhaps so. My parents had slept in the same room, but then we'd always lived in small houses with only a few sparsely furnished rooms. In contrast, Adelina's room was ornate and elegant, with fringed lamps and patterned wallpaper.

When I stared at myself in the long mirror, I looked too small, too drab, for somewhere so grand. My little case with its few possessions had been brought into the room and left by a large wardrobe. But when I opened the wardrobe, I saw that it still contained, pushed to the far side, some of Adelina's clothes – beautiful dresses in silks and cambric. I ran my hand over them and breathed in the smell of naphthalene mixed with some other scent, jasmine perhaps. Her perfume. Her shoes were still lined up at the back of the wardrobe. When I sat at the walnut dressing table, I saw crystal glass bottles and a set of enamel-handled brushes and a comb. Had these been hers? Would Dante really have left them here?

Greta came in and found me sitting there. 'Good morning. Did you sleep well?'

'Yes. I must have been very tired.'

She stared at the bottles and brushes. 'Did you want me to take those things away? I asked Signor Cavallera, but he said you might want them.'

'Oh. I... Maybe we should just put them in the drawer. Here.' It seemed wrong, somehow, to displace Adelina entirely.

'If that's what you'd like.'

I stood up, drawing my dressing gown round myself, and Greta began to move the bottles and perfumes and brushes into the drawer.

'Did she...' I hesitated. 'Did she and he always have different rooms?'

Greta stared at me, then looked away. 'I wasn't here at the

beginning.' She shut the drawer. 'He said you'd be helping with the housekeeping from now on, and the ordering.'

'The ordering?'

'The food and such. Deciding what I should order with the budget.'

'Oh, I see. I'm sure you're far better versed in all that than I am.'

'He's expecting it nonetheless.'

'Right. Well, maybe we could discuss later and you can tell me how it's usually done.'

She nodded. 'Very well.'

'Where is Dante, by the way?'

'At the tennis club. That's where he goes every Saturday morning.'

Every Saturday? Even the day after his wedding?

'I see. And the children?'

'At *sabato fascista*. They'll be back this afternoon.'

'Oh yes, of course they are.' All good children went to Fascist school every Saturday to march and play sports and sing. 'Well, I suppose I'll unpack my things. Make myself at home.'

I did not feel very much at home, however, as I wandered from room to room. I felt like a usurper, or like a child in a museum. Everything was very neat, very ordered. After Greta had gone to the market, I sneaked into Dante's room and, although he must have left in a hurry earlier that morning, his pyjamas were folded on the chair, the bed remade. Perhaps Greta had already been in and tidied. It was nothing like the messy apartment I'd shared with Mirella and I found that I rather missed it. I'd brought Bruno, however, in his cage, which was now in the kitchen. I found him there and fed him some seeds and whispered to him, but he was very quiet: suspicious, perhaps, of this new place with its new sounds and smells. Nevertheless, his presence was reassuring – something

144

familiar when I myself felt different and strange and sore.

Dante returned at around midday, by which time I had bathed and was feeling a little more myself. He brought a bunch of purple irises and was full of cheer and affection.

'Settled in, I see. Good, good. I do hope you like your room. I wasn't sure what your tastes were – if you had particular tastes – so I left it as it was. She had it done rather finely, I thought, and, of course, it cost an awful lot at the time.'

'Yes, it's very fine.'

'You must buy a few things of your own, of course. And some new clothes. I'll allow you a budget now that you won't be working.'

'That's kind of you, my darling, and of course my income is not so very much, but I really don't mind continuing with my classes. Indeed, they're expecting it – my pupils, the school.'

Dante frowned. 'I very much doubt that. People know that when a woman marries she gives her time to her husband, to the home. They will understand.'

I didn't want to argue with him – didn't want us to have a row, especially on our first day of married life – but this wasn't what I'd agreed to, was it? Or should I have expected it? I felt as though I'd signed a contract without properly reading the terms. Once again, I felt foolish and ignorant and wished I had someone to advise me. Then I fastened onto the thought of Signora Silvio at the school. She was married, wasn't she? She taught. 'Some women continue to teach after their weddings. There is a lady at the school—'

'Yes, some women,' he said easily. 'Women who need the money. You, fortunately, my dove, are not one of those women. In fact, I've been invited to apply for a new position, so it may well be that our finances are about to improve considerably. Oh, by all means continue with some of your private lessons if you want to and it keeps you occupied, but you really can't continue to work at that school all hours. We need you here. The children need you. With their mother gone, I regret that I had become a little lax as to their learning, but you can take charge of that now: give them private tuition at home, ensure they catch up in the subjects where they are lacking. You're such a gifted teacher. Alessandro has fallen behind terribly, but I'm sure with your assistance he'll improve in no time. He's keen to please you. We all are.' He smiled and kissed me on the cheek. 'Now, what are we having for lunch?'

The children, when they arrived home, put on a decent show of making me feel welcome, but I was quite sure that Dante had instructed them on how to behave, even on what to say. Our conversation was hesitant, awkward, though I tried my best to lighten the mood, introducing them to Bruno, asking them about their routines, what they liked for tea. We felt like players in a rehearsal still working out our parts. I knew Alessandro was watching me and I wasn't sure what he thought of me; I wished Chiara and I could regain what had at first felt like a friendship.

Still, it was early days. Things could, I thought, only improve.

That night, I put on the satin nightdress I'd so carefully chosen before the wedding and lay in bed, trying to read. At around eleven o'clock, Dante came to me again as I'd assumed he would and I felt my body freeze, though I willed it not to. After all, this was the man I'd desired for so long. This was my husband, the man to whom I'd bound myself before God.

Dante, however, didn't seem to notice my reticence, or, if he did, it didn't bother him. Perhaps he thought it the natural reaction of someone as inexperienced as I, and for all I knew, it was. He was gentler with me this time, but it was still painful at first, and I hated myself for my resistance, hated my body for not knowing what surely it was supposed to do. He knew what to do, though, and gradually I lost myself in our movement, in the sensation of his fingers, his tongue; the heat rushed through my body and when I closed my eyes, it was as though there were lights behind my eyelids, as though a flood of sparks had been released. And I thought, *Oh, so this is what it is like.*

He stayed with me briefly afterwards and kissed me. 'You must lie here resting for a while.'

Then he was gone and the room seemed very large and quiet in his absence. I had a sense that it did not want me there.

When I finally fell asleep, it was into a shallow, confused slumber into which strange rustling noises intruded now and again. Though I told myself it was only the noise of the water pipes, it felt as though the house were whispering to me.

At the end of February, as the mimosa began to bloom, Dante announced that he was travelling to Milan 'about a job'. I was to take care of the house and the children and he would miss me terribly, but there was nothing for it. I'd always wanted to go to Milan and I considered suggesting that I could join him, but I had the clear impression that he didn't want me there; that work was work and to be kept separate.

I wasn't at all sure how I felt about being left alone in that house. Not that I was on my own, exactly. Chiara and Alessandro were there, and Greta, and Bruno of course, who had taken to shouting 'Bravo!' in imitation of Alessandro. But sleeping in that room on my own made me uneasy. I had a sense, though I told myself it was ridiculous, that there was something in the walls.

I decided to make use of the time to discreetly get rid of some of Adelina's belongings and make the place more my own, thinking that might make me feel less anxious. The very night that Dante left, I took down some of the prints that hung on the wall. I would, I thought, replace them with something lighter, more colourful. I would buy something tomorrow from one of the stalls along the Tiber. Perhaps I would take Chiara with me, see if I could get her into conversation. I moved the clock too – the heavy carriage clock that had perhaps been a wedding gift. I pushed it to the back of the shelf and in its place I set a glass vase filled with freesias from the garden. Already, the place looked less gloomy, less like a museum to the wife that once was. I didn't dare get rid of her clothes, though. Not yet. I would need to speak to Dante about removing them, but I would leave that a little while until I was surer of my footing in the house.

I convinced Chiara and Alessandro to play a game of table tennis, and both soundly thrashed me, for I hadn't played for years. It was the first time I'd heard them laugh, I realised, and I thought, *maybe it will be all right. Maybe my being here will help. If they are broken, I will heal them.*

At nine o'clock, they said goodnight and I retired to bed to read. The strange noises in the walls continued. I would need to talk to Dante about bringing in a plumber. Evidently he'd grown used to the sound over the years, but I could barely concentrate on my book and instead imagined other noises within the hissing – spiteful whispers and quiet laughter – until I abandoned the book altogether and instead lay on my side, wondering what Mirella might now be doing, wondering how Ettore was faring, what exactly he'd got himself involved with, whether he'd seen Pietro again. I wanted very much to call him – to ask what he thought would happen in Spain, what would happen here, what might happen to me – but I knew I could say little over the telephone given Ettore's previous warnings and the ramping-up of the OVRA's activities. Alongside that, I feared that he'd detect that, despite all my protestations, I wasn't quite as happy as all that.

I must have drifted off to sleep with the light still on as I jerked awake sometime later to hear the sound of the piano. At first, I thought it must still be evening and that Chiara had returned to her practice, but I saw from my watch that it was gone one o'clock. Was I imagining the sound? Or was it coming from outside the house?

I slipped out of bed and opened the door to my room. I could hear the piano music even more loudly now – this was no dream, no imagining. The hallways and the stairs were unlit, but there was enough light to make my way down to the piano room, the moonlight picking out the curve of the banister, the gleam of the wooden floor. Was it Chiara playing? It must be, but it wasn't a piece I'd heard her play before. As I walked closer to the room, I had a horrible fear that it wasn't Chiara at all. That it was something else. An iciness spread down my spine.

Entering the room, I saw the outline of narrow shoulders, bobbed hair, and I breathed a sigh of relief. It was indeed her, but why on earth was she playing in the dark, in the middle of the night?

'Chiara?' I said gently, but she did not turn, only carried on with the waltz.

I walked softly up to her and stood by her side, but still she did not turn to look at me.

A noise, from behind me.

It was Alessandro, standing at the bottom of the stairs in his pyjamas. He put his fingers to his lips. 'She's asleep,' he whispered when he was closer to me. 'Best not to startle her.'

I looked again at Chiara. Her eyes were open, but there was something dreamlike, automaton-like, about her movements. Alessandro was right: she was asleep, yet somehow playing. 'She's done this before, then?'

He nodded, but did not smile, did not make light of it as

I thought he might. Instead, he gently took her hands and removed them from the keyboard, then pulled on her arms, encouraging her to rise with him. Then, still holding her by the shoulders, Alessandro guided her back towards the staircase. She walked along blindly, docile as a calf, up the stairs to her room.

Alessandro said nothing the following morning about Chiara's midnight piano-playing and Chiara herself smiled at me when I suggested we go to buy paintings, so I decided I too would remain silent about the affair. It unnerved me, though. Dante had mentioned that she'd begun sleepwalking again, but this was hardly just sleepwalking. Once more, I wondered at Chiara's state of mind. I wanted to ask her about the piece she'd played, but I couldn't betray that I'd seen and heard her. I wondered if she had any awareness of what she'd done, or if she'd remembered it only as a dream, if she'd remembered it at all.

I decided to try Alessandro later on that day. 'Does she often do that? Play during the night?'

'Only occasionally.'

I sat down opposite him. I noticed he gave off a smell, of unwashed adolescent boy. He had his schoolbooks splayed out of the table and I could see he'd been reading a page of textbook. 'I can help, if you like.'

'Boring as hell,' he informed me. 'I don't know why they make me bother with it. I'm only going to be in the army.'

I took the book from him and began to read the text: 'Benito Mussolini began to say that it was time to free Trento, Trieste, Fiume, Pola and Zara; all the countries Austria was lording over, despite the fact that God had made them Italian in the mountains, rivers and seas of Italy.'

'See what I mean?' Alessandro said.

I shrugged, aiming to give nothing away. 'Does Chiara do

other things in her sleep ever?' I tried to sound casual, light, but he was not fooled.

'Well, I suppose you'll find out, won't you? Living here.'

I thought there was something snide in the way he said it, an insinuation, or maybe I only took it that way because I felt like an interloper.

'I suppose I will, yes. I've a lot to learn about all of you.'

He met my eye, his gaze a study in blankness. 'Yes, you have.'

I did something then which at the time seemed like a clever little game. I hadn't been able to find the sheet music for the Ravel piece Chiara had played in her sleep anywhere in the house, which struck me as odd. Where had she learnt it or heard it? Then, as I was leafing through second-hand music at the Campo de' Fiori, I saw a copy of the waltz, and it seemed a sign. I bought it and I began to practise it. I thought it might coax out of Chiara that she knew the piece and how. I played only a few bars, looking for recognition in Chiara's face, but though I thought I saw a flash of something, she didn't say anything, didn't ask me what I was playing or why. She only asked had I bought any other new music and where from, and could I buy some new duets. The whole thing was perplexing.

In the first week in March, Dante returned, tired but exuberant. 'I'm very pleased to be back with my beautiful family,' he announced the first night we were back together. I felt a warmth course through me when he said that. A family. I was part of a family.

After we had made love, he ran his hand over my stomach. 'Do you think you might be?'

'Not yet. I don't think so.' I wished I was pregnant. It would, I thought, make me a proper wife, a proper Italian: to have a baby, a child of our own. Maybe then I wouldn't feel so anxious all the time. Maybe no one would question me.

'Yes, let's hope so. A new little Italian. What a glory that would be.'

I thought Dante might stay with me that night, but when I woke in the morning, he was already gone and I felt a tug of sadness and also of annoyance. Couldn't he have stayed with me just for once? It was Saturday morning and he was out at tennis again, no doubt.

I went down to the kitchen still in my dressing gown to make coffee. There was no one else up. I guessed the children were still in their rooms. As I waited for the water to boil, I wandered back into the living room and sat at the piano, absently playing the first bars of the waltz Chiara claimed not to remember, thinking of when I would tell the school I could no longer work there.

My hand was suddenly jolted away, the lid of the piano slammed.

'You will not play that piece. Not in this house.' It was Dante, his face white and pinched. He looked like a different man altogether. 'I imagine you think this is some kind of joke.' His voice was a violent hiss.

My heart shrank with dread. 'Joke? No. I just …' I didn't know what to say, didn't know whether to tell him of Chiara's night-time playing.

The silence stretched, interminable, between us and then I began, pathetically, to cry.

He closed his eyes. 'You really didn't know, did you?' He knelt down beside me. 'It was my wife's piece.' The anger had gone out of Dante's face and voice and he now looked merely tired. 'It was the piece she always played. And when I heard you playing, I thought just for a moment … Ridiculous, of course.'

'Dante, I'm so sorry.'

'You weren't to know.' He forced a smile. 'A horrible co-incidence, I suppose. I just can't bear to hear it, that's all. It brings it all back: our life then.'

He had imagined it was her, Adelina, in her silk wrap and slippers, playing her favourite piece.

'My darling, your face!'

Blood had begun to drip from his nose, horribly fast.

'*Maledizione.*' He pulled out a white handkerchief and pressed it to his skin, soaking up the red. 'Please, please.' He put his hand up. 'Don't fuss. It's just a cold, that's all.'

'You must sit down and I'll get you some ice.'

I ran to the kitchen, broke off a piece of ice from the sheet in the larder, and wrapped it in a serviette. I felt miserable, wretched, and not just because I'd upset him. *He still loves her*, I thought. *He still loves her, even though she's dead.* He'd wanted me to be her. He'd wished it was her there, playing, not me at all. I was a pale, inferior imitation.

Back in the piano room, I held the ice to Dante's nose and made him sit back.

'What would I do without you?' he said. 'My little nurse. You'll make us all better, I know it.'

I smiled, but my heart remained small and shrivelled, for I knew he no longer believed that.

I played no more games after that, but I remained alert and watchful, for I felt that the house watched me. I couldn't help but suspect that it, or *she*, had tricked me into playing the piece. And why had Greta not warned me not to play it? Why hadn't the children? I began to wonder if they were all working against me. At times, I felt the air thicken as though with hatred, and I wasn't sure whether it came from them, or my mind, or from the house itself.

I'd shut away Adelina's brushes and books and shoes, but occasionally I sensed they were lined up against me, watching, waiting. I knew that was ridiculous and that it must be a product of my own anxiety, possibly a resurgence of my old illness, but with no one to tell of my fears, they remained pent up within me, coalescing with worries past. I suppose I could have told Carmela or Serafina, but I didn't want to admit to them that my seemingly perfect life was not what I'd thought it would be. Nor did I want anyone to know that the illness of my youth might be returning. When the girls invited me to come out with them, I mostly declined, claiming responsibilities to my new family. When I wrote to Mirella, I couldn't bring myself to tell her what was going on. Her troubles were so much more real than mine, and I couldn't even articulate what mine were.

It was difficult, too, for me to separate what was happening in the house from what was happening outside it. With every day that passed, hostility towards outsiders increased and with it my fear that I would be found out; that I would be arrested or exiled, or worse. In the middle of March, Hitler's troops marched into Czechoslovakia and no one stopped them, least of all Italy. Il Duce gave a speech talking of how 'the Axis is not just a relationship between two states; it is an encounter of two revolutions which present themselves as the clear antithesis to all the other concepts of modern civilisation.' We were alone against the rest of the world and it terrified me, despite Dante's continued assurances that Mussolini knew what he was doing and that it would all play out well for us.

Was I even part of the 'us'? I'd thought before that I might get away with it, but each week brought some further polarisation, further hostility towards those who were not truly Italian – not just Jews but Roma peoples – gypsies, as they called them – brown-skinned people, homosexuals, anyone who didn't quite fit. The language of the newspapers had now seeped into the language of the people that I overheard in cafes and shops, into the comments of friends and colleagues. I still hadn't given up my job at the school and I saw the attitudes harden before me. Those whose eyes had filled with tears the day the Jewish children were removed from schools now seemed to accept that Italy had to be stronger, bolder, tougher; that to become the great empire of which Il Duce spoke, sacrifice was needed.

'Look at the Germans,' my old suitor, the once melancholy maths teacher, told me, now puffed up with a new sense of purpose. 'They didn't get where they are by pussyfooting around. They're brutal yes, but they've needed to be given what the other countries did to them – and to us – after the war. Germans first. Italians first. No more of this being treated like second-tier citizens.'

When Dante came home from work that evening, I decided I must talk to him about it – this strange and seemingly inevitable slide into hostility. But it turned out I had mistimed it entirely. 'Eva,' he said after I'd spoken, 'you sound like one of those liberal pamphlets students pump out on illicit printing machines. You must be more careful. I know it stems from your soft nature, but you have no real understanding of what's going on, nor of what's necessary to pull this country out of its post-war slump and towards its true potential. These are not normal times and what Il Duce expects of us is hard, yes, but it is essential.'

'Why, though, must making Italy strong involve turning race and nationality into a weapon? Why must it mean turning Italians against anyone who is in any way different? It feels like he's trying to nourish a hatred that Italians don't really feel. I don't understand.'

'No, you don't understand. Perhaps few women truly do. It's about becoming more warlike, more unified. It is about

155

rooting out those elements of society that have weakened Italy, and about driving Italy towards the future.' He smiled at me with what was clearly an attempt to be patient. 'You see?'

I nodded, but I had no idea what he was talking about. Was that because I was young, foolish, female, foreign? Or was what he was saying deluded?

'Anyway, I have some good news. The job I interviewed for, you remember? I got the call today, and they're appointing me.'

'My darling, that's wonderful. Congratulations!'

'Thank you. I confess I'm rather pleased. I didn't want to tell you about it at the time in case I didn't get the role, but, you see, it isn't just a town council post, it's within the Party itself.'

'Oh yes?' I felt my heart falling, my face freeze.

'Yes, I didn't want to get your hopes up until I was sure I had the position, but I'm to be one of the team advising Count Ciano, the Foreign Secretary. I have Massimo at least partly to thank.' He gave a radiant smile. 'Isn't that something, my love?'

For a long moment, I couldn't say anything at all. 'It certainly is.'

He kissed me on the cheek. 'So, you see, my darling one, there can be no more of this sort of talk now, you understand? Absolutely none. We must have faith. We must be the best we can be. And you, my beautiful wife, must buy yourself a new dress, because we're invited to a drinks reception at the residence of the Chief of Police, Arturo Bocchini.'

'Bocchini.' Chief of the Fascist Police.

'Yes, this Thursday. Don Arturo's place is quite extra-ordinary, apparently. It's quite an honour to get an invite.' He touched my face. 'Something peach, perhaps, to bring out the glow of your skin. We need to make a good impression, and I know you will. The other wives will die of jealousy.'

13

I tried to tell myself that it would be all right; that, in fact, this was a fortunate thing. Hadn't I wanted to burrow in, make myself safe? Well, now I was within the Party itself. Maybe I could use that to help Ettore and Pietro, help others. Maybe it would all be all right. After all, that was how some Slovenes and Croats had survived in my youth: by becoming fascists themselves. But I was no longer properly capable of deceiving myself, because I saw by that stage what was happening in our country; I saw what it was doing to my own friends. I'd no wish to be part of it, but now it seemed I had little choice, and some aspect of me knew I hadn't burrowed to safety but was now trapped in the eye of the storm. Still, I continued as was expected of me, toasting Dante's success and buying a new gown, to play the model wife.

Dante had told me Bocchini's house was exquisite, but he hadn't prepared me for the size or scope of the place: it was like some kind of palace, with soaring frescoed ceilings and gold Venetian mirrors. Immense torches had been placed outside the house, leading up the stairway and onto the mosaic-covered landing so that it felt we were entering a Roman villa.

Perhaps it *was* a Roman villa, I thought, looking down at the ornate mosaics covering the floor, horses racing across them. The illusion ended abruptly when I studied the hunter's face, for it was Il Duce, picked out in stone.

'Spumante, Signora? Signor?'

I looked down. A dwarf dressed in black silk was offering us glasses of champagne from a silver tray.

Dante took two, then led me along a mirrored corridor towards a group of people standing about talking and smoking.

A tall man with grey hair and a black cravat spread his arms. 'Dante, at last! Excellent news, isn't it?'

'The best of news.'

'We knew it was coming, but a relief nevertheless.'

'To Franco!'

'To Franco.' The group raised their glasses. He'd won the war in Spain, that's what the newspapers were saying. Dante had explained it as a reassuring thing, which I didn't believe, but it would at least mean an end to fighting, wouldn't it?

'Forgive me,' the man said, 'this must be the new Signora Cavallera. It's Eva, isn't it?' He took my hand and kissed it.

I smiled at him. '*Piacere*, Signore.'

'This is Giuseppe Volpi,' Dante explained to me. 'You must watch out for him. Wolf by name, wolf by nature.' They laughed.

'Nonsense, I'm a settled man now. Eva, I must introduce you to my wife.' He turned and called: 'Irena!'

His wife looked away from the clutch of women to whom she'd been speaking. She was a rake-thin, beautifully dressed woman in a small, feathered hat. She and the three women with her all eyed me closely, taking in my clothes, my hair, my make-up.

'But Dante, she's absolutely charming,' one of the women

said, putting her hand on his wrist. 'How on earth did you find someone so untouched in Rome?'

'I'm a lucky man, what can I say?' He put his arm round me and gave me what I knew was supposed to be a reassuring squeeze. 'You see?' he murmured in my ear. 'I knew you'd be the belle of the ball.'

He crossed the room to talk to a man in German military uniform, leaving me in the company of the sharp-eyed women who closed in around me. When, they wanted to know, had Dante and I got married? How long had we been engaged? What did I think about Dante's new job?

'I'm afraid you'll now see rather less of him,' said Irena. 'The legal team all work like absolute demons. Giuseppe certainly does. Always away doing something or other. My advice to you is to develop a hobby, some kind of activity to keep you occupied while he's off working or with the boys. Mia creates the most beautiful scrapbooks, don't you, darling?'

'Oh yes.' Mia wore a fox fur, the whole animal. Its dead eyes stared at me dully. 'And we have regular bridge mornings. Do you play? You must come.'

I was seized with slight panic at the thought of these bridge mornings and the endless questions. They would uncover me far more quickly than Dante was likely to, for I was bound to let something slip. 'I'm afraid I can't say I really play.'

'Well, you must learn. There's very little else to do. Cards. And tennis, of course. You play tennis? We're all members of the Royal Club. You know, the one the Cianos frequent. They do the most marvellous cocktails.'

I couldn't admit I didn't play tennis either. I supposed I would have to learn, though I'd never been much good at sports. I felt the sourness of anxiety seep into my mouth and accepted another glass of champagne from one of the waiters, hoping it would numb me against the inquisition. Dante, I noticed, was now talking and laughing with a woman in a grey fur. After a moment, I placed her as the woman I'd seen him with at the cinema, that first time we'd gone together to the Imperiale. The recognition gave me a shivery feeling.

'You're terribly young, aren't you?' Irena said, taking my arm and walking me to the other side the enormous room. 'Twenty? Twenty-one?'

'Twenty-five, actually.'

'Well, you're dreadfully lucky. Your skin is quite perfect – soft as silk.' She said it as though she wanted to stretch it out and have it made into a pair of gloves. 'And I hear you play piano very well. You must show us.'

I realised with horror that she was guiding me towards a white grand piano. 'Oh no, I couldn't possibly.' I looked about for Dante, but he had vanished.

'But you must. Mauricio here is so decidedly dull,' she murmured. She reached the piano and smiled at the over-weight, morose-looking pianist who was playing Cole Porter. 'Mauricio, did you know that Eva here, Dante's new wife, is a piano tutor? Quite brilliant, he tells me. Eva, do play us a song. Something upbeat that we can dance to.'

My father had done this once he'd accepted that I would play: dragged me out to the wine bar and made me strike up a tune on their aged piano so that he could show the other men that his daughter had something their children didn't. I hated it then and I hated it now – being made to play like a performing monkey. But other people were waiting around by this stage, expectant, and poor Mauricio had stood up and shuffled away from the piano, so I smoothed my skirts and sat down on his chair, placing my hands on the keys. What on earth would I play? Something 'upbeat', she'd said, but I couldn't play Gershwin in a house full of people celebrating the triumph of the Nationalists. I plumped instead for a foxtrot and thought, *Please God, let Adelina not have played this piece.*

I did my best to concentrate on the music and ignore the crowd around me, though I could feel sweat collecting on my brow, and was acutely aware that Dante must be somewhere in the room, possibly annoyed that I was playing at all. When I finished, there was clapping, cheering. I looked up to see a circle of faces, alien, hard, and I wondered how I'd had ended up in this room with these awful people.

'Bravo! Another!' one woman shouted.

'*Giovinezza*!' demanded a giant of a man in the Fascist uniform. 'Play *Giovinezza*!'

Others joined his cry and I felt a sickness in the core of me. 'I'm afraid I don't know how to play it,' I attempted, but Irena was there, insisting that Mauricio must have the music. The truth was that I did know it — of course I knew it — but I had no desire to play it then and there, the sole Slav in a room full of Fascists and Nazi officers. Mauricio, however, had dutifully found the sheet music and placed it on the piano and there was nothing for me to do but play.

The voices around me joined in: *Dell'Italia nei confini, Son rifatti gli italiani* — and in the midst of all that sound, I understood that I was not one of them. Nor did I want to be.

At last, the piece was over and I let my hands rest in my lap. I would play no more.

When I looked up, I saw that Massimo was staring at me. He often stared, but there was something in his look that I couldn't at that time read.

It felt as though the evening would never end. By two o'clock, I was exhausted. I couldn't understand how Dante had so much energy. It seemed he would never stop talking, of the Nationalists and Il Duce and the 'empire', as he and everyone else there now referred to Italy. There was much animated conversation about whether Italians were truly 'Aryan', with Dante and others insistent that there was such a thing as a pure Italian race. There was another man, equally drunk, with a monocle fixed firmly in the flesh around his right eye, who ranted on about ancient civilisations. By that time, I felt quite ill. The champagne that had initially made the whole thing bearable had given me a headache and I wanted desperately to go home. But though I whispered to Dante that I was very tired, and hadn't we better leave, he merely kept saying that, yes, yes, we would leave soon, but there were things he needed to say.

The next thing I knew he was in spirited discussion with the man with the monocle, who was objecting to the practice of sending homosexual men to the islands as a form of punishment. 'So we deprive our armies of any man who prefers a *pisello* to a *figa*? It hardly makes sense.'

'But of course it makes sense,' Dante was saying. 'They're an insult to the Italian race and its prestige. They are not part of us. Drown the buggers, so far as I'm concerned. It's not as though we're wanting for valiant men to fight. It's the munitions that are an issue, though, of course, it'll all be sorted out by the time we have to get involved. Il Duce has made sure of that. No, spare me the sentiment. Italy will only be made stronger if we each become stronger – if we accept our own role in rooting out anyone corrupt, anyone who is not truly part of our nation.'

I was suddenly very sober and very afraid. Did he mean it, or was this just drunken talk intended to impress his new colleagues?

'Well said, Cavallera,' another man said. 'Couldn't agree more. Enough of this namby-pamby liberalism. Look at Germany. Look at what they've achieved through bringing people into line.'

'*Germany*,' the man with the monocle practically spat. 'We

are not Germany. Never will be. Nation of halfwits and pen-pushers.'

'I'd be careful who you say that to, old man,' Massimo said smoothly. He seemed less drunk than the others. 'Unwise to malign our new friends, especially at the moment.'

'Well, yes, they're the only friends we have! Them and the Spanish. And the Japanese, of course, but I wouldn't trust them as far as I could throw them. Odd-looking chaps.'

'The fact remains,' Dante said, his speech slurred, 'that Il Duce is the one leading the show. Not Hitler. Oh, he'll go along with him to keep him happy, but it's Il Duce who knows what's what. Always has been.'

'So you don't think this anti-Jew business is a sop to the Germans?' said the man with the monocle. 'Bit of a coincidence, isn't it? Just as they're turfing Jews out of the country, we're forcing them out of their homes and jobs here, telling them they're no use to us?'

'Mussolini knows the Italian people. He knows what'll make them stronger and bring them together, what will make Italy a great nation once more, and it's making the Italian race as pure as the driven snow. We've been being slowly corrupted for years and this is simply him saying enough is enough. No more. Our civilisation is Aryan. Our population is Aryan. Let's make it pure. You see?' Perhaps Dante had caught sight of my expression. 'At any rate, we're boring my wife. Let's get another drink, for God's sake.'

I was nauseous with exhaustion and anxiety by the time I went to bed, but the house did not want me to sleep. From within the walls came first a slithering sound, as though a snake were trapped behind the bricks, and then an almost-voice: not the indistinct gurgling I'd heard before, but something closer to a human voice, rasping, whispering. I couldn't, though, work out what it was saying, for it seemed the sounds were not quite words but strange noises, like someone or something learning to speak. Where was it really coming from? The pipes? Next door? Or was it only in my own mind? There was a clawing, too, as though a rat or some larger animal were trapped in the wall and trying to get out. It went on and on until I became so frightened that I almost went into Dante's room to shake him awake and ask could he hear it too? But, ultimately, I didn't dare, because what if there was no noise, save in my own head? Certainly no one else was up and awake.

I thought back to the episodes that had begun when I was fourteen – the peculiar sounds and feelings that came to me, as though I was inhabited by another being. For years I'd tried not to think of that time and the things that had happened to me then. I thought of them that night, though; I couldn't *stop* thinking of them. I remembered the time I'd woken in my narrow cot to a terrible itching on my skin, the sure and horrifying sense of insects crawling all over my arms and legs, beetles or flies that had somehow got into my bed. I remembered screaming and scratching at myself, only stopping when my mother rushed into my room with a lamp to show me that there was nothing on me at all, only scratches caused by my own fingernails.

Was it that again, only different? Had my mind – strained by events and worries and alcohol – once again decided to play tricks on me? I tried over and over to shut it out, but every now and again a sound would come, like a machine struggling to speak or an animal struggling to escape. Only at about four in the morning did the sounds finally stop and allow me a few hours' rest.

I felt terrible the following day, my head fuzzy with champagne and lack of sleep. Dante was irritable and greyish-looking,

164

and insisted that he was staying in to work, despite it being a Saturday. He had, he told me, a big piece of advice to complete for Ciano.

In the afternoon, he asked could I be a marvel and take Chiara out so he could have some silence in the house. 'Why don't you go to the Azalea Festival on the Spanish Steps?'

Chiara herself looked rather drawn, I thought, but she agreed to come with me. I wondered if she was troubled by Dante's appointment. Alessandro had greeted the news of his father's new position with apparent glee and a barrage of questions: Did this mean he'd be allowed inside the party headquarters? Would they get to meet Il Duce himself? Chiara had also claimed to be pleased, but she must have some idea of what was happening in Italy for she'd seen her Jewish classmates disappear, heard the rising vitriol in our newspapers, on our radio, and she was an intelligent girl. I didn't dare, however, to ask, so we talked instead of other, inconsequential things.

The Piazza di Spagna certainly looked beautiful, with the deep pink flowers flowing up the white steps, and the flocks of girls all in white dresses or colourful smocks walking arm in arm up and down, men turning to look at them. But it was almost too dazzling; the brightness of the dresses and the sunshine hurting my eyes. There were so many people: tourists, soldiers, vendors, all chattering and laughing, and I couldn't stop thinking about the voice and the scratching of the night before. I couldn't stop thinking of what Dante had said.

I went about the place in a half-dream, trying to get my mind to focus. As we reached the top of the steps, a group of young Fascists marched past, one of them knocking the hat from the head of an old man who'd failed to salute quickly enough. I felt suddenly nauseous and too hot.

'We don't have to stay, you know,' Chiara said. 'If it's too much.'

'Perhaps we could go and sit in the church for a moment. I'm rather tired.'

We entered the white walls of the Trinità dei Monti and I was immediately glad of the cool and calm, the smell of incense and snuffed-out candles. At the front of the nave, a mass was being said in French. Chiara and I sat on pews further back and listened for a while in silence. I felt the sweat dry on my brow and for a moment I closed my eyes. I thought of going to church with my mother when I was young, the safety and boredom of the priest's services, the closeness of my mother's body. I'd thought at the time that it would always be like that; I'd no idea that one day merely giving a Slovene service would be enough to get a young priest shot. I'd no idea that a choir-master would be kidnapped and tortured because his choirs continued singing in Slovene.

'I'm going to light a candle,' Chiara said.

'Of course.' I watched her as she walked to one of the walls, lit a little candle and then mouthed a prayer, crossing herself.

I smiled at her as she returned. 'Is she buried here?'

'Who?'

'Your mother.'

'Oh, no. No, she's buried in the family vault at Cimitero del Verano.'

'Would you like to go there?'

'No. Thank you. I don't really think of her as being there.'

'What do you mean?'

'I mean, I think of her as still being in the house.'

The nausea returned to me suddenly, the bile rising in my throat, because Chiara was right. Adelina, or some part of her, was still there. Still in the house.

Chiara stood up. 'I suppose we should get back for dinner.'

★

That night, the voice came again, and it *was* a voice now, though still not quite a human one, and it made my stomach turn over with fear. It was saying something again and again, but I couldn't work out what it was. At around midnight, it stopped and I was drifting off to sleep, but then came a note: a note from the piano. Then another, higher. It must be Chiara again, playing in her sleep, mustn't it?

Shaking, I forced myself to climb out of bed and walk down the stairs as I had before, telling myself this was nothing new, though I could feel the blood pounding in my ears. When I reached the piano room, I found it silent and empty. No, not empty exactly. There was something there, or had been, but of Chiara there was no sign. Was she playing a trick on me? Was Alessandro? Well, I would not have it.

I walked barefoot to Chiara's room and opened the door a crack. She was there in her bed, apparently asleep. I noticed, however, that her body trembled. A nightmare? Or had she just run back upstairs and pretended to be asleep? Why would she do that? Had Alessandro set her up to it?

I returned, still shaking, to my room and lay for a long time in the silence. The sounds did not come again.

At breakfast, the following morning Dante peered at me over his newspaper. 'Are you unwell, my darling? You look rather pale.'

'I'm fine, *mio caro*, just not sleeping very well.' I hesitated. 'There were some odd noises last night. You didn't hear them?'

'No, I slept like the dead, but then I always do. What noises?'

I shook my head. 'Maybe just the pipes again.' I thought of the slithering sound; the whispering.

I caught Alessandro looking at me, but I could not read his expression.

'Ah, yes, mea culpa,' Dante said. 'I said I would speak to

someone and I haven't. I'll do it today. We can't have you missing out on your beauty sleep.' He smiled and I thought that he himself looked rather unhealthy, the skin around his nose raw, the skin taut over his cheeks.

Chiara had kept her head in in her book the whole time. Was she listening to us? Was this all a game they were playing with me?

'Greta, turn up the radio, will you?' Dante said. 'There's an important bulletin at ten.'

There came the martial music that announced a government bulletin, the instruction that you must stand to attention; then the strident voice of the announcer: 'At 9.30 a.m. today, Italian government troops entered Tirana, Albania, and quickly captured all government buildings. This measure was judged necessary to safeguard the peace of the country and quell the armed bands patrolling Albania. Currently, there is no attempt at resistance and the population is cordial and grateful to all the Italian troops.'

Dante clapped his hands. 'There it is. Albania. Il Duce is finally taking control of our territories. He is rebuilding the Roman Empire.'

'Bravo!' Alessandro shouted. 'We'll show them.' His voice was rather high, however. Unsure. He was saying these things, I understood, because he wanted to please his father, his only remaining parent.

I was bewildered, still trying to make out what the radio announcer was saying. He was talking about troops advancing to protect the people of Albania. 'What are they protecting them from?'

'From rebels,' Dante answered, as though that were obvious, getting up and pouring himself more coffee.

Rebels. But it was the rebels in Spain whom we were supposed to support, the rebels who'd overturned the communist government.

'What happens now, Father?' Chiara asked. I thought she too seemed nervous.

'Now Albania becomes part of Italy, just as it once was. It was already our protectorate – it's a natural step. Really, it's no more than Britain and France have done in Egypt, Algeria and many other places.'

He'd known, then. He had known what was going to happen and what would be announced. Yet there had been no prior announcement here, no warning. Is this what he'd been advising Ciano on? The legalities of annexing another country?

'What will it mean, though?' I asked. 'For Italy?'

'It will mean, my darling, that the world will have to start taking notice of Italy and answering to our territorial claims. It shows them that it isn't just Germany who means business – that we're no sleeping partner in this axis. The spirit of Rome will rise again. We will take our rightful place in the world.' He smiled. 'In more practical terms, it means that we should all go and have a gelato in the Villa Borghese gardens. Oh, I know it's Good Friday, but I think a little celebration is called for, yes?' He looked up at us expectantly and I did my best to look pleased. Really, though, I was tired – tired of pretending to agree with him, tired of pretending that everything was fine. I wanted very much to be on my own, to try to understand what was happening, or to be with someone who understood me. 'Chiara, should you like that?' he asked.

'Yes, Father.' Her face was solemn. I wondered again what was going on behind those light brown eyes. I wondered how much she understood.

'Bravo!' Bruno squawked from his cage.

Dante laughed. 'You see? Even that damn bird knows this is a thing to celebrate. Let's go and put on our finest.'

When I returned to my room, I saw that Adelina's brushes had been moved back out of the drawer and placed again on the dressing table. A thread of fear ran through me. Who had moved them? Greta? Dante? It seemed a very odd thing to do. What was it supposed to mean?

That evening, after the liturgy at St Peter's Basilica, Dante went out for some celebratory drinks with his colleagues. As soon as the children were in their rooms, I went into Adelina's old sewing room with Zefiro and I shut the door. There was a radio in there that I supposed she must have listened to when she was working on the many cushions and curtains that filled the house, or the outfits she made for her children. Very quietly, I turned it on and tuned it to Radio Londra. I needed to find out what was really going on, and the Italian media wouldn't tell me. Nor, clearly, would my own husband.

On the hour there came the familiar notes of Beethoven's Fifth Symphony and then the clipped tones of the radio announcer as he spoke of the 'sudden invasion' of Albania on 'the day which to most Christians is the most sacred day of the year'. Then an account of the occupation, talk of a 'loss of international confidence' and 'questions about what this means for the Mediterranean'.

'There is great concern that three nations in Europe – Czechoslovakia, Austria and Albania – and one in Africa – Abyssinia – have now lost their independence, while vast areas of China have been occupied by their ally Japan. Reports, which we hope are not true, insist that further acts of aggression are contemplated against still other independent nations.'

When the report ended, I turned off the radio and sat in the silence. Zefiro stared at me balefully. It was as I'd thought: Mussolini was snatching land, just as Hitler was, and there seemed little glory in that. Rather, it was an act of aggression, intended to provoke, like a bunch of drunk men on a Friday night, looking for someone to pick on. It was the same as all the talk of race and purity: it was an 'our gang is better than yours' mentality and it sickened and confused me that my own husband should buy into it. More than that, it frightened me. I wasn't in their gang, no matter how much I'd tried to believe I was. Underneath it all I was a Slav, and if Dante realised that, what exactly would he do? What would happen to me then?

My eyes fixed on Adelina's sewing basket. Had she sat here at night, I wondered, when Dante was out, working on clothes and listening to her radio? Had she had her favourite programmes? Had she too listened to the foreign news to try to work out what would happen next, or had she been the good wife, who never questioned her husband? I wished I could have known her, spoken to her, found out what marriage was like for her. For although her belongings were still littered about the house, although her husband was now my husband, and her children effectively my children, I had little understanding of what she'd been like, as Dante rarely spoke of her. In fact, now that I thought of it, I realised that on the rare occasions when he talked of her at all, he never used her name.

Then, almost as if by thinking of her I had summoned something, there began again that scratching in the walls, as though of a large rat. It was not just in my mind, could not be, because Zefiro's ears had risen. Rats then, it must be rats. I imagined them scurrying behind the wallpaper. But Zefiro didn't run to the wall and sniff and bark as I would have expected him to do. Instead, his legs began to shake, then his whole body, and he retreated away from the wall.

The scratching came again, but from a different place this time, over towards the sewing machine, as though the thing in the walls had moved. Was this a trick, or some animal? I felt a rising tide of ice-cold fear. Zefiro gave a low whine.

'It's all right, Zefiro. It's not going to hurt you,' I told him, but my voice evidently sounded as thin to him as it did to me, for he backed further away into the corner.

The scratching came again: louder, viler, from a point further along the wall. I wanted to get away from it, whatever it was, at once.

'Come on, out of here.' I tried to drag Zefiro by the collar, but he strained away from me, still whining, refusing to move from the corner. 'Enough, Zefiro! It's nothing. Stop being such a silly dog!'

There came the sound of the front door opening and closing. Footsteps on the stairs. Thank God, Dante was home.

Zefiro finally left his corner and ran to find his owner. I walked more slowly after him, trying to calm my racing heart.

14

The man arrived two days later: a handyman who Dante said had sorted out all sorts of issues in the past. He went about the house knocking at walls, turning on taps and fiddling with the radiators, then knocked on the door of Dante's office. I crept closer to Dante's room so that I could listen in to their discussion.

'There's no problem that I can find,' I heard the man telling Dante. 'Nothing wrong with the pipes or the radiators. Your wife said there were sounds coming from the bedroom at the end of the corridor and in the small workroom, but I didn't hear anything.' A pause. 'It might be something next door, I suppose. Or vermin. But I didn't see any droppings anywhere.'

'No, I don't think it's that. Well, thank you all the same for coming. It's a relief to have it confirmed that there's no problem with the house, at least.'

But there was a problem. Dante must sense that, surely. Or did these things really only happen to me?

I returned to the front room where I'd been rehanging the curtains. I heard Dante paying the man and showing him out. Then footsteps towards the room where I was pretending to be busy. I turned as the door opened.

Dante stood with his hands in his pockets. 'No issue that he could find.'

'Right.'

Dante walked closer to me, then stood, rocking on his heels. 'You know, you mustn't overdo it, my angel. Mustn't put strain on yourself.'

'I'm not imagining it, Dante. Zefiro heard noises too.' My voice came out too sharp. 'I'm not mad, if that's what you think.'

'I never said that, my love. I merely mean you are in a new house, a new situation. The mind plays tricks.'

For an instant, I thought again of the sense I'd had as a fourteen-year-old that the organs within my body were shifting; that something was trying to get out. Was he right? Was my mind playing a horrible game, just as it had when I was younger? But then how to explain Greta's concerns, Zefiro's frightened whine?

'My darling, could you be...?' He smiled. 'It's common for women to become emotional if they are carrying a child.'

I stared at him. It wasn't the time for my courses yet but might that explain in part the strangeness I had felt? The odd energy? 'I don't know. I don't think so. But I suppose it's possible.' Yet pregnancy no longer seemed a positive thing; the prospect now filled me with fear.

He kissed me on the cheek. 'Let's hope that's what it is. All the more reason for you to take it easy. I'll tell Greta to do this.'

'Really, there's no need. I'm fine. Honestly.'

He nodded. 'Well, if you're sure. I'd better get back to work.'

I watched him as he left the room. In the doorway, he looked back at me and gave a smile. It didn't reach his eyes.

★

The noises diminished over the next few days, the scratching stopped, but the voice still whispered at night, attempting words I couldn't fathom, filling me with icy dread. I didn't dare mention that to Dante. In fact, I saw very little of him over the next week as he was, he said, working on several important projects and stayed late in the office every night, often not returning until after I'd turned in for bed. I grew nervous that he was avoiding me. It did, however, allow me to secrete myself in Adelina's sewing room night after night, listening to Radio Londra – to the reports that Britain and France had condemned Italy's actions in Albania, that Hitler had meanwhile celebrated them; to the news that the European countries still couldn't reach an agreement as to what was to happen to the Jewish people that Germany was threatening to expel.

One evening, just as I was readying myself for bed, the phone in the hall began to ring. I hurried towards it, not wanting it to wake the children. It would be Dante, I thought, calling to tell me why he was so late again.

'*Pronto*?' I said into the receiver. It was one of those heavy, black Bakelite phones.

No reply. Just the static of electricity.

'Hello? Dante, is that you?'

Still only a crackling sound. A bad line, I thought. Some problem with the connection. I wondered if it might be Ettore, trying to ring me from Bari.

I replaced the receiver and walked down the corridor back towards my room. As I reached it, the phone began to ring again.

I hurried back to the receiver. 'Yes? Hello?'

This time, there was something there – not just the crackle of electricity, but a breath. I felt the hairs rise on my arms.

'Hello? Who is this?'

Still only the breath: rasping, horrible.

175

I slammed down the phone, my hand shaking.

'Eva?'

I jumped, but it was only Chiara in her nightgown.

'Who was it?' she asked.

'I think it must just have been a wrong number,' I said. 'Or a problem with the line. I'm sorry it woke you.'

'I wasn't really asleep.'

We looked at one another. How much had she heard of the noises in the house? I wondered. Had she heard the hideous voice too?

I thought she might say something else. I almost prayed that she would. But she only said, 'Goodnight, then,' and shuffled back to her room, leaving me with my heart beating frantically, like the wings of a hummingbird.

The following morning, I told Dante about the phone ringing. 'I was sure I could hear someone breathing on the other end. Was it you, trying to get through?'

He looked up from his paper and frowned. 'No, I didn't call. I assumed you'd know that if I was out, it was because I needed to be.'

I didn't say anything to this, merely carried on trying to eat my roll. My throat felt incredibly dry so that I couldn't swallow. 'Well, whoever it was called twice,' I said.

He raised his eyebrows. 'Odd. A mistake, I suppose. Or a prank caller. Let's hope he doesn't bother us again. I've been meaning to tell you, by the way, that I'll be in Berlin next week.'

'How long for?'

'All week, I'm afraid. Several legal meetings and we're visiting the Reich Youth Leader to take a look at their organisations, how they organise the ranks over there. I'm intending to take

Alessandro. I'm sure he'd love to know what they get up to, and he needs to work on his German. He might even make some German friends. You can take care of Chiara, of course?'

'Of course,' I said flatly. 'Although' – and here I brightened – 'perhaps we could all go. I could explain to my private pupils.' By this stage, I had given notice at the school, but I was damned if I was giving up all my lessons.

'That's a nice idea, Eva, but Chiara has her recital, hasn't she? And I thought it might be nice for me to spend some time with Alessandro, just boys together. Try to sort out some of his behaviour.'

My heart fell. He was right about the recital and about Alessandro, who had become increasingly disruptive. The school had called Dante in to complain about the boy's behaviour – he'd been found with matches in the school stables. Further, I had no real wish to go to Germany. Nevertheless, I was stung. I thought of the promised honeymoon. The summer seemed so far away.

Dante must have guessed at my thoughts, as he said, 'Of course we must plan another trip away together. The problem is that, having just taken this position, I can't take any proper time, but perhaps a long weekend in late May. Should you like that? Amalfi, perhaps. Or Positano.'

'Yes, I'd like that very much. I've never been to the Amalfi coast.' The thought of being alone with him made me anxious, but I wanted, more than anything, I realised, to be away from the house.

'Never been to the Amalfi coast? Good lord, did your parents not take you on holidays?'

A mistake, I realised, for we'd spent all our holiday time back in Trieste. I had to be more careful. 'They did, but mostly to the lakes.'

'I see.' He looked at me closely and I had a horrible fear

that he saw right through me. Hadn't I told him we'd never been to Lago di Bolsena? 'Well, we must plan something soon. Though, of course… your health may not permit it.'

'Oh, that. Actually, my darling, I found out his morning that I'm not in fact, as we'd hoped… not yet in any case.' My period had come on suddenly with cramps and a great rush of blood that made me wonder if I had in fact been pregnant, if only for a few weeks.

He smiled, but I could tell he was disappointed, annoyed even. 'Well, there's still plenty of time.'

This struck me as a peculiar thing to say. Of course there was plenty of time. I was only twenty-five.

A long pause and then he said, 'I'm afraid I'm likely to be back home late this evening, as well. There's a function at the Palazzo Chigi I need to attend. Dreadfully tedious, but I have to put in a decent appearance.'

I put down my roll. I had the clear feeling he was not telling me the truth. Was he avoiding me, or was he spending his time with someone else? I thought of the woman with the grey fur, her hand on his arm.

'Do you really have to? What if there are more phone calls?'

He sighed, irritated now. 'If there are more calls, then you must tell whoever it is that you'll inform the police, and then you must dial the operator and see if you can find out the number. I'll do that this morning, in fact, though it may now be too late. With any luck, it was just some bored youngster calling numbers at random and they won't bother us again. All right?' He kissed me on the cheek, ending the matter, and returning to his paper.

With any luck; but this house had no luck, just as Chiara had said.

I was supposed to have been the luck and I began to think Dante judged me a dismal failure.

That night, I lay in bed, wide awake. I didn't know how I knew, but I was certain that the phone would ring again. At around midnight, the air seemed to thicken and I was seized with a terrible feeling of loneliness and rage. Then came the ringing of the telephone, a jangling that seemed to wake every nerve in my body like the shudder of a dentist's drill. I walked towards it this time, not running, not hurrying, barely daring to pick it up.

I put the receiver to my ear. The breath was there again, rasping, evil.

'Whoever you are, you're to go away,' I said unsteadily. 'There's nothing for you here.'

A gathering of breath and then, far too loud, far too real, came that hideous hissing, whispering sound that I'd heard coming from the walls – the voice that was not quite a voice trying to speak – only now it was much clearer and closer, as though the presence was right there, next to me, its tongue and teeth in my ear, and I felt sick to my stomach. I dropped the receiver and backed away from it. Then, gripped with terror and anger, I wrenched the wire out of the wall so that it might not ring again. Dante would be furious with me no doubt, but it wasn't him who had to live with the damn thing. He was always so conveniently absent.

I returned to my room, my mind whirring. For a long time, I lay on my bed, trembling, finally falling into a confused slumber. From the depths of my consciousness, I became aware that the phone was ringing again. I must still be dreaming, I thought, because the phone could not be ringing. I'd disconnected it. Befuddled and exhausted, I sat up. It was not a dream. The phone was ringing. How was that possible?

I threw open the door and hurried out onto the landing, nauseous with fear, but I was too late. Chiara was already standing in the hallway with the receiver to her ear. Her eyes were round with horror.

'Chiara?' I said, rushing up to her. 'Chiara?'

The girl did not respond, nor did she move the phone from her ear. A lone tear was making its way down her cheek.

I wrenched the receiver away from her and shouted into it: 'Leave us alone, you hear? Leave us alone! We don't want you here! Go away!'

Alessandro was now in the hallway as well, his eyes bleary with sleep. 'What's going on? What is it?'

I took Chiara's hands. 'I won't let it hurt you,' I said, and in that moment I was furious; that this thing should try to frighten not only me, but the children.

'Who is it?' she whispered. 'What is it?'

'I don't know. I don't know, Chiara. But I promise you I'm going to stop it.'

The tears were spilling down her face now. 'What if it's Mother?'

I froze. Had she heard something completely different to me? What I'd heard was vile, frightening, not human. 'No, Chiara, darling, it's not your mother.'

'But what if it's her, trying to tell us something?'

'It wasn't Mother, you idiot!' Alessandro shouted at his sister with sudden violence. 'Mother's dead! It's someone playing a rotten joke, that's what it is.' His voice was brittle, very much that of a boy. 'Father said it was a prankster, didn't he? Well, we'll show him, whoever he is.'

I didn't have it in me to point out the disconnected wire, and perhaps after all I hadn't totally broken the phone and it was somehow still able to function. Perhaps it was someone – someone who hated Dante for working for the Party, or who hated me – winding us all up. Could it be? Well, they'd got to us, all right.

I looked at Alessandro's pale, frightened face, the downy hairs on his lip. I should have been paying him more attention, I thought, trying to get closer to him, rather than fearing him. He was just a boy who missed his mother and had no way of dealing with his grief.

'Well, whoever it is, we'll get them to stop,' I said. 'You're not to worry, all right? I'll get rid of them.' I had no real idea, of course, how I was going to do this, but I was the adult. I had to try to reassure them. 'For tonight, I'm taking the telephone outside. I don't want it in the house. Not until we've got rid of whoever it is. Now, you must both go back to bed and try to get some sleep.'

I picked up the phone and carried it downstairs and into the garden. I walked right to the back of the garden and put it in a box in the shed. There. It could ring all it liked and we wouldn't hear it.

When I returned to the house, I peered around Alessandro's door and saw that he had his eyes shut, pretending to be asleep. In the next room, Chiara was sitting up in bed, her face still wet with tears.

'Maybe she was trying to talk to me and I couldn't say anything at all. I could hardly even bear to listen.'

'It wasn't your mother, Chiara. I'm sure of it.'

'Will you stay with me?' she asked. 'Just for tonight. I don't want to be on my own.'

'Of course I will.' The truth was that I didn't want to be on my own either. I climbed into bed next to her. 'Now, you must lie down and try to go to sleep. Tomorrow we'll work out what to do.'

Obediently, she lay down and turned on her side away from me. After a moment, she said quietly, 'Whoever it is, I don't believe they'll go away. I think they've only started.'

★

When Greta arrived the following morning, she of course noticed the missing phone, the straggling wire. 'What happened, Signora? Some accident?'

'No, Greta, no accident.' I'd considered keeping the whole episode from her – I didn't want to frighten her – but I was gripped with the urge to tell someone what had been going on. I told her then of the phone and of the noises in the walls: the terrible voice and the hideous rat-like scratching. She listened to me in silence.

After I had finished speaking, she nodded. 'It's as I told Signor Cavallera weeks ago, it's as I told you: there is something in this house; something that is moving and breaking things.'

'Like the vase.'

'Exactly. The vase. And, before that, a plate that I know he thinks I dropped, but which I swear to you jumped from the shelf. The wasps too. That wasn't normal. Then there was the water, wasn't there? Coming from nowhere. I've found things moved, too. Last week, just after I'd finished cleaning the kitchen, a toy soldier appeared on the windowsill. It had been in Alessandro's room – how did it magic its way down there? And now this, this phone business.'

I thought of Adelina's brushes, of how they'd reappeared on the dressing table without explanation and a chill ran through to my bones. 'Could it be someone playing a prank? Someone breaking things, moving things?' The children, I meant. Could it be the children? I didn't believe it, though.

Greta shook her head. 'I don't see how.' She paused. 'You've spoken to him about it?'

'Dante? No, not really. He thinks I'm imagining the noises. He claims to have heard nothing.'

'Yes, he claims.' Greta met my eye and I saw reflected there the fear I myself was feeling. For a long moment, neither of us said anything, but then Greta seemed to gather herself. 'I tell you what I'll do: I will speak to Rosalie, a woman I know. She understands these things better than most. Maybe she'll know what it is. Maybe she'll tell us what to do.'

'Who is she?'

'A woman who knows things. I went to her after my husband died; and my daughter has been to her for healing.'

She must mean a wise woman such as they used in the countryside. I'd always assumed it was superstitious nonsense, but what other option did I have? 'All right. If you think she might help, then please ask her as soon as you can. I can't... I can't bear it.'

She gave a nod. 'I'll go to her today. But it's important that Signor Cavallera doesn't know of this. Agreed?'

'Yes, agreed. Thank you, Greta.'

'Good. I'll go and see Rosalie. See what she can do to help.'

We waited until the day Dante left for Germany to bring Greta's friend to the house. I'd told him nothing of my ongoing fears, nor of Chiara's idea that it had been her mother trying to contact us. He seemed ever more excitable and agitated at that time – forever talking about the importance of his work, the rebirth of the Rome, the regeneration of Italy – and I doubted we'd be able to discuss it rationally. I'd brought the phone back into the house and managed to reconnect it. I thought at first that I would be frightened, but when I touched the phone, I sensed that it had lost its energy. It would not ring again. Whatever it was would torment us by a different means; one we were not expecting.

For almost a week, the house remained silent: no whispering noises from the walls, no blood from the taps, no water from the ceiling. I wanted to believe that was the end of it, but in my heart I knew that whatever it was remained in the house, lurking, biding its time.

When Rosalie arrived, I understood why Greta had insisted Dante mustn't know of her visit. She was a stooped woman in a faded black dress and black shawl mostly covering her long dark hair. Her eyes, though, were luminous amber and about her neck hung a tangle of gold necklaces. She was a Roma woman. Greta brought her into the kitchen and began making tea while Rosalie sat down at the table. I stared at the gold rings on her fingers, wondering at how she could still be wearing the traditional dress of her people at a time when they were being identified and persecuted. I'd heard of terrible things done to so-called gypsy people: children taken from their families, men beaten to death or sent to labour camps. Did it not make her want to hide who she was, just as I had done? I'd been convinced it was better to try to camouflage yourself and hope they'd shoot at someone else, but I was beginning to realise it wasn't that simple. I didn't read any fear in her, either, though she must have known this was the house of a Fascist official. Her amber eyes – light against her tawny skin – were intelligent and calm. She smelt of some kind of herb – marjoram, maybe – mixed with the smells of her own skin.

'So, Signora,' she said, once Greta had brought her a cup of tea, 'You sense that there are spirits here.'

'I don't know, Signora. I'm not even sure I believe in spirits. But there is something here. Something which is doing things, moving things, whispering. We were hoping you'd be able to help.'

No answer.

'Can you?'

The woman sipped her tea. She was in no hurry.

'I am not a spirit reader. But sometimes I see things. I will see what the cards show.'

She took a pack of Tarot cards from a net bag and began shuffling them with an expert hand. I felt faintly ridiculous, like a gullible girl on a visit to a fortune teller at a fair. It was a mistake to have allowed Greta to bring this woman here. She wouldn't be able to tell us anything.

Rosalie set down the pack and turned over the first card. It was a tower, alight, lightning streaked throughout it.

I felt quite cold. 'What does that mean?'

'It means chaos,' Rosalie said levelly. 'Destruction, disaster. And that is what I sense here.'

I stared at the card, the flames bursting from the windows. I envisaged the fire licking at the Narodni Dom, felt the ash in my throat. I looked at Greta, who was watching Rosalie intently.

She turned another card. This time, it was a series of arrows, birds flying between them. 'The eight of wands, reversed. I see it as a terrible burning anger that is being pressed down.'

'In the house?'

'Yes, in the house.'

And that's what I'd sensed time after time, I realised: an incandescent rage bursting to get out.

'There is something being pushed down,' the woman said. 'That is what I think.'

'What? What is being pushed down?'

She shook her head and turned another card: a crescent moon, upside down.

'I don't know. This means confusion, fear. And that's all I see. It is clouded and dark, blurred with smoke.'

'Well, can't you turn another card?'

The woman looked at me steadily and held my gaze as she set another card on the table: a priestess seated in a throne. But the card was upside down. 'It does not want to show us its true self.'

I felt an immense sense of frustration and disquiet. 'Well, can you get rid of it, whatever it is?'

She shook her head. 'These things only leave when they want to leave.'

'But surely there must be something you can do to drive it out!' I said, aware of how foolish this sounded. What even was this thing we were to drive out?

'*People* you can drive out — Jews, gypsies, other unwanteds. But this? This is not so easy. It will only go away when the anger has died.'

'Anger about what?' I asked.

'That I can't tell you. You'll need to work out it out for yourself. You'll need to listen.'

'Listen to the thing? It's been hissing in my ears since I got here! It doesn't want to help me; it just wants me to leave.' I thought of the voice spilling its bile from the telephone receiver, the gurgling and whispering coming from the walls. I didn't want to listen to that anymore; I couldn't. In fact, now that I thought about it, acknowledged it, I'd sensed a hostility in the house ever since the beginning — the thickening of the air, the swarming wasps. Yet now I was supposed to lend it my ear as though it were some kind of troubled friend?

'I know, it's hard to listen to anger, particularly when there's hatred all around us, but that is all I can tell you.' Rosalie took another sip of her tea and began to pack up her cards.

'Is it to do with the first Signora Cavallera?' Greta asked suddenly. 'Could it be her spirit?'

'I know that's what you think, Greta, and it's possible, but I don't see her or hear her. Often I see spirits, but today? Nothing so clear. No, it's not so simple as that.'

Greta nodded but didn't seem convinced. She passed Rosalie a paper bag, which I could see contained food. 'For the grand-children,' she muttered.

Rosalie took the bag without comment, then looked at me.

'You can work it out. You have the gift. But you need to stop lying to yourself.'

That night, I woke in an instant, knowing something was wrong. A sound, I was sure, had woken me, but now it was gone, sucked into the silence. I sat in bed, listening. Nothing. The silence was too thick, too heavy. So was the air, which seemed too dense to breathe. Minutes went by and the only sound was the beating of my own heart. I knew, however, with cold certainty, that the house, or the presence, was watching and waiting.

At last, there began a quiet susurration, a growing rustling, like dry leaves in the forest warning of an approaching storm. The dread was visceral, revolting. I wanted to scream at it to leave us alone, but I remembered Rosalie's words.

'All right,' I whispered, though my stomach was tight with dread. 'I'm listening. I'll listen to whatever it is you have to tell me. I will try my best to help you.'

The rustling sound grew louder, thicker, until it was a violent hissing, like tongues of flame licking at the house. Then I felt it: an invisible energy moving closer to my bedroom, followed by the very real noise of the door latch rattling, lifting. As though with a breath, the door opened, the milky light from the corridor following it into the room so that I could see the doorway, empty.

I wanted with all my might, with everything within me, to run, or to shrink in on myself, to disappear. I felt my scalp prickling, the fear spreading through my veins.

'What do you want?' I whispered back to it. 'What are you trying to tell me?'

That thickening again of the air, that appalling sense of a rage more powerful than anything I'd ever felt: a searing, burning pain, of something shut out and alone. From the walls, the sickening hissing, like the walls were filled with snakes. In my head, an image, very clear, of a woman lying on the workroom floor, face down. Adelina, it must be Adelina, upside down like the priestess card, but where had that image come from? From my own mind or from the thing that was in the room with me? Then came a gush of wind, cold as winter, and the door slammed. It was gone.

Dante and Alessandro returned two days later. Alessandro was oddly quiet, while Dante was full of their exploits and adventures in Germany.

'Their organisation is something else, Eva, I tell you. We definitely have the edge when it comes to fire and enthusiasm, but the Germans know how to manage their youth organisations, keep them all working together. I wish you could have seen it.'

I smiled, feigning interest.

'And how have my girls been? All well, I trust?'

I hadn't meant to tell him. I'd meant to keep it to myself, keep trying to work it out, find a solution. But I found his arrogance, his assumptions, infuriating. No, it was not all fine, and I thought he must sense that, must have some idea he'd left me in a house that was brimming and hissing with rage and hate.

'In fact, Dante, things have been rather difficult.'

'Difficult. What do you mean?' He was still smiling.

'I mean the things that have been going on in this house, Dante. The things that have been going on for some time.' I knew that I would annoy him, but my own anger made me bold and I told him of how it was: the noises that had become a voice, the piano playing on its own, the hissing on a disconnected phone.

For a time, Dante stared at his hands. Eventually, he looked up. 'Eva, I regret to say that you are unwell.'

'No.'

He gave a tight smile. A muscle pulsed in his jaw. 'You'll recall that a man came here. That he couldn't hear or find anything. That I warned you that you were making yourself stressed.'

'I'm not unhinged, Dante. Greta has heard things too. Things have moved—'

'Greta is a superstitious old woman whose mind started giving way some time ago.'

'What about your own daughter? Chiara heard the voice on the phone. She knew there was nothing natural about it. She knows there's something here, in this house, just as well as I do. Just as *you* do.'

He slammed his hand against the table. 'Oh, for God's sake: Chiara heard the prankster who rang you to try to frighten you!' He was almost shouting now. 'And instead of trying to reassure the poor girl, you've been nurturing in her a belief that there's some kind of supernatural phenomenon floating about and trying to make contact with us! Do you think that's responsible behaviour?'

I backed away from him. 'I'm not inventing it, Dante. She heard it just as I did. It wasn't a prank caller. It couldn't have been. It's not as easy as that.'

'Let's ask her, shall we?' He moved to the stairs and shouted up to her. 'Chiara! Chiara, come down here, please. I need to speak to you!'

Chiara appeared a few moments later, her face tense, her hands clasped in front of her. 'Yes, Father?'

Dante gave her an unconvincing smile. 'Eva has been telling me about the phone ringing. She said that she believed it to be some kind of ghostly voice and I explained to her that that wasn't possible – that it was merely a prank caller trying to frighten you. She seemed, however, to think that you supported her view that it was some type of "supernatural communication". Can you confirm what you heard?'

Chiara stared at him, eyes wide, her glance flicking to me, then back to him.

'Well?' Dante said.

'I didn't really hear anything,' she replied.

'No?'

'No, not… No, I didn't hear anything, Father.'

'Good. Well, it was just some joker who'll hopefully not bother us again, and you mustn't worry about it, all right?'

Chiara nodded.

'And you do know, don't you, that there's no such thing as ghosts, spirits?'

'Yes, Father.' She would not look at me. 'I was just upset.'

'Of course. That's only natural. And when we are upset, we are liable to imagine things.' He looked at me pointedly. 'Thank you, Chiarina. You may go.'

'Yes, Father.'

Dante waited until she'd left the room and we'd heard her footsteps retreat back up the stairs.

'Jesus Christ, Eva,' he hissed. 'I thought bringing you here as my wife would mean I had some more help with Chiara – that she'd be soothed. If I'd known you were just as neurotic as she is – more…' He stopped himself. 'It will not do, you understand?' he said more quietly. 'You need to pull yourself together. I need you to be a capable mother.'

Rage coursed through me. 'Naturally. You need me to look after the children at all times. Keep everybody happy. That's why you married me, isn't it? Why employ a tutor or a cleaner or a whore when you have me?'

'What in God's name has got into you?' His face was white with anger.

'I am trying to tell you what is going on in this house and

you are refusing to listen! And of *course* Chiara told you she hadn't heard anything. How could she say otherwise? You've brought her and Alessandro up to always agree with everything you say, everything you do. How could she dare challenge you?'

'Enough! I will not hear this.'

'You will hear it! You will!'

'Keep your voice down.' His hand was on my arm. 'I'm going to speak to the doctor.'

'I don't need a doctor.'

'I think I'll be the judge of that. I don't believe you're capable of knowing what's best for you at the moment.'

'I'm not mad, Dante. I'm not making it all up. There is something *here*. Something that is furiously angry. It isn't just me who thinks so. Greta's friend came. She said that she sensed the anger, she said that the house was trying to talk to us.'

'What friend?' His voice was very cold and I knew at once that I had made a terrible mistake.

'Just a woman who knows about these things.'

'Some crank, you mean? A spiritualist? A fraud? And you let this woman into the house? You encouraged this nonsense in Greta and in my daughter? I should never have left you alone.'

'No, you shouldn't have.' I was crying now. 'You shouldn't have left me night after night with this thing, whatever it is, in the house. But you are out, always out, wherever it is you go, and—'

'You are to stop talking now, Eva.' He had hold of my shoulder. 'You are to stop talking and go to your room. You are unwell. I am calling the doctor.'

I could feel his fingers digging into the muscle. I thought of my father, the way he would sometimes push me or my mother out of the way as though we were merely pieces of furniture. I went to my room and I lay on the bed and I wept until I

191

was numb. I'd destroyed everything. I'd acted the part of the hysterical woman in which Dante had cast me. I'd frightened Chiara, betrayed Greta. I was pathetic and stupid and weak.

By the time the doctor came, I'd already given up the idea of resisting. It was the fat little man who'd administered to Massimo after the wasp attack. He took my temperature and pulse and looked into my eyes. 'I am going to give you something to help relieve the anxiety,' he said. It was presented not as an option, but as a decision. 'You will go to sleep and by tomorrow everything will seem much better.'

I didn't say anything to him at all, just let him prepare the needle, pull up my sleeve and administer the injection, whatever it was. I even relished the pain. Within a few seconds, I could feel the drug spreading like ink through my veins, slowing my heart. Yes, I would sleep, but no, things would not seem better tomorrow. If anything, they would be worse.

I slept until late the following morning and when I woke, my head was heavy as though it had doubled in weight. I felt washed out, alien. It was as if some other woman had taken charge of my body. I went into the bathroom and retched. My face in the mirror was bloated and blank. I thought of my mother's often swollen and bruised face, thought again of her words, 'There's no use fighting. It only makes it worse.'

I think I knew even before I went downstairs what I would find.

Greta was washing up the breakfast things and she was crying. Dante had told her to leave. Her case was already packed.

I sat down at the kitchen table. 'I'm so terribly sorry, Greta. I can't explain why I told him. I wasn't thinking properly. We were arguing. It was stupid.'

'Stupid,' Bruno repeated from his cage.

From Greta, only silence.

'What will you do?'

'I will go to my daughter in Milan. She won't want me, but what other choice do I have? I won't get another job in Rome, not at my age.'

'Has he paid you?'

'Oh yes, he's paid me. He's paid me to shut up.' She came and sat opposite me and I saw that her eyes were red-rimmed but clear. 'You must leave this house too, Signora. You hear me?' She spoke quietly, but firmly.

'I can't leave, Greta.'

'Yes. Yes, you can leave. You must leave. Because this thing, whatever it is, whatever it wants to say, it is not to me, it is not to you, it is to *him*, you understand that? It is him it wants to tell, and he will not listen. He will not change. And so everything will be destroyed.' She took off her necklace and put it in my hand. It was a thin silver chain with an amulet of red coral in the shape of a horn.

'I can't take this, Greta! It's yours. And it's all my fault you're leaving.'

'Please.' She closed my fingers over my palm. 'Take it, for protection. It's the least I can do. I should have done more. Been braver.'

'What do you mean?'

She blinked. 'I mean that I don't like how things are going and that you must get out. Take the children if you can, but get out.'

'Greta, there's a car waiting. Please hurry up.' It was Dante, standing in the doorway. Had he heard anything of what she'd said?

I wanted to hug her, thank her, apologise for not having believed her right from the beginning, to ask her what exactly she meant, but there was no time. She picked up her case and was gone.

15

May passed as though in a dream, or a nightmare. Dottor Falluci had prescribed a set of small blue pills which I must take morning and night to 'steady my nerves'. They didn't steady so much as numb me. I was often tired, sometimes falling asleep midway through the afternoon, and I found I no longer had the energy to argue with Dante – to protest that I was not imagining what was going on in the house, to tell him I didn't want the life he was making for me, nor the Italy that this country had become. None of this languor was unwelcome. For the first time in weeks, I was able to sleep properly at night, sinking into an even deeper numbness where the house's whispers and shrieks couldn't reach me, nor the torment of the outside world. I still heard the noises now and again, piercing through the membrane that surrounded me, but I let them wash over me like a wave and slipped back into unconsciousness. 'I'm not listening,' I told the house. 'I'm not listening anymore.'

As for Chiara, she kept to the line that she could not have heard anything. Were she to claim otherwise, it would have meant disagreeing with her father and thus certain punishment, and Chiara was an obedient girl. Like myself at that age, she'd learnt it was easier to go along with what was asked of you and drown the rest out. Generally, she avoided me. Occasionally, I would catch her staring at me as though confused, trying to place me, or remember something, but we never spoke about what had happened, nor about what was happening now.

Meanwhile, events in the wider world marched onwards, with reports flooding in of more dissenters denounced, people arrested on the spot for the wrong thing said, more people locked up or sent into *confino*. From France, a letter from Mirella telling me of government leaflets instructing people what to do if war should come, and asking me what was happening in Italy, what I intended to do. I didn't reply. I couldn't. Nor could I bring myself to contact Ettore.

Later in May, Italy and Germany signed the *Patto d'Acciaio* – the Pact of Steel – making the Rome–Berlin Axis agreement a thing set in metal. The two countries were tied together, for better, for worse, till death do us part, and I was filled with a queasy dread, despite the little blue pills.

'Does it mean we must go to war?' Chiara asked her father when she heard it announced.

'My darling, you mustn't worry your pretty head about it. Il Duce signed the agreement only after obtaining a promise that there won't be any war within three years. He's keeping us safe, just as he always does. When war comes, we will be ready for it, and we will succeed. Now begins the preparation.'

Alessandro had abandoned his comic and stood up. 'In three years' time, I'll be eighteen. And I'll be ready to fight!' His words sounded strained and unconvincing.

'Exactly, my boy.' Dante patted him on the back. 'War will, as Il Duce says, put the stamp of nobility on all who have courage to meet it.'

I watched them as though they were characters in a film.

Did Dante not remember what war was like? Would he really send his only son to fight? Sacrifice him for the fatherland and some vague idea of nationhood? And poor Alessandro would go along with it, so desperate was he to prove himself a man, a loyal Fascist and a loyal son, just as so many Italians followed Il Duce, believing him to a strong and caring father. But Mussolini didn't care about them, about us. I knew that by then, even from behind my narcotic haze. I just couldn't bring myself to really think about it, or to work out the cause or meaning of my own husband's increasing fervour.

Dante's talk now was always of the Party and the empire and the great strides Germany was taking; how we should follow close behind until we were ready to overtake; how the spirit of Rome would rise again. While I felt ever sleepier, he seemed never to stop. He was always up and working, or out at some bar or function, from which he'd return reeking of smoke, sometimes entering my room in the middle of the night and then entering me. Often, I only became aware of him once he was inside me, and I would wake believing I was still in a nightmare. Sometimes I dreamt that it was others who penetrated me – Il Duce, Hitler, a strange horned beast – and awoke in a state of horror. Dante was affectionate afterwards, though, more than he'd been a few weeks ago. It's easier to love someone who doesn't resist, doesn't argue, doesn't make you question yourself.

At the end of May, Dante announced that we were to go to another party together, this time in the Palazzo Braschi, the Fascist headquarters. A celebration of the Pact. It was a great privilege to be invited, he assured me, confirmation of his rising status. Many important people would be there, Count Ciano and Edda Mussolini included. I must look my very best.

'You'll forgive me for saying you're not seeming quite as

sprightly as you were, my love. And you're losing your beautiful curves. Perhaps some exercise would do you good. Why don't you buy yourself another dress? Something expensive and elegant.'

I looked at myself in the dressing-table mirror. He was right. My skin was dull, the whites of my eyes bloodshot, and I could see the outline of my ribs high in my chest. I looked like a woman who had given up. I looked, in fact, like my mother.

When Dante had gone, I drew kohl around my eyes, dabbed rouge on my cheeks, and forced my lips into a smile. 'Sprightly enough for you?' I asked the mirror, which told me I looked like a ghastly clown.

When I opened the door, I found Chiara standing in the hallway just outside my room, as though considering whether to come in. She too appeared wan, her lips cracked, that terrible pained look again in her eyes.

'What is it, Chiara? What's wrong?'

She remained silent, her fingers worrying her lip.

'Are you ill?'

'I don't think so.' She met my eye. 'Have you heard things, Eva?' she whispered. 'Seen things?'

My heart slid. 'No, sweetheart. Because I'm no longer listening or looking. I can't. You can't. It will drive us all insane.' I smiled. 'Want to come shopping with me? Get out of this house. Get ourselves something nice?'

She shook her head and I hated myself, but my attempts to acknowledge the thing had only made it worse, for me, for her, for all of us.

When I returned later with my new dress and hat, I felt that the air in my room was cooler and I had again that powerful sense of rage that broke even through my sedated state. There was nothing out of place, though: the cupboards were still all neatly shut, the bed made, the pile of books lined up. It was only when I went to the dressing table that I saw them: all of my tiny blue pills. They'd been placed in concentric circles, one perfect circle inside another. I felt the cold breath of fear. Had Chiara or Alessandro done this? No, I thought, staring at the circles, the pattern was too neat, too symmetrical. No human hand had done this.

I dropped my shopping bags, picked up the pill pot and swept all of the blue pills into it, my heart racing. I ran to the bathroom, poured them into the toilet bowl and pulled the flush. I watched as the little blue pills whirled around the bowl and disappeared. Then I closed the lid and sat there for a moment. I had no more pills, but I didn't want them. I needed to wake up again. I needed to stop it all.

The sense of panic and foreboding stayed with me all day and into the evening. I took a bath in the copper tub, scrubbing violently to wash myself clean of the pills, the fogginess. *Wake up, Eva. Wake up.*

The woman in the shop had assured me the new dress suited me, but when I tried it on and looked at myself in the full-length mirror, I realised it was all wrong. It was the sort of dress Adelina would have worn. I might just as well have taken one of the dresses that hung limply in the wardrobe. Only on me it looked silly – the dark green colour made my skin look doubly pale.

Dante refused to let me change into one of my other dresses, however. I couldn't possibly wear the same dress as I'd worn to the Bocchini party.

'Besides, it makes you look sophisticated. Demure.'

'It makes me look not like me.'

'Nonsense. Of course you look like you. Who else would you look like?'

I glanced at Dante. He himself looked exhausted, I realised, the skin beneath his eyes bruised. It occurred to me that he was ill, had been ill for some time, and was hiding it from me. I thought of the nosebleed, the feverish rhetoric. What exactly was wrong with him?

'Are you sick, my love?' I asked.

'Sick? No, of course not. Why ever would you think that? I'm on fine form. Full of energy. Come, you are being morose. We're going to have a splendid evening. Here. I bought you something.' He removed a box from his pocket and opened it before me. 'Go on. Take it.'

It was a necklace – a gold choker in the shape of a snake, its eyes small glinting rubies. It must have cost a fortune.

'My goodness, Dante, you didn't need to. Not for me.'

'Do you like it? Rather lovely, isn't it? Certainly very modern. Edda, Ciano's wife, was wearing one at the club and I thought it would look perfect on you.' Dante stood behind me and put the choker around my neck, fastening the clasp at the back. Then he put his hands on my shoulders and stared at us both in the mirror. We looked, I thought, like ghosts. 'There. I knew it would suit you.'

I touched my fingers to the necklace. It felt cold against my skin. 'It's beautiful, thank you, darling.' I smiled.

'Yes, it works, doesn't it? Right, let's get going. Won't do to be too late.'

The party was in full swing by the time we arrived, the chatter and laughter of the guests booming off the vaulted ceiling and mixing with the strains of the jazz quartet, rebounding off the mirrored walls of the ballroom. Over the glistening parquet floor swarmed women in satin and sequin dresses and men in dark uniform – Italians in black with gold braiding, Germans in brown, the light flickering off their tiepins and medals as they whirled past painted friezes and flags. Above us hung immense chandeliers of glittering crystal, casting golden light throughout the room.

I recognised some of the faces from the Bocchini party, and some from newspapers and portraits. A small crowd surrounded a man I knew to be Count Ciano, the Foreign Secretary, the man for whom Dante worked. Standing beside him was a dark-haired woman in a jet-black, satin dress with a diamond brooch pinned at the cleavage: Edda Ciano Mussolini, Il Duce's daughter herself. I was right in the wolf's den. Half of me wanted to laugh.

'Let me introduce you,' Dante insisted, dragging me forward, and the next thing I knew we were within the circle of admirers and flatterers, Dante shaking hands with Ciano and gesturing to me, and Ciano smiling – a flash of white teeth – and taking my hand.

'She is indeed a beauty,' he said to Dante, before directing his attention to someone else.

Dante smiled at me approvingly and I felt a coldness creep up my arms and legs, because it was just the same as my father, parading before his friends the daughter who could play the piano. I'd thought Dante so different, but I understood then why he'd pursued me, why he had married me: he wanted me as a trophy, a pretty, untouched wife to prove what a great man he was. He hadn't even really desired me. I was like the new chandelier, the new necklace: an adornment, a status symbol.

'Eva, there you are!' I turned to see Irena, the terribly thin woman who'd dragged me to the piano last time. She clasped me by the arm and inspected me more closely. 'But I must say you look dreadfully pale. And you're losing that puppy fat. Have you been dieting? Cider vinegar? Or is it' – she was watching my expression – 'something else?'

'I'm fine, Irena.' I looked desperately about the room for

someone who might rescue me, but Dante had already moved off.

Irena was still studying me. 'A drink?'

'Thank you, no. In fact, I must go to the bathroom.' My head still felt woozy from the little blue pills, or perhaps the removal of them.

There was no shaking the woman, however, and she followed me into the marble-walled bathroom. Once I'd left the cool and calm of the toilet cubicle, she whispered hoarsely: 'You're pregnant, aren't you? Well, I must say, I am pleased for you. Slightly relieved, if truth be told. I know Dante was so eager to have more. It's all about showing willing, isn't it? And poor us to have to put up with it. Don't worry, though: you can get a nanny in once it's born. I insisted on it. I said, "Giuseppe, if you're going to make me have all these babies, you can't also expect me to look after them!" I have the name of an excellent woman. She'll sort you out.'

'Please, Irena,' I said with alarm, 'you mustn't say that, mustn't say anything at all.'

'Aha, you haven't yet told him. Well, don't worry. I'll keep it to myself. But you really should tell him sooner rather than later or he'll carry on pawing at you. Not that I'd mind being pawed at by Dante, handsome as he is, but when you're not feeling so well...' She put her hand again on my arm. 'Poor lamb. Don't look so upset! Lord, it's not as bad as all that. You'll start to feel better once you're three months in. Not everyone does, of course. Poor Margareta was dreadfully ill, throughout. Ended up on a drip.' She pouted and put on her lipstick. 'But then at least she didn't have to diet afterwards.'

I watched her with horror. Was she right? Was I pregnant? I'd had a spotting of blood only recently so discounted the possibility, but now I wondered if I'd been wrong. It was what I'd wanted for so long, to make myself a family, to be part of one, but now the idea that I would have this man's child struck me with an icy fear.

One of the cubicle doors opened and I saw that the woman emerging from it was her: the lady in the silver fur. She wore no fur tonight, though, but rather a high-necked dress of golden taffeta and ivory lace.

'Oh hello, Lucia,' Irena said. 'What a gorgeous dress.'

'Thank you, darling. Hides a thousand sins.'

Was she being ironic? I could barely breathe.

'Ah, you have one of those necklaces too,' she said, nodding at me in the mirror. 'Edda has set off quite a trend.'

I'd become mute, it seemed. I struggled to think of something to say. 'Dante bought it,' I said stupidly. Of course he'd bought it. I'd hardly have bought it myself.

She smiled at me patiently. 'Those lovely high cheekbones of yours. Do you have Germanic heritage, perhaps?'

I went quite cold. Was she saying I looked Slavic? 'Thank you. No, no German, that I know of.'

'They're terribly good-looking, those German officers, aren't they?' Irena said. 'Those piercing blue eyes. That uniform. If I was younger… Well, we'd better go back out and face the music, hadn't we?'

'Hadn't we just?'

'Ladies?'

I found Dante in the centre of the room where he'd already been sucked into a heated discussion between a group of Italian and German officials in imposing suits and uniforms. I slid in next to him, but he barely noticed me, so focused was he on the conversation.

'And you boys have a useful word for all of them, don't you?' one of the Italian men was saying. '*Untermenschen*. Underman. That's right, isn't it? Covers them all.'

'Yes,' a German officer said. He was a rotund man with a cavalry moustache, its ends waxed into sharp points. 'Underman, or subhuman perhaps is closer to the Italian. Covers all inferior peoples: Jews, gypsies, Slavs, blacks.'

'The physically inferior too,' another man added casually. 'The cripples, for example.'

'The principle,' the German officer said, 'is that not all of those who appear human are in fact so, nor should they be treated as such. Of course, in Italy they've infiltrated the population far more insidiously than in Germany. The Jew in particular. This is why Italy has a problem. There are still Jews in the Fascist Party, I hear.'

'It's true,' Dante was saying, 'that they've managed to assimilate far more successfully here than in many countries, but things have ratcheted up a notch these past few months, I can assure you. Il Duce is taking firmer measures; public attitudes are hardening. Italian people are now on the lookout in a way they weren't only last year. They're far more aware of their racial superiority. And remember that we have a long history of racial purity, longer, I daresay, than Germany's. In the borderlands, for example, there was a highly successful campaign of forced Italianisation of the Slav population during the 1920s.'

I felt as though my heart had stopped in my breast. Somehow I'd refused to let myself think that Dante might hate Slavs, despite his increasingly extreme pronouncements. I'd refused to engage with the idea at all. Now it was set out before me, clear as water.

'Well, that's where the Germans and the Italians differ,' the officer replied. 'There would have been no Germanifying of those barbarians. They would have been cast out or squashed like insects, as they have been in Poland. Now how do you even know where they are?'

'Oh, one always knows,' Dante said, taking another drink

from a tray. 'There are lists, to prevent half-breeds. Poisoning of the blood.'

'Perhaps, perhaps, but this is Italy's problem. It has always been too soft, too accommodating of non-Aryans.'

'Well, there's no accommodating now, that's for sure. Il Duce's stance has altered. He is, after all, the head of an empire now, and he is readying his empire for war. The *Untermenschen*, as you term them, can no longer expect Italy's hospitality.'

There was some polite laughter from the Germans, then more conversation, but I was no longer paying attention to what was said. I was instead staring at Dante. Did he really think these things? Had he always thought them, or had the venom infiltrated his veins in the months since we married? I stood frozen. '*Highly successful campaign of forced Italianisation.*' Had he any idea what it had been like, to be told as a child that you couldn't speak your own language, sing your own songs, love your own people? To be told you were an inferior race?

After a moment, I became aware that I was being watched. Looking up, I realised that Massimo's eyes were on me and I feared then that he knew, he'd worked out what I was, and dread cut through me, cold as a blade.

I moved quickly away from the men and to the bar, where a woman was standing on her own, smoking a menthol cigarette from a long, jewelled cigarette holder. She looked at me for a moment and then gave an odd smile. 'You're her, aren't you, Dante's new wife?'

I did not reply.

'Oh, forgive me.' She stretched out a hand. 'Clementina.' She paused for a moment, assessing me. 'Well, it looks like you need a drink at any rate.' She leant across to the bar and ordered us two exquisite-looking Martinis, then raised her glass to mine. '*Salute.*' To your health. She raised a quizzical eyebrow. 'I thought you might be like her, but you're not.'

'Adelina, you mean.'

'Yes. Adelina.' She said it with warmth.

'She was your friend.'

'She was.'

'I'm glad. I'd hoped she'd had friends.' And I had, I realised. I'd feared she'd been alone, just as I was, sitting in that sewing room, afraid.

The woman nodded, half-smiling. 'Not many by the end. No doubt he's told you she was a "difficult woman".'

'No, not at all. Dante's told me fairly little about her, and all of it's been positive.'

'Hm. Easier that way, perhaps.' She finished her Martini. 'Those were rather delicious, weren't they? Another?' She didn't wait for my reply, but spoke once again with the barman.

'And was she?' I asked when I had Clementina's attention again. 'Difficult, I mean? I'd always had the idea she was perfect.'

'None of us is perfect. Adelina was not perfect. But she was a damn sight cleverer and more independent-minded than he'd have liked.'

'What do you mean?'

'Well, men like Dante want to possess a woman and then want to be able to control her, and Adelina was not a woman you could control, not really, though she played along for many years. And when she stopped playing along... But, heavens, I'm frightening you. You must forgive me. Perhaps with you everything will be very different. I hope it will be.'

I thought back to Greta's pronouncements. 'Was she angry?'

'Angry? Well, sometimes she was angry with him, frustrated with the constraints he tried to put on her, though not angry enough, if you ask me. I wouldn't have put up with half the nonsense Adelina did, but then that's probably why I'm still here, still single.'

And still alive.

'Clementina, I didn't expect to see you here.' It was Massimo, standing only a foot or so away from us.

'Didn't think I'd get invited? Max, darling, you underestimate me.' She was smiling, but I could tell there was something – a tension – between them.

'Oh, I never underestimate you. What have you been talking to lovely Eva about?'

'Lovely Eva and I were just getting acquainted. These parties are dreadful when you don't know anyone. Or when you only know Irena and the vultures. Now, I must go and say hello to Margareta over there. Eva, delightful to have met you.'

I looked with dismay at her retreating back.

'You mustn't listen to anything Clementina tells you, you know,' Massimo said fluidly. 'She's what our German friends would call *eine dreckschleuder*. A shit-stirrer.'

'Is that so?'

'Yes.' I could tell he was staring at me, though I refused to look at him. 'And you, I think you're what the Germans would call *eine Slawin*, aren't you?'

I froze, feeling the blood drain from my face.

'Yes, I thought so. Oh, don't worry. I won't tell Dante. It would upset him dreadfully.' A pause. 'But then, you know that. That's why you've kept it from him.'

My voice came out stiff, alien. 'I don't know why you would think that.'

He continued as though I hadn't spoken. 'The thing with Dante is that it's all about appearances, isn't it? He only cares about surfaces, never looks beneath. And you certainly look the part: young, beautiful, accomplished, Aryan. It's really only your reactions that give you away. That and the fact your little maths teacher friend told me he thought your parents might be Slovene.' He smiled and I felt deathly sick.

Maths teacher. He must mean Mr Melancholy, my old

admirer, the man we'd all laughed about and mocked; the man whom I'd only been to dinner with out of a misplaced sense of pity.

'Yes. Met him at a Party meeting, realised we both knew you. Only he knew some things I didn't.' Massimo took a glug of his drink.

I felt fear wash through me, cold as the sea. It had finally happened: what I dreaded more than anything. The whispering of others had finally outed me. I could think of nothing to say.

'Well, now it's our little secret, isn't it?' Massimo smiled again. 'Something we can share.' He put his hand on my waist and held it, too tight.

Another man approached Massimo and I managed to get away from him and lose myself in the crowd. I could feel tears burning behind my eyes and my head was pounding. What would Massimo do with this information? Why had he told me he knew? Where on earth was Dante? Maybe it was the effect of emerging from the blue-pill haze, maybe it was what Massimo had said, but I felt as though reality was sliding out of my grasp. As I circulated the ballroom, everything – the lights, the dancers, the mirrors – seemed to swim before my eyes. I couldn't find Dante anywhere. Nor could I see Clementina, though I'd hoped to speak to her again. Sweating, nearly crying, I left the main room and hurried along a corridor, trying to find somewhere where I could be on my own. I came at last to a doorway which led onto a patioed garden with a fountain and I'd never been so grateful to be outside in the cool evening air.

After a moment, I realised that I was not alone. Behind the trees, I could make out two people moving, scuffling. A woman in a cream dress was, I saw, trying to free herself from a tall man in a dark uniform. In the darkness and in my distress, it took me a few seconds to realise who they were, and then the sweat dried on my face and I stood very still and very quiet.

'Fine, be a bore,' Dante said. 'I'm going back inside, anyhow.' He was drunk, I could hear it in his voice, and he strode away across the patio back to the main building, not noticing me at all.

Lucia came a minute later, correcting her dress from where Dante had pulled at it. She stopped when she saw me and gave a mirthless laugh. She, too, I thought, was drunk.

'Well, if it isn't the little spy!'

'He's my husband,' I whispered.

'Yes, and you can keep him.' She tried to light a cigarette and I saw that her hands were shaking. Seeing that I'd noticed, she laughed again. 'You poor bitch. I can walk away. You can't, can you?' She managed to get the cigarette to light. 'He needs to stop taking that wretched stuff.'

'What do you mean, "stuff"?'

'Good God, don't tell me you didn't know! *Cocaine*, darling. They're all doing it. Only Dante now takes so much that it's making him demented.'

I froze, thinking of his increasing fervour, his pallor, his nosebleed.

'My, but you're a naive little thing, aren't you?'

'I don't need your pity,' I said coldly.

'No,' she blew out a gust of grey smoke, 'but you'll need some good friends. Possibly a good lawyer. You'll need to get out if you can't control him. Go back to live with your ma, or something.'

'I don't need your advice either, thank you very much.'

She scoffed. 'Well, do as you please. It's not my concern. Only don't say I didn't warn you.'

I was determined to leave the party, whether Dante came with me or not. 'I'm not feeling well,' I told him shortly, 'I need to go home, lie down. Don't worry about me – I'm happy to walk.'

'Don't talk utter rot. Of course you can't walk alone.' He was drunk and loud, his pupils very large. It must, I thought, be the drug. The never sleeping, the sore skin. I felt like such a fool. 'Let's call you a taxi, if you must go. Come – this way.'

He took me by the arm and strode down the steps and out of the building into the street.

We couldn't immediately see a car, so Dante took me to a line of taxis not far from the hotel and immediately started shouting for a car. 'Via Giulia! At once!'

'*Ehi*! Wait your turn, *ragazzo*! We were here first!'

'The lady is sick,' Dante hissed at the man who'd dared to challenge him. He turned to me. 'Let me handle this. Wait here. I'll tell them we'll pay double.'

I stood on the street, my shawl drawn around me, feeling a mixture of embarrassment and fear.

'Eva?' A man stepped forward into the lamplight.

'Ettore?' I couldn't quite believe it. 'It *is* you!' I was so ridiculously happy to see his face. I wanted to grab him, to laugh, to cry. 'How good to see you! When did you get back? Why didn't you contact me? How are you?'

He gave a small smile. He looked so much older. 'Only a few days ago. I'm sorry I hadn't called. Things have been difficult. But you, Eva?' He looked towards Dante in his Fascist uniform, gesticulating at the taxi driver.

We stood staring at one another. Seeing Ettore, I remembered everything that had been – him, Mirella, me, laughing; it seemed like a different lifetime. 'I...' I couldn't think of anything to say. Anything that wasn't a lie.

'Quickly, Eva!' It was Dante. 'Before some other chap nabs the car.' He took my face in his hands and kissed me roughly on the cheek. 'You'll be all right? I won't be too late. Go and get some rest.'

'Yes, darling.'

'Here!' he shouted to the taxi driver. 'Look after her, will you? Good man!'

Dante was already walking away. He hadn't noticed Ettore, who still stood, hands in his pockets on the street, watching me.

Ettore did not stop watching me as the car door slammed and we pulled away. I put my hand to the glass to wave to him. He did not wave back.

When I woke, I felt wretched and I prayed that it was the aftermath of the blue pills and not, as Irena had presumed, the beginnings of a child. After taking my morning coffee, I retched, then splashed water onto my face. *Come on, Eva.* I felt terrible, but at least my mind was no longer cotton wool. For the first time in weeks, I was thinking clearly. Now I needed to work out what to do.

I considered briefly going to Dottor Falluci, telling him about Dante's addiction, asking him what to do. But I could guess what he'd say: that it was his body, his life, his decision as to what he should do with it. How different when the patient was a man. I also worried that he'd detect that I'd stopped taking the pills, against the wishes of my husband. Worse, I feared he'd somehow see that I was pregnant. And then there was Massimo, with his snide little smile. What would I do when he next approached me? I needed to stop him from telling Dante, but I thought I could guess the cost. The thought made me retch again.

Ettore. I would go to Ettore and I would tell him everything. We would work out together what to do.

I got myself ready and took the tram to Trastevere to Ettore's old apartment, desperate to see him again, planning what I was going to say: that he had been right, that I should have listened to him, that I would do what I could to help the movement, no matter what the risk.

Except that, when I got there, I found it was no longer his apartment. The concierge, a greasy little man whom I'd met several times before was distinctly nervous when I asked him about Ettore, pulling at his lank moustache.

'He wanted to come back, but there was talk,' he said. 'Talk of him and his… activities. I can't be having someone like that living here. He had to go elsewhere.'

'Well, do you know where he's living now?'

'No. I didn't ask. Best I don't know.' Then, perhaps seeing how disappointed I looked, he added: 'If I see him, though, I'll pass on the message you're looking for him.'

I gave a tight smile and nodded. Little use that was.

As I walked back, I saw that someone had splashed the words DEATH TO JEWS in white paint across a wall. No one had tried to cover it up. Death to Jews, death to the outsiders. It was clear now what was coming and my stomach clenched with dread. How had I thought I could sleep through it all?

I returned, exhausted and frightened, to the house. The weight of the place seemed to press down on me. I felt, once again, that the house was waiting. What exactly did it want?

I was in Adelina's sewing room, listening to Radio Londra, when it happened. Dante was at his club and Alessandro at a friend's house. I heard the familiar notes of the Beethoven Symphony, the voice of a colonel talking of men being called up into the army and then sudden static, a heavy buzzing like that of the wasps, intermingled with odd whispering and piercing sounds. It was horrible: a thick ugly noise, and no amount of turning the dial on the radio or pressing the buttons would make it go away. To my growing alarm, I could find no other channels, nor turn the wretched thing off. Then – behind the buzzing – screaming. Not from the radio, not from the room, but outside the workroom door. It was Chiara.

I ran to the door and wrenched at the handle, trying to get to her, but the handle was stuck fast. Could the door somehow be locked? But no, it wasn't that – it felt as if someone was holding the handle from the other side, preventing me from turning it, and horror washed through my brain.

'Stop!' Chiara was shouting. 'Please, stop!' She gave another awful scream. There was barking too and growling – Zefiro was trying to help her.

'What is it, Chiara?' I yelled through the keyhole. 'What's going on?'

'I don't know! I don't know! I want it to stop! Please!'

I wrenched again at the door handle, the thump of blood in my ears now competing with the sickening buzzing that still emitted from the radio. It would not turn, however, and I knew that the thing, the energy, was holding the doorknob to prevent me from escaping. I could feel the pungent hatred of it on the other side of the door. 'Let me out! Leave her alone!'

Not knowing what else to do, I grabbed Adelina's rosary from the worktable and held it up before me, towards the door, beginning to say the Pater Noster.

'Our Father, who art in heaven, hallowed be thy name—'

The next thing I knew, the rosary was swiped from my hand and thrown through the air, ricocheting against the door, and I was pushed backwards, against the wall. I could still hear Chiara still screaming and I ran again to the door and beat upon it.

'Chiara, it's all right! It's going to be all right! I'm going to make it stop!'

She was still screaming, still shouting, Zefiro still barking, and I thought my heart would jump out of my body I was so frightened, when, just as quickly as it had started, it ceased. The doorknob suddenly twisted in my hand and the door burst open, revealing Chiara, kneeling on the ground, clutching at her head. Zefiro was next to her, whimpering. About Chiara's neck, I could see red marks: the distinct imprints of fingers. I ran over to her and put my arms around her, both of us trembling and crying.

'It was pulling me by my hair, up the stairs.'

'Shh,' I whispered, rocking her.

'My hair was twisted in front of me, and it was pulling, pulling, pulling.'

'It's over now.'

'No, it's never over,' she sobbed. 'It's never over.'

'What do you mean?'

'I don't know. It's as though I've seen all of it happen before, in a dream.'

I stroked her hair gently. There were beads of blood from where it had been torn at. 'Come with me. Let's go downstairs and I'll make us a tisane.'

I led Chiara down to the kitchen and sat her at the table with a blanket around her shoulders and Zefiro on her lap. In a pan, I mixed together some wine, sugar and herbs, trying to stop my hands from shaking. My mother had made something similar for us on nights when things had been bad; when I'd witnessed something I shouldn't have, or heard things meant for her alone. Bruno was uncharacteristically quiet. I noticed that he'd shed several black feathers that now lined his cage.

As Chiara sipped at her drink, I held a cool cloth to her neck. The fingerprints had almost vanished now, only reddish marks remaining. I took her hand in mine. 'I'm so sorry, Chiara. I've been... absent. I should've been looking after you.'

'You were angry with me for denying I'd heard it.'

'No. I wasn't angry, *cara mia*. I was afraid.'

'I wanted to believe him,' she said. 'I wanted him to be right.'

'You were trying to be a good daughter, I understand that.' Dante had taught his children that goodness meant not questioning him, just as patriotism meant not questioning Il Duce, even when he was wrong.

'But what is it, Eva? Why is it here? It isn't my mother, it can't be. My mother would never hurt me.' She looked up at me. 'Would she?'

'No, my darling. I don't believe she would.'

Chiara hugged Zefiro, who was still shuddering. 'There were the scratches first – you saw them.'

I thought of the claw-like marks on her arm. 'Yes, I saw them. I thought maybe you'd made them yourself. Or that it was Alessandro.'

'No, Alessandro would never do that, never really hurt me. He looks after me, in his way. They just appeared, fresh with blood, out of nowhere. It's something that hates. That hates me.'

Hatred, anger, fire, destruction. 'Has anything happened since then, Chiara?'

She paused. 'I should have told you.'

'You tried to tell me. Tell me now. I'm listening. I promise.'

Chiara spoke then of the other terrible things that had happened to her in the past weeks: on one night, a rippling across her bedclothes as though from a breeze, even though the air was hot and still; on another, the mattress pushing up from under her. 'It was as though someone were beneath the bed. I could feel it, but there was nothing there!'

I felt the feather-stroke of fear. 'Chiara, I'm so sorry. I should have been there with you. I should have helped.' I'd been so preoccupied with protecting myself, with not angering Dante, that I'd allowed this force to abuse his daughter.

214

'I'd hoped at first that it was Mother, come to be with me. That's why I didn't say anything. But that thing is not my mother.' She began, again, to cry and I put my arm around her and hummed the song my mother used to sing to me: 'Green Grows the Linden Tree'.

That was how Dante found us when he entered the kitchen a moment later with Alessandro.

'*Santo cielo!*' he said, overly cheerful. 'What's all this? Fighting while we were out, were you?'

Chiara remained very still, her head on my shoulder. Alessandro didn't laugh, did not even smile. *He knows*, I thought. *He knows. He too has heard the thing. That's why he's been behaving so strangely.*

'Well?' Dante said. 'Will neither of you tell me what's going on?'

'Yes,' I said quietly. 'I'll tell you. I must tell you. And you must sit down and listen.'

'Must I, indeed?' His tone had hardened. 'What is it, exactly, that you need to tell me?'

'Something that's been happening in this house that we can no longer deny.' I told him of what had taken place that night, and then – very quickly so that he couldn't interject – of the things that had occurred up until that point. 'We've both seen and heard them, Chiara and I, and—'

'Stop! Just stop! What utter nonsense are you spewing? With what craziness have you been filling Chiara's head now?' He turned to his daughter. 'Chiarina, you know that all of what Eva is saying is not possible, don't you? You do know that?'

She looked up at him, her eyes full of tears. 'But they are possible, Father. They're happening and they're getting worse.'

'Jesus Christ. This is hysteria. This is what happens when women are left alone. This is what you have done to my daughter!' He grabbed tight hold of my arm.

'Don't touch her, Father, she's telling the truth!' Chiara was standing up now, crying. Alessandro, I noticed, was very still and very pale and had backed away from the table.

'You're madwomen, the pair of you!' Dante shouted.

'Ask your son,' I said. 'Ask Alessandro whether he thinks this is impossible nonsense. Ask your son if he thinks this is just the lies of hysterical women. We've *all* seen and heard it. We're all terrified. You can't pretend—'

With one violent movement, Dante knocked the table to the ground, so that its contents – the little cups, the glasses – went smashing along with it, tiny pieces of china skittering across the floor. 'I will not listen to this.' His voice was icy cold. 'You've whipped yourself up into a frenzy. You can stay here with your delusions and ghosts. I, however, am going.'

'Going where?'

'Out. Away from you all.'

'Away from *it*, you mean.'

He stared at me for a moment, his eyes strangely bright, and I realised in that instant that he *did* know. He knew it all, and somehow that was worse.

After Dante had left, Alessandro simply stood, staring at the ground: at the broken table and the broken china. His sister stood up and put her arms round him. He didn't move, didn't hug her back, but didn't push her away, either. I left them like that and took Zefiro out into the garden. In the dark blue sky, the moon was a thin crescent, shining like one of the fragments of pottery.

Later, after the children had gone to bed and I'd swept the floor, I sat down at the kitchen table and I began a letter to Mirella. I started at the beginning of the year and I told her everything that had happened and that was happening still. I wrote all the things I should have written months before. I wrote and wrote and wrote until my hand was cramped and sore. I didn't expect her to have any answers, but I wanted just to get it all down, to accept that what was happening was real. I wished desperately that I could see Mirella and talk it through with her, find out how she was and what was happening in her life. Find out how I could help. I wished so much that I could hug her close, smell the familiar scent of her: lavender and resin and soap. But I could not because the Party that my husband worked for and revered had sent her far away.

16

The following day, an envelope appeared on the mat by the front door. An envelope addressed to me.

I'm in the usual cafe. Come when you can.

It was not signed, but I knew who it was from and something inside me soared.

When I arrived in the Caffè Panella, I found Ettore sitting at a table in the far corner, a cigarette in his mouth.

'You look terrible,' he said as I approached.

I laughed. '*You* look terrible!' I hugged him and we stayed like that for a long time, me with my chin on his shoulder. 'Tell me,' I said. 'Tell me everything that's happened.'

'No, you first. I want to know about *Principe Azzurro*, your charming Fascist husband.'

Principe Azzurro: Prince Charming. I felt my whole body grow heavier. 'Remember I thought I would be safe with him?' I laughed again. 'So stupid!'

'You're not stupid, Eva. It's not stupid to want to be safe. Not now.'

I lowered my voice to a whisper. 'Well, now he works for the Foreign Secretary, Il Duce's right-hand man. He was appointed a few months ago. Since then, it's seemed a slide into deluded fervour. Italy this, Rome that. We must be warlike and heroic and racially pure.' I sighed. 'I don't know. Maybe he always thought those things; he just realised it was best to hide them from me, just as I hid my origins from him.'

'And he still doesn't know?'

'No. But he might do soon.' I thought, with a sickening lurch, of Massimo, his insistent gaze, the feel of his insistent fingers. 'And then I don't know what he'll do.' I swallowed. 'Do you think,' I whispered, 'that if the Party knew I'd lied to him, that it would be considered some kind of crime?'

Ettore's expression was grim. 'Maybe, given he's a Fascist official. They make the rules up as they go along. I don't know. What will you do now?'

'I've no idea. I feel like... like I've only just woken up, but woken into a nightmare.' I told Ettore of what had been happening: the wasps, the water, the telephone, the vicious attack on Chiara. 'There's something evil in that house. I know it seems insane, but I truly believe there is.'

Ettore didn't answer.

'You think I've gone mad, don't you?'

'No, Eva. I don't think you've gone mad. I believe that there's something evil in that house. I think it's him.'

'Oh Ettore, it's not Dante! It can't be. Things often happen when he isn't even there – in fact, almost always, now that I think of it. It's not his doing. There's something else, something that's trying to speak. I can't bear it. I'm so frightened.'

For a while, Ettore was silent.

'I have a friend, from the movement,' he said eventually. 'Marcello. He's a priest. Maybe he can help. Maybe he can do something, I don't know. I think he's done such things before.'

'An exorcism, you mean?'

'Yes, something like that.'

I shook my head. 'I can't quite believe we're having this conversation, but yes, please, ask him as soon as you can.'

'Today. I will go to him today, as soon as I've left you.'

'Thank you, Ettore. And now you. Tell me about you now. How are you? How is Pietro? Is he back in Rome?'

He gave a thin smile. 'No. They've moved him to an island, Tremiti, where I can't go. Where no one can go.'

I took his hand. 'Oh, Ettore. I'm so sorry. For how long?'

He shrugged. 'A year? Three years? Forever?'

We stared at one another. His eyes were full of tears, but he said: 'We're the lucky ones, you know. Others are faring far worse.'

'Like who?'

'Like Lucio, one of the younger men in the cell. Dead. Tortured first. When they brought back his body, it was missing several fingers.'

I closed my eyes. Very quietly, I said, 'I can't believe I ever thought this government cared about the Italian people – that it ever cared about anything other than its own power. I wanted to believe Il Duce when he said that wasn't what the Party was. I wanted to believe he knew what he was doing. I wanted, I suppose, not to have to think about it at all. I buried myself in lies.'

'You and millions of others.'

I looked at him. 'What can I do? Tell me what I can do. I want to help. I should have done so months ago.' We were very close to each other, whispering.

'You have no idea how dangerous it is. Nor how difficult it will be to make a difference.'

'You forget what my childhood was. I have some idea of what they might do to me, but I can't just stand and watch anymore, even if we can't win. If Dante recognises me for what I am, then I may be an enemy of the state in any case.'

He smiled finally. 'Welcome to the club.'

I smiled back. 'So, where do I start?'

'You start by buying me a drink and then we talk about what happens now. We talk about how you get out.'

'I can't leave without the children.'

'They're not your children, Eva.'

'I can't just abandon them to that house, Ettore. It isn't that simple. I need to help them.' I felt terrible that I had failed to protect them, that I had failed to see Alessandro for the frightened child he was.

He sighed. 'Oh, Eva. Have you written to Mirella? Told her any of this?'

'Last night. I wrote it all down. But I hadn't written to her for ages. I didn't know what to say. And you? Have you been writing?'

'A little. Not as much as I should have. Thank God she got out when she did. You heard about the ship that sailed from Germany with nearly a thousand Jews and no country will let them in?'

'But I thought America was letting them dock?'

'That's what Roosevelt said at first, but he's changed his mind; bowed to pressure from the loudest section of the public – the anti-immigrant brigade.'

Again, that sense of despair and fear. 'What will they do now, all those people?'

He shrugged. 'They'll have to return to Germany.'

We sat quietly together.

'And we know now,' Ettore said. 'We know what happens when they go back, because people have talked about the camps at Sachsenhausen with their watchtowers and machine guns and their SS men with whips and sticks.'

'But how can the other countries not let them in? How can they let this happen? If they know?'

'Because it's the same as you, Eva. The same as the old Eva, I should say. They pretend not to see, not to know. They put their heads in the sand and hope it will go away, that someone else will deal with the problem. But it will not go away. It will get worse, until people begin to wake up and stand up, and they'll only do so when it touches their own lives.'

'Then I must help now,' I said, 'in whatever way I can.' I screwed up my face, suddenly aware this sounded ludicrous. 'But I'm not exactly a fighter. I don't have any useful skills. What am I going to do? Play the piano for peace?'

Ettore laughed, then – a proper laugh that shook his whole body. Quietly, he said: 'You'll start as a *staffetta*, a messenger. They'll be very grateful to have you. It's early days, but it's important. We've a long battle ahead.'

The priest came to the house with Ettore two days later, early evening, while Dante was still at work. He was a gentle-faced man with clear blue eyes that looked as though they'd seen too much. He, too, I understood, worked with the anti-fascists, one of many priests who would eventually join when, during the war, the Resistance fully took shape.

'Eva, this is Father Marcello Bruni,' Ettore said. 'I've told him everything you told me about the house.'

'Thank you for coming, Father. You think you can help?'

The man fixed me with his blue eyes. 'I'll certainly try, as Ettore has asked me and he is a good friend to me, but I must warn you that this is not something I've attempted before.'

I glanced at Ettore. 'But I thought—'

'Oh, I've carried out rites on possessed individuals before,' the priest said. 'But this is different. Here, we're talking about a presence within the house itself, as I understand it. Is that right?'

'Yes, that's right. Please, come through to the living room. I'll explain.'

Chiara sat next to me, Alessandro remained standing, as I told the priest of what had happened since I came to the house: the constant whispering from the walls, the ongoing sense of rage and loneliness, the appalling scene I'd witnessed last night. 'It was pulling on the handle, I swear it.'

'And there's no sign that anyone in this house is possessed? No one's been seized with demonic rages, talking in tongues, levitating, for example?'

'No, nothing like that. My husband' – I glanced at Chiara, then Alessandro – 'sometimes he's terribly angry. Sometimes I am too, though I mask it better than him. But that isn't possession, is it?'

'No. If everyone who was frustrated with their spouse was deemed possessed, I would be a very busy man.' The priest smiled. 'What you've described is something else. But I'll do my best. I'll start with carrying out a blessing throughout the house.'

He took a flask of water and a beautiful silver crucifix from a cloth bag, then began scattering water on the walls and uttering the Pater Noster and the Hail Mary.

Alessandro stood with his arms folded, watching him sceptically. 'This is just a lot of old rot, isn't it?' he muttered.

I didn't reply. I noticed that the goldfish had swum to the bottom of their bowl. Zefiro's ears were folded back, as though he were afraid.

The priest went into the hallway. We could hear him speaking in Latin, his footsteps as he went from room to room, and as he did so, I felt something growing. I sensed again that blistering anger, gathering force, thickening the air. Chiara felt it too, for she clung to me, shaking. Zefiro was whining. Alessandro was no longer scowling. A whispering sound came, and a hissing, growing louder. Then a shout, half-human, from behind us, and I turned to see with horror that – on the wall

– handprints had appeared, black handprints, as though something had singed them into the wallpaper, as though burning hands had touched it, clawing at the wall.

Chiara screamed and I grabbed hold of her arm. Alessandro was swearing under his breath. I heard Father Marcello running back to us.

'What is it?' he asked. 'Where is it?'

I pointed at the wall, unable to speak.

The priest stood staring, his eyes widening, and I prayed that he would not run and leave us. He crossed himself, still gazing at the wall. After a moment, he said: 'I will need your help. If I'm to drive this anger out of this house, you will have to help me. All of you.' He looked at Alessandro. 'You will do it?'

The boy nodded. 'Yes.'

'We'll do whatever you ask,' I said, 'all of us. Only get rid of the wretched thing.'

We were to stand in a circle holding hands, with our eyes closed, and we were to recite the Lord's Prayer, over and over again. Whatever happened, we must not break the circle. We must not open our eyes.

We began, our voices low:

'*Our Father, who art in heaven, hallowed be thy name ...*'

As we did so, I could hear the priest walking from one corner of the room to the other: 'Depart, then, transgressor. Depart, seducer, full of lies and cunning, foe of virtue, persecutor of the innocent.'

'*... And lead us not into temptation; but deliver us from evil ...*'

The priest's voice grew louder and louder until he was shouting: 'Give place, abominable creature. Give way, you monster! Give way to Christ!'

Chiara gave a shout of pain and pulled her hands away from ours.

I opened my eyes to see that bite marks had appeared on her

chest, on her shoulder, the teeth marks wet with saliva.

'Help me!' she screamed.

I hugged Chiara to me to protect her. 'Leave her alone!' I shouted. You hear me?'

Alessandro moved away, towards the wall, his face white with fear.

Then came a voice, not Chiara's voice, but the voice of the thing, rising deep from her throat, that mechanical inhuman whispering voice I'd heard before, from the walls, from the telephone, but now a thousand times more vile because it was spewing from Chiara's mouth. 'GET OUT!' it hissed. 'GET OUT! BEFORE IT'S TOO LATE!'

Instinctively, I backed away from Chiara, terror washing through me like a tide. Was it talking to me? To all of us?

The priest was holding the crucifix before Chiara and shouting the prayer now: 'Give place, abominable creature, give way, you monster!'

Alessandro was crying and saying: 'Stop! Please, God, make it stop!'

'I'll go!' I shouted at the thing. 'We all will! Only leave Chiara alone!'

'Give way! Give way to Christ!'

And then, like a fire that had suddenly blown itself out, it was gone. We could almost feel the presence leaving the room.

'Has it worked?' Alessandro asked, his voice cracked. 'Is it gone?'

The priest put his hand on the boy's arm. 'It's gone for now.' He approached the wall where the handprints had appeared and I watched, barely daring to breathe, as he put his own hand to the prints, then inspected his fingers. 'Soot,' he said. 'It's as though something has burnt the wall. It's still hot.' He took out a white handkerchief and rubbed his face, then his hands. 'I'll come back in two days, with my colleague. Something else is needed, something stronger. Sometimes it can take many exorcisms before the devil leaves.'

'Does it always leave?' Ettore asked him flatly.

The priest looked at him gravely. 'Not always, brother. Not always.'

After Father Marcello had gone, I tried to make Chiara and Alessandro promise that they wouldn't tell their father that the priest had visited. 'Just until I've managed to get him to accept that we need to do something. You understand? I'll hang something to cover the mark on the wall.'

'But if I tell him,' Alessandro said, 'if I tell him what we saw today – if I show him the handprints – then he'll get someone to make it go away, won't he? He must know people. He knows everyone.' He'd reverted to the brusque tone he often used, but I saw through it now. I saw the confused little boy beneath.

'I don't know, Alessandro. I'm not sure he can, and at the moment he won't even accept it's necessary.'

Alessandro scowled, wrong-footed, his precious papa suddenly powerless. In a low voice, he said, 'He'll be angry with me. I'll get a proper thrashing and it'll all be your fault.'

'It'll be Eva he's angry with,' Chiara said, suddenly, perceptively. 'So you mustn't breathe a word.'

Her brother glared at her. 'Since when did you get to tell me what to do?'

'Alessandro, don't be pig-headed. We're not playing games anymore.'

'Fine. Suit yourselves. I'm going to my room.'

The stomping of feet, then the slamming of the bedroom door. Chiara stared after him, then at me. 'He's upset and frightened. Let me try again.'

Once we were alone, Ettore shut the door and sat down

opposite me. 'You can't stay here, Eva. You heard what Marcello said. It may not be possible to drive it – whatever it is – out of this place.'

'I can't leave them, Ettore. You saw what they were like. You saw what happened to Chiara, how frightened Alessandro was, for all his bravado. And you've seen what kind of a man Dante is.'

'Then take them with you.'

'Take them where? And how? You think they'd come with me? And even if they did, Dante would track us down, have me arrested. I can't do that!'

'My people – soon to be your people – they might be able to help.'

'They might?'

'Possibly. But you'll need to be very brave.'

'I'm trying to be brave, Ettore, honestly I am. I realise now how cowardly I've been most of my life. But to take this man's children with the help of the people who are resisting the Fascists?' I was whispering now. 'I don't know if I have that kind of courage.'

'I think you do. I think you've always had the courage but assumed you didn't. I think you didn't really know who you were.'

Tears were burning behind my eyes. 'I wish Mirella was here with us.'

'I'm thankful she isn't, given what's going on. But yes, I miss her too. I miss what our lives were. But even then, you know, it wasn't freedom. Even then, we were afraid. So all this' – he waved his hands to indicate the whole world – 'it will at least bring things to a head. Make Italy realise she can't continue to follow this man, this ideology, this hatred.'

'My Ettore. Always the idealist.'

'We're owed a better future, Eva. One where we don't have to hide who we are.'

I wasn't sure I believed such a future existed. At that moment, it seemed impossible. 'Can we meet again, tomorrow?'

'Same place at eleven?'

'Yes.'

We smiled at each other. Despite everything that had happened that day, I felt more hopeful than I had for a long, long time.

17

I'd opened the windows to get rid of the smell of the incense and burning, and moved a painting to conceal the handprints, but when Dante returned, he was instantly suspicious.

'Someone's been here.'

'No one's been here, darling. You're tired and agitated. Come and sit down. I'll get your supper.'

I tried to seem calm and normal as I went about the kitchen preparing an omelette, but I could feel his eyes boring into me, the sweat beginning to collect between my shoulder blades and trickle down my back. Would he be able to tell just from looking at me that I was pregnant? I felt fairly sure now that I was. My breasts had swollen a little and my stomach was no longer flat, but I'd drawn in my corset to hide it.

In the next room, Chiara had begun to play the piano. A Bach cantata, not a note wrong. It felt comforting – as though she was supporting me, covering for me. I set a glass of wine on the table before Dante. As he lit a cigarette, I noticed that the veins on his hands were standing out. He was ill, I saw. He'd made himself terribly ill. Had he been taking the stuff to steel himself against the presence he knew to be in the house, or had something else prompted it? He was so different now to the desirable man I'd first met, but perhaps that had all been a facade — the vulnerability, the tenderness, the charm: it was all a mask for a man who cared only about appearance and control. Part of me still wanted to help him, but a much larger part wanted to run.

'What are you keeping from me, Eva?'

'I'm not keeping anything from you, Dante.'

I continued about my task, trying to keep my hands steady, not spill anything, not show fear.

'I begin to worry, Eva, that I can't trust you.' He paused. 'A man must be able to trust his wife.'

'Of course you can trust me, darling. You're being silly.' And the gall, I thought, the absolute gall of the man to accuse me when he'd been unfaithful for the whole of our marriage, when he'd misrepresented throughout what he was, when he'd only pretended to love me.

He stared at me over his wine glass. 'Am I? I hope so. For your sake as well as mine.' His voice was thin, but still I felt ill with dread. What if Massimo were to tell him what I truly was? Would he turn me in to the Party? Would I be considered a traitor, to be put to death before a firing squad?

I finished making the omelette in silence and set it down before him with some bread. I didn't look at him again. I couldn't bear to. I took off my apron and walked into the piano room where I stood learning against the wall watching Chiara play. She looked up at me and our eyes met — conspirators.

That night, I went again to Adelina's workroom to listen, very quietly, to Radio Londra, opening the window to let in the velvety night air. I knelt close to the radio with one of Alessandro's *Balilla* shirts, sewing on a button so that, if Dante found me, I'd have a pretext for being in there.

I worried that the radio would once again hiss with its hideous buzzing, but there was only the sound of the radio announcer talking of the British Foreign Office warning Japan of serious consequences if they maintained their blockade in China. Then, as I knelt there, I heard a noise, very close to me: a whirring, clicking sound. It was the sewing machine. Adelina's old Necchi sewing machine had begun to move.

I turned off the radio, stood up and backed away from it, my breath stopped in my chest. The pedal was moving back and forth, driving the wheel, as though an invisible foot were pressing on it. Faster it went and faster, whir, click, whir, click, whir, and the horror grew in me until I wanted to scream at the top of my lungs, but I didn't dare. Instead, I ran forward and shoved the thing away from me as hard as I could, just as Dante had shoved the table, desperate for it to stop, to leave me alone. The machine shifted, then fell with a clunk onto its side, the wheel still turning, but slowing, winding down, until there was only my breath, heavy in the silence, and the pounding of blood in my brain.

For a long moment, I stared at the machine, the shining black paint with its gold embellishments, but then my eyes were drawn away from it, to a spot not far away. When I'd pushed the Necchi, it had dragged along with it the rug on which it had stood. There, in the patch the rug had left, was a stain darkening the wooden floor. I turned on the lamp and brought it closer to the floorboards. In the lamp's glow, I could see that the stain was a murky brown with patches of maroon seeped into the veins of the wood, and I felt fear settle around my heart. The mark wasn't new, it had been there for some time, had been scrubbed at and cleaned and then finally covered, left where it was thought no one would look. Only I *had* looked. I had no way of determining how old the stain was or where it had come from. I couldn't even be sure what it was. But the thing in the house had wanted me to see. It had wanted me to know.

After a long moment, I pulled the rug back over the stain and righted the machine. The presence, whatever it was, had gone. I made the decision then and there. I would take the children if I could, and I would leave, as soon as possible. I would speak to Ettore tomorrow.

It was a hot, humid night and I slept little, my brain and body having entered some kind of fugue state, and woke at dawn, my mind still whirring like the sewing machine. I gritted my teeth when Dante told me he'd be working from his office at home that morning. I would have to make some excuse for meeting Ettore and I fixed at last upon an imagined visit to one of Mia's bridge mornings – events which the wives had pestered me to attend but which I'd so far managed to avoid.

As I walked to the cafe, thinking, I became aware that the day was darkening, and a minute later, the skies opened, releasing a torrent of rain. Around me, umbrellas sprouted like fungi, but I'd been too preoccupied to think to bring one, and by the time I arrived at the cafe, I was drenched and panicked. Ettore was already sitting at one of the little tables smoking a cigarette, a paper spread out before him. 'Thank goodness, you're here,' I breathed.

He raised an eyebrow. 'Well, of course I'm here. Where else would I be? Sit down.' He nodded at the proprietor. '*Due caffè.*'

I took a seat, the rain dripping from me in rivulets.

'Well?' he asked.

'Something happened last night. I can't … I don't want to go into it, but I think I need to leave as soon as possible. Your friends: will they help me? Us? Because I can't leave the children. I'm not yet sure how I'll persuade them to come,

Alessandro in particular, but I don't think any of us are safe.'

Ettore regarded me with his dark eyes. I noticed the ends of his fingers were yellow from the cheap, rolled-up cigarettes he'd taken to smoking. Had he always smoked so much? 'I'd already spoken to them about you. About your willingness to assist. They may offer some help, if I ask in the right way. But we'll have to be extremely careful. You mustn't tell anyone at all, you understand? Not even the children. Not until we have a plan.'

'Yes, I understand.'

He nodded, swallowed. 'Then we'll get to work at once. I'll speak to my people. You'll need new papers. You have money?'

'No, but I can get some.' I thought of the gold necklace, Adelina's jewellery. I'd sell it.

'Good.' Ettore rubbed his face. He needed shaving. 'You're sure about this?'

'Am I sure I should follow this course? No. But am I sure that I can't stay there any longer, that I can't stay silent any longer, that I should help? Yes.' The presence in the house had showed me that stain for a reason. 'I'm pregnant too, I think.'

He breathed out. Tapped the ash from his cigarette into his saucer. 'Does Dante know?'

'I don't think so. I pray to God he doesn't, anyway. Of course, it should be everything I ever wanted. A family, a real family. A real Italian family.' Laughter bubbled up in me, uncontrollable. 'I'm sorry, Ettore. You think I'm losing my mind, don't you?'

'No, I think you're finally figuring things out, Evalina. And I'll help you as best I can. You come back here again in two days' time and I'll tell you what I've been able to work out. Try to have the money by then. As much as you can, yes?'

I nodded.

'I can't promise anything, you know. It may be too much – the wife and children of a senior Fascist?' He shook his head. 'Can you imagine what they'd do to us? But I'll try. I promise you that.'

'Thank you, Ettore. And, like I say, I'll do what I can to help your friends, whatever they need me to do.'

He shushed me. 'Not here. But I know. They know. First, we need to get you out.'

It was still raining as I walked back, though less heavily, re-flections forming in the watery tarmac. In the piazza, I saw a line of men, some with women or children clinging to them, standing before a military vehicle, several soldiers at the front taking notes. This must be a line of conscripts, I thought, and the fear rose to my throat. One and a half million men had been called up already, I'd heard on the radio. The government were preparing for war, even if they denied it. They wouldn't commit such expense unless it was essential.

War. It felt as though we'd always been at war. The Spanish Civil War, the conquest of Abyssinia, pushed into one armed conflict after another, supposedly to make us stronger. Even government programmes had to be battles – the Battle for Grain, the Battle for Births – and now this, the battle to a pure race, the battle to the very end. When would my end be? I wondered. Would I make it out of Rome, or would I be discovered before then, hiding in plain sight?

When I got back to the house, I was relieved to find Dante had gone into the ministry. In his absence, I went through Adelina's jewellery and my own and selected the pieces I thought likely to be of some worth. I began to pick out clothing too, that I would take with me when I could find somewhere to run to. In the wardrobe, I came across the lace shawl I'd worn on the evening of our wedding and a sudden rush of guilt swept through me. I remembered what my mother had said when I asked her once, as a teenager, why she didn't leave my father. 'I am his wife, Eva. I stood up in church and told God and all my family and his that I would stay by this man, through thick and thin. And he is your father. So I make the best of it, that's my role. You mustn't ever ask me again.'

I sat on my bed – Adelina's bed – and I asked myself if I was jumping to conclusions. The bloodstain, if it were indeed blood, might be a mark from where Adelina fell, when the haemorrhage took hold. Because, now that I thought about it, there must have been blood. Had I imagined she'd been perfect in death just as she'd seemed to be in life? It was understandable, too, that Dante wouldn't have wanted me to know that her blood still stained our house.

I ran my hand over the fabric of the shawl and thought again of my mother in her worn dress with her worn shoes and her secret, Slovene songs. I thought of how she'd lived her life in fear, telling herself that if she stayed quiet, if she didn't fight, she would at least survive. I loved her, but I was not her. I wasn't Adelina either. I felt I was only beginning to work out what I myself was, but it wasn't a woman who stood still, watching as the place burnt down around her.

I stood up and I continued packing: making my plans to get out.

Dante seemed calmer that evening, but I sensed suspicion and resentment beneath, like a current running through a dark stream. Throughout dinner, he affected the role of caring father, talking to Alessandro about munitions Italy was ordering in, and trying to draw Chiara into conversation about her school work. With me, he was polite but distant, smiling as I passed him his plate, complimenting me on the roast lamb.

'What a feast you've made for us, Eva. What a lucky family we are.'

Both of the children watched me over the dinner table, clearly not sure what to make of their father's change of mood. I wanted to reassure them, make it all right, but I wasn't deceived by him any longer. He hadn't forgiven and forgotten; he was watching me like a coiled snake, working out when to strike.

Things continued like that for the next two days, the summer heat descending, the air growing heavier, and when the time came for me to meet Ettore with the money, I was wound up tight as a spring. I'd kept expecting Dante to say something or do something, but he'd continued quiet and watchful. I'd thought Massimo might turn up and harass me once more, but for now he stayed out of sight. The house, too, had been unsettlingly silent, as though plotting its next trick.

It seemed hotter than ever that morning, the heat rising from the pavement through the soles of my shoes, the sun beating down on my head, as I walked towards the Caffè Panella. I kept my bag close to my chest, feeling too visible, too obvious. I feared an OVRA agent would spot me and somehow know me for a subversive, simply from my movements, and I was desperate to see Ettore, to move to the next stage of the plan.

But when I reached the cafe, he was not there. The proprietor nodded to me as I entered and after a while brought me a coffee. I kept glancing at the door, but time went on and only two women entered, then a man with a small dog. I began to grow agitated. Had Ettore changed his mind about helping me? Or had I misunderstood when we were supposed to be meeting?

After a time, I walked to the bar and asked the proprietor if he'd seen my friend – the man with whom I'd met previously.

The man remembered Ettore but said that, no, he hadn't seen him. 'Men, eh?' he said. 'We're a feckless bunch, even with a beautiful woman like you.'

I smiled. Better for him to think Ettore and I had been meeting for some lovers' tryst than to construct a plan for me to join the anti-fascists and flee my lawful husband.

I waited another ten minutes, my body tense, then left, telling the proprietor that I must have made some mistake.

Had I made a mistake? I didn't think so, but I'd been so flustered the last time I saw Ettore. I determined to visit his new apartment, which he'd told me was in the Aurelio district. I hailed a cab, wanting to get there as soon as possible, to quash my sense that something was wrong. The drive seemed to take forever, the traffic achingly slow, the taxi stiflingly hot. When we were a couple of streets from his apartment, the traffic came to a complete standstill and I told the driver I would continue on foot. I couldn't work out why there were so many cars and vans, unmoving, drivers beeping and swearing at each other. I understood the cause when I reached Ettore's road. The street had been shut off to traffic.

My heart was now pounding, everything seeming very clear and slow. I didn't want to run, didn't want to draw attention to myself, so I walked as quickly as I could, the sweat trickling from my face, towards the far end of the street. Numero 35, Ettore had said. I searched for the house numbers. *Please let it not be the address around which a small crowd had gathered; please let that be some other disaster, some other person's nightmare.*

As I came closer, I saw that there were policemen outside the door of the apartment building. Had they come to arrest Ettore? Had they worked out his role with the anti-fascists? I thought of his tortured friend with the severed fingers. Had he given Ettore away?

I walked even faster, hurrying past the police and into the

stairwell, up the winding stairway, ignoring their shouts to stop.

The door to the apartment was open and there were more policemen inside and then there was blood, so much blood, blood on the floor, spatters on the wall, and the hideous, nauseous smell of it nearly knocking me to the floor.

'Signorina, you can't be in here.' A tall officer was trying to block my view, but I could see Ettore, on the ground. Or at least I could see what had been Ettore; what had been his face.

A wail began, a low wail, that I realised was coming from my throat.

'Signorina, you must leave.'

I was led, dragged, out of the foul-smelling room and back down the spiral staircase. 'Who did this?' I kept asking. 'Please tell me who did this.'

No answer.

I was deposited back in the hallway, but the ground continued to swirl beneath me. I grabbed hold of the banister to stop myself from falling. Ettore's face, not a face anymore, just a mess of cartilage and bone.

'Here, come with me.' Someone was leading me away by the arm. It was an older woman in a grubby-looking house dress, who took me into a dimly lit kitchen and sat me down on a chair. 'You were a friend of Ettore's? I'm his landlady.'

'Yes. A good friend.'

'You're the girl he sometimes met at the cafe?'

'Yes.' I gulped for air. 'They won't tell me who did it.'

The woman lit a cigarette on the cooker. 'Blackshirts,' she said very quietly. 'That's who. Blackshirts came here last night. Brutes. I saw them, but the police don't want to know.' She blew out a trail of smoke.

My head was thumping. It was unbearably hot. I thought I might be sick.

'Lean forward.' The woman handed me a cool glass of water

238

and waited until I'd gathered myself. 'I don't know what he was involved in,' she said. 'I didn't want to know. But the police, they know. I would get out of here, if I were you, once you've caught your breath, before they think to start asking questions. You can't do anything for him now.'

I thanked the woman and stumbled away from the apartment and towards home, through the unbearable midday heat. The landscape of Rome seemed to have become alien, frightening, the stone animals on the buildings hostile beasts snarling in the blinding sunlight. It was as if all the hatred that had been gathering in the world, in the house, was coming to a point, swirling in the air about me like the furious swarm of wasps. I tried my best to think logically and calmly, I tried to work out a plan, but it was as if the whispering in the walls and the buzzing of the wasps had entered my head and I could think only of Ettore and what he must have endured in the awful minutes before he died. In my mind's eye, I saw him curled in on himself like the man in the green jacket I'd seen at the parade that day, shuddering beneath the Blackshirts' blows; bones, teeth, breaking. I put my hands to my head, trying to shut it all out of my mind, burrow down into numbness as I had before, but I found that I couldn't any longer and the pain was searing and raw.

18

When I returned it was to a silent house and for that, at least, I was grateful. On the mat by the front door, an envelope with my name on it and a French postmark. I opened it to see Mirella's handwriting: *Eva, why did you not tell me?*

I refolded the letter and put it into my handbag. I could not bear to read it now. I sat for a minute in the cool of the kitchen trying to collect my thoughts. I would have to hide the money until I'd managed to form a new plan to get away. I would go to Father Marcello and see if he could help – if he could put me in touch with Ettore's people.

I climbed the stairs, my shoulders feeling as though they were weighted down with armour, and went to Adelina's sewing room to put the money in her old sewing box. I was dimly aware that the room was darker than usual and I had a dull sense that someone had been there recently, or that the presence was nearby, waiting. The sewing machine stood still, however, and the radio remained silent. I approached the sewing basket and unlocked the lid.

All at once, the door slammed shut behind me.

I whirled around, ran to it, twisted the doorknob. I felt an awful sense of familiarity as the handle refused to budge just as it had that night Chiara was dragged by the hair, and I sensed again a presence on the other side of the door. Then came a new sound: the click of the key turning. I'd been locked in from the outside.

I retreated from the door, my heart thudding. Someone, or something, was standing on the other side. I could see a shadow moving beneath the door and my heart convulsed with dread.

Then came the steady clip of footsteps: a man's heavy shoes on the floorboards.

'Dante?' I ran to the door and hammered at it.

The footsteps continued, moving away.

'Dante?' I said again, less loudly.

No answer. I heard the thud of his office door closing, then the sound of him typing on his Olivetti, as though nothing had happened at all.

Half an hour passed and no further sound came. I didn't call again because, as the seconds ticked by, I took in the changes to the room. The shutters had been closed and locked shut. In the corner stood a metal bucket that he must have intended me to use as a toilet. The room was now a cell. He had planned this all perfectly and I felt as cold and sick as death.

When the door eventually opened, my heart jumped into my throat. It was not him, though, but Dottor Falluci, perspiring, his leather case in his hand. 'Please,' he said. 'Sit down.'

I remained standing.

The doctor frowned, uncomfortable. 'I need to examine you, Signora Cavallera.'

'I don't permit it.'

The doctor opened up his case. 'Your husband has commanded it.'

'My husband does not own me.'

241

The doctor rubbed at his eyes behind his spectacles. 'Please, Signora. Don't make this difficult.'

I stared at his doughy face as he took out his medical equipment. The bloodstain on the floor, the medical report. Had it been he, I wondered, who'd signed off Adelina's death certificate? He who'd found the supposed haemorrhage?

'Please lie down on the daybed.'

'Why should I do anything you tell me?'

He pressed his fingers against the top of his nose. 'Please, Signora. Either lie down or I will call your husband. I won't hurt you.' He put the emphasis ever so slightly on the 'I'. *I won't hurt you, but your husband might*. That's what he was saying.

I lay on the daybed and stared up at the ceiling, thinking again of Ettore's face, the mess of blood and bone. '*Blackshirts came*,' the woman had said. Yes, but who had sent them?

The doctor ran his hands over my stomach, nodding to himself, then asked me questions about when I'd last had my courses, how regular they were. I answered as briefly as I could.

When he'd finished, I sat up, watching him. 'Why is it that you always do his bidding?' I asked very quietly. 'What do you think Dante will do if you don't go along with what he asks?'

Dottor Falluci pushed his glasses up his nose and finished packing up his equipment. 'I'll do what I can to keep you safe and well, to keep your baby healthy. But I can do nothing if you refuse to comply with your husband.' He made for the door.

'You didn't keep Adelina safe though, did you?'

The doctor froze for an instant, but he did not turn to look at me. He closed and locked the door.

I stayed there, motionless. Another half an hour or so passed. The house remained silent, but in my mind the wasps continued to buzz. Ettore dead. Adelina dead. A house full of angry whispers. I thought again and again of Ettore. I thought of the man in green.

Then footsteps – Dante's footsteps – and I felt a queasy feeling of fear and revulsion in my stomach. I heard the click of the lock and then he was there, standing before me: the man for whom I'd stayed in Italy, the man I'd thought I loved. How had I not seen that his face was cruel?

He gave a smile, false and cold. 'Eva, why did you not tell me you were with child?' He walked around the room, circling me.

I remained sitting there, silent.

'I'm hiring a new housekeeper. Someone to keep the place in order, make sure you're properly fed, not overtired. It was a mistake keeping Greta for so long and not procuring you any help. I should have realised sooner how it was with you.'

As he walked, I was looking at the door. He hadn't locked it behind him.

He caught my gaze. 'My darling, you are to stay here and you are to rest until your mind is more ordered. Dottor Falluci thinks you've become overexcited. Hormonal. This may explain your hallucinations.'

'No,' I said quietly. 'That's not it. You know that's not it. You've seen things, heard things too.'

His voice was louder this time: 'You are not to talk in this way anymore, Eva. Not to me, not to anyone. You are making yourself unwell.'

A long pause.

'What will you say to the children when they come home from school?' I asked. 'How will you explain why you've locked me up?'

'I'll tell them the truth, *cara mia,* which is that you've become overexcited and unwell, and need to spend some time recovering.'

243

'They won't believe you.'

'I'm their father. They'll do and think as I tell them.'

I envisaged Alessandro and Chiara: brought up to be obedient and unquestioning. '*Obbedire, credere, combattere*'. How much did either of them suspect of their mother's death? Did they understand, deep down, what their father was?

'Adelina didn't do as you told her, though, did she?'

He narrowed his eyes. 'You will not mention her name.'

No, because to give her a name was to make her a real person, and she could exist in Dante's mind only as the woman he'd wanted her to be: the perfect wife and mother who'd never dared question him, never asked for more than he could give.

'I'll bring you some food, which you will eat. Then you must rest. It's the child we must think about now, Eva.'

The child. The child that was a half-blood, a dirty, foreign Slav. If he knew that – and Massimo might tell him at any time – Dante would kill me. I was sure of that now. That was what the house had been trying to tell me.

Once I could hear that he was in the kitchen, I began going through the drawers and cupboards, my hands shaking, praying that there'd be a spare key to the shutters secreted somewhere, or that I'd find something I could use to pry open the lock. The sewing scissors had disappeared. Dante had already thought to take them.

As I ran my hand along the top of the wardrobe, my fingers brushed against something – a parcel. I brought it down and unwrapped the dusty brown paper. Inside was a narrow gold watch and some passports. Touching them, I felt the breath of fear. I opened the one on top and saw a photo of a dark-haired woman with a name I didn't recognise – Lilliana Mareschini. I looked closer at the photo. It was Adelina.

I looked at the other identity documents, my pulse racing.

The names were unfamiliar, but the faces I knew: a younger Chiara and Alessandro. I felt a coldness settle over my neck and shoulders and trickle down my spine. Adelina could only have procured these for one reason: she had intended to run away. She had planned to take the children and start her life afresh. What had caused her to decide to leave? I looked back at her photo. Had she realised how repugnant her husband's views were, how deep-seated his hatred for others? Had his behaviour grown steadily worse, more controlling, so that she knew her life was at risk? And so she'd decided to run. Only, when she'd finally left this house, it had been in a wooden box.

Shivering as though it was bitterly cold, I wrapped the papers and the watch back up and, through some instinct, I put them my bag. A short time later, I heard the children return home and some mumbled conversation. I wondered what they would think of Dante's explanation as to why I was closeted in the sewing room. I thought Chiara might try to come to me, but she did not. She must have known it was dangerous. Instead, she played the song I'd first taught her how to play – 'It Ain't Necessarily So' – and I thought she was playing it for me. She was telling me she knew it was lies.

When Dante brought the food to my room – bread, salami, olives, wine – I ate and drank it all. I would, as he said, need my strength, but not just for the reasons he intended. Afterwards, I found that I was very tired, though whether it was from the wine or the stress or something else, I didn't know. I lay on the daybed and fell into a half-sleep where I imagined that I hadn't returned to the house after seeing Ettore's body but had instead run straight for the border, knowing Dante was coming after me. As I reached the Slovenian border and fumbled for my passport, I saw not my own photo, but Adelina's. I was seized with a stifling panic, believing that the border official would turn me away, passing me back into the hands of my husband:

the man I knew would kill me. But he did not. The official glanced at the photo and let me through. Which is when, with a gathering, screaming fear, I realised I'd become Adelina.

I woke, distraught and sweating, shreds of the dream still clinging to my skin, and ran towards the looking glass. There, staring at me from the little mirror, was the woman that I'd replaced, her eyes hollow with death, and my mind was a swarm of insects, buzzing thick and deathly. 'No! I am me! I am *me*! I am Eva! I am Iva!' I ran to the door and hammered at it. 'Dante! Please! Dante!'

He did not come, however, no matter how much I shouted. No one came; though, from her room, I could hear poor Chiara crying.

When I looked in the mirror again, it was just me, pale and clammy-looking, my hair plastered to my forehead.

I lay back down and slept again. This time I did not dream.

I awoke early, my clothes sticking to my skin, a few shards of light piercing through the shutters. It was already hot. As I began to peel off my blouse, I found the letter from Mirella that I'd folded away the day before. I smoothed it out on the table. The sight of her sloping handwriting brought me a moment of comfort.

My darling Eva,

Why did you not tell me? Why did you not write to me before of what was happening? I know the answer to that, I think. You wanted to pretend that it would be all right and it would all go away, just as you wanted to believe the Nationalists overtaking Europe would somehow turn to dust. No such luck. But I'm not chiding you, I promise. I'm so glad you finally wrote.

Dante is a brute, or perhaps something worse. He tricked

246

and deceived you and now he seeks to control you. Well, damn him. You have done enough – more than enough – for that family. You need to look after yourself now. You need to leave, and quickly – not just the house, but Italy. It's clear that there will be war, and that Italy will take Germany's side. You must get out before that happens. Come to France. I can put you in touch with people who can help. You would like it here, I know you would, and how wonderful it would be to see you!

As for the strange events in the house, I truly don't know what to think. I'm passing on some information I've obtained, but lord knows what you'll make of it. I think I've mentioned Oscar before. He's one of the other boarders – English, terribly proper and hopelessly awkward, but truly kind-hearted. Anyway, he's much interested in the supernatural so I went to him the very night I heard from you. Rather than reciting here the conversation we had, and in order to save time, I'm enclosing a letter that Oscar tore from the magazine for the Society for Psychical Research. It seems madness to me, but then what on earth do I know? I wish to God that I was with you so we could talk about it properly and have a decent drink.

Please, Eva, get out as soon as possible. Let me know what I can do to help.

All my love,
Mirella

I replaced the letter in my shirt and began to read the article, stumbling over some of the English words.

Haunted Minds: A Letter from America
Dear Sir,
Members of the Society will have heard about the recent

resignation of Dr Nandor Fodor, parapsychologist and former chief ghost hunter at the International Institute for Psychical Research. What is less well known is the source of the controversy. This is, as I understand it, a book-length manuscript that Fodor produced following his investigations into a woman known as 'Mrs Forbes'. I believe that Dr Fodor's work may be significant.

Mrs Forbes, a housewife in Thornton Heath, England, had sought help after experiencing an escalating series of strange happenings in her suburban home: rappings, whisperings, household items flying about the house and being smashed, apparitions in mirrors, marks and teeth marks appearing on her body. You will recall similar phenomena were recorded in the case of a thirteen-year-old Romanian peasant girl, Eleonore Zugun, who was brought to London by psychical researcher Harry Price. When Zugun was tested at Price's Laboratory of Psychical Research, the investigators saw red ridges bloom along her arms, like the welts left by a whip, and dents appear in her flesh, as if she had been bitten. Objects wandered around the room when she was in it and a 'Dracu' spoke through her voice. Despite a host of investigations by different specialists, no one was ever able to firmly locate the cause of the phenomena. Countess Wassilko-Serecki, however, speculated that the activity was spurred by an inner conflict, possibly abuse by the girl's father, which the girl had been trying to repress.

In the Thornton Heath manuscript, Mr Fodor takes that idea further: having carried out various examinations, he speculates that Mrs Forbes had suppressed memories of similar abuse in her own past. That trauma, having no other route, was expressing itself in supernatural disturbances: bitings, burnings, the production of objects. He attributes to those early repressed memories her other concerning behaviour, namely attempts to supplement the apparently real hauntings with fraud.

Fodor's theory has, it is understood, found a supporter in Freud himself, who has approved the notion of carrying out a psychological study of the subject. The idea does not, however, meet favour with the spiritualists, who have little desire for the private lives of mediums to become the subject of investigation and debate. We must hope that Mr Fodor will find America's paranormal research community more welcoming than the distinctly frosty British ghost-botherers, and that he has further opportunity to develop his theory. For, if he is right, it would mean that the phenomena which until now have largely been attributed to a mischievous or evil spirit are in fact the product of repressed memories and suppressed trauma, bursting from the body or mind in a form of destructive fire.

One other point of note is that Mrs Forbes is unusual as the medium or focus of poltergeist energy as she is thirty-four years of age. In most reported cases, the focus has been found to be an adolescent. This, of course, fits with Fodor's theory of repressed energies because puberty is a tumultuous time for many and may give rise to desires or experiences that the adolescent wishes to suppress. At a time when the world appears to be marching towards war, and our boys and girls are under more stresses than they have ever been, one wonders whether we will see an increase in the chaotic phenomena that have been termed 'poltergeist'.

Yours sincerely,
J. Ellory
Seattle

I read the article twice, desperately trying to understand it and focus on the details above the buzzing in my own brain. The rappings, the clawings, the bitemarks, the whispering: they were phenomena that others, it seemed, had witnessed. Phenomena which, if this was to be believed, burst from the repressed emotions of humans.

I was still clutching the article when Dante entered the room, carrying a breakfast tray. I pulled my knees up to my chest.

'What do you have there, Eva?' He spoke to me as though I were a child.

I swallowed, my throat dry. 'Nothing important.'

He set down the tray and the cup rattled in its saucer. I watched the tea slop over the edge of the porcelain. He held his hand out for the piece of paper.

'Dante, I would rather—'

'Do not try my patience, Eva.' He ripped it from my hand.

I watched his dark eyes as they ran left to right over the sentences, watched the crease on his forehead deepen as he reached midway down the page.

When he'd finished reading, he crushed the paper in his hand. 'How the hell did you get hold of this?'

I'd promised myself I would be brave, no matter how frightened I felt. 'It doesn't matter,' I managed. 'What matters it what it says. The things described are so similar, Dante. Surely you must see that.'

He pressed his hand to his eyes. 'I see that I was right to remove you from society.'

Perhaps I should have stayed silent, but I couldn't bear it; couldn't bear his pretence not to understand, not to see what was before his eyes. 'The noises, Dante. The wasps. The water coming from nowhere. All of the things we've seen and heard. If that article is right, then they're the product of a mind. The mind of someone in this house.'

He took his hand away from his face and it was very still and very white.

I pressed on, even though I was shaking, even though I knew I was making him furious. 'According to that article, in most cases it's been an adolescent who is at the heart the happening, a child making the transition to adulthood. An adolescent who is in turmoil.'

'What exactly do you mean, Eva?'

For a moment, I couldn't speak.

'Well?'

'Alessandro,' I breathed.

'Alessandro.'

'He's been troubled, you've said that yourself. Unsettled. Sometimes violent. Could this somehow be coming from him? He doesn't mean to, of course. He isn't even conscious he's doing it. But you yourself have said how difficult he's been recently, how awkward. And then his mother dying. All that, all pent up, and—'

With a sudden sweep of his arm, Dante knocked me backwards so that my head smacked against the wall. 'SHUT. UP.'

I put my hands over my head, trying to stop the pain.

Dante leant forward so that his face was level with mine. 'Look at yourself. Listen to yourself,' he said quietly. 'Listen to yourself as you talk of the things that have happened in this house and how they are the product of a disturbed mind.'

I was backed up against the wall, my heart kicking against my ribs, my head throbbing.

'When did these phenomena you speak of begin, Eva? When did the whispering start? When did the wasps attack? When did the telephone ring?'

I felt as though I might explode, as though I might die.

Dante was very close to me now so that I could smell the coffee on his breath, the sour smell of his stomach. 'If there is such a thing as a poltergeist, Eva, if there is such a creature at all, it is nothing to do with my son's mind. It's the disgusting product of yours.'

Part Three

19

Dante left. He didn't return until many hours later, and only then to bring food for my foetus: the thing that grew inside me. Despite my pleas, he wouldn't open the window to allow me some air, only turned on the ceiling fan and locked the door again behind him.

Left alone in that room, it became for me the pit of hell: hot, dark, airless, hopeless. The whirring of the fan matched the circular motion of my mind as I went over events again and again – the cracking vase, the swarming wasps, the dripping water, the scratching, whispering sounds. Had I always been close by when these things had happened? Had I always been anxious or disturbed before the events began? I remembered walking to the house crying before the strange pools of water. I remembered my deep sense of uneasiness before the arrival of the wasps. Could it have been my mind causing and doing these things? Could it have been me who'd hurt poor Chiara, caused the bite marks on her flesh?

I thought back to my periods of paranoia as a girl – the screaming walls, the crawling insects, the vile stretching of skin. Then, from my mind, I dragged memories, like long-buried maggots, of the weeks I'd spent in the psychiatric hospital, being doused in cold baths, tied to my bed, shocked with electric cords. For years, I'd tried not to think of that time: the time when I'd believed my parents had left me alone to be experimented on; to die. Stress, the doctors had said, acute mental stress. It had led to psychotic episodes and they needed to shock them out of me; they needed to reset my brain. Had I somehow projected my madness not inwards as I'd done as a child, but outwards, onto others?

The more I thought about it, the more I believed that Dante might be right. The longer I stayed in that room, I felt that I'd left off reality altogether and descended into my own hideous nightmare, reliving the pain of the hospital, the screaming, searing fear.

I tried turning on the radio to at least hear the voices of others, but it was news of gas masks being distributed in London, civilians digging trenches for air-raid shelters: the ghastly prelude to war. Then, all at once, the voice morphed, changing from that of the presenter to the hoarse and half-formed growl that had come from Chiara's throat, from the telephone, from the walls: GET OUT, it told me, GET OUT OF THIS ROOM! GET OUT, OR YOU WILL DIE!

Then the buzzing came again, thick and dark as a clot of wasps, and I couldn't tell whether it was coming from the radio or from my own mind. No matter which way I turned the dial, it wouldn't stop, wouldn't quiet. When I ran to the door to pummel on it once again, I could feel the thing right there, right next to me, close as death, breathing hotly down my neck.

'Let me out!' I shouted. 'Please! I can't bear it in here! Something's in here with me!'

I heard footsteps and the doorknob turned but the door remained shut. 'What's wrong, Eva? What's wrong?' It was

Chiara, poor Chiara, on the other side of the door. 'Eva, I don't have the key!'

Then Dante's voice: 'Get away from there. Don't listen to what she's telling you. She's unwell.'

'But Father—'

'But Father nothing. I'm protecting you. I don't want her contaminating your mind.'

'Father, we can't just leave her in there!'

'Do you want to be locked in your room as well? Enough now, Chiara. Go!'

Retreating footsteps, then silence again and I felt that the wood of the door beneath my palms was squirming, as if it the surface had turned to rats. I retreated away from the door and back towards the gloom of the room, shivering, shaking, terrified. In the looking glass, something else was moving, like deep sea fish in the depths of the mirror. A face. A face that was not my own. I put my hands to my head, which still throbbed and ached from where Dante had hit it against the wall. Was it my mind that was causing this? I needed to still it. I needed to find a way to calm down. 'Stop it, Eva. Stop it, stop it. It's going to be all right.'

Dante returned a minute later with a bottle of blue pills. I'd thought they were all gone, but evidently Dottor Falluci had given him more. 'You will take these,' Dante said stiffly, holding two pills out on his hand, as though he were feeding an animal. 'You will not cause any further ruckus. You're distressing the children. Or is that what you want? Do you want me to also lock them away, because that's what I'll have to do?'

I shook my aching head.

'Well, then.'

I took the pills from his hand.

He stood and watched as I put the blue pills on my tongue and swallowed.

257

'Open?'

I opened my mouth to show him the pills were gone.

He nodded and left.

As soon as I heard the click of the lock, I coughed the pills back up. I was terrified but I couldn't be numbed again. I needed to find a way out.

I returned to the bed and I began, very quietly, to sing to myself. I sang the Slovene song that my mother had sometimes sung when I was young to get me to sleep. I thought I would have forgotten the words, but they were still there, still part of me: *Lipa zelenela je tam v dišečem gaju, s cvetjem me posipala.* Green grows the linden tree, In the scented grove flowers rain down on me.

When I finally fell asleep, I dreamt again of the burning: the rows and rows of faces in the Narodni Dom, the flames rising, the smoke choking. As always in the dream, I knew I had to run, knew I had to help, but my legs refused to move, my throat refused to scream. This time, however, I opened my mouth, I tasted the smoke, I coughed, coughed again. I opened my eyes. I was awake, but the fire was still there. It was real. It had finally come for me.

I sat up. The lace curtains were alight, giving off an acrid smoke that had spread throughout the room. This was no dream, but reality.

I ran to the door, beat upon it, shouted, screamed. 'Fire! There's fire! Please! Let me out!'

It must have been the middle of the night, but, please God, they would hear me and believe me. The fire was spreading, taking hold of the carpet, and gusts of black smoke were billowing towards me.

I grabbed my bag and ran back to the door, hammering on it, my heart racing, my throat choking. 'Fire! Dante! Chiara! Someone!'

'Stop it, Eva!' Dante's voice. 'You're frightening the children.'

'Dante, please! I'm telling the truth. You have to let me out!'

Hurried footsteps. The doorknob was rattling again. 'Eva! Eva!' Chiara was there.

'Let me try!' Alessandro's voice. He was trying to wrench the door open, but it was no use. 'Father! Please! I can smell the smoke!'

'Then she has set the fire herself.'

'No!'

There came a sudden gust of smoke and energy and the door burst open, seemingly of its own accord, the lock snapping, the smoke swirling into the corridor.

I ran, barefoot, blinded, out of the door and down the stairs, but I wasn't fast enough. As I reached the landing, Dante grabbed hold of my hair from behind and twisted, pulling me back towards the stairs.

'You don't want me!' I shouted. 'I'm an *untermensch*. I'm a Slav.'

'You're a liar!' He hit me full in the face.

'No. I'm telling the truth. I'm an Italianised Slovene. Your child is a half-breed. Let us go!'

He did not let me go, though, but continued to pull me by the hair and I thought I should faint from the pain. I could hear Chiara and Alessandro screaming and shouting at him, Zefiro barking furiously, the crackling and hissing of the fire. The pain in my head was awful, unbearable, the buzzing was there again, and I was still coughing, still barely able to see. I couldn't take in what the children were shouting above the buzzing and hissing and pain, when all of a sudden Dante let go and I fell like a broken thing to the ground.

I heard then what Chiara was saying.

'You killed Mother! You killed Mother! I saw it. I saw you pull her upstairs by the hair. I saw you drag her into that room. I saw you!'

'You're out of your mind.'

'No, Father. I'm remembering.'

'You're confused and upset. Alessandro, run and get help. The fire's spreading. Chiara, get water. Do what I tell you. Do it now!'

Chiara, however, ran to me – I could feel her hand on my back – and Alessandro said, 'Did you do it, Father? Did you hurt Mother?'

'What are you talking about? I never hurt your mother.'

I blinked up at them, trying to raise myself up from the ground.

Alessandro looked at his sister, looked at me. Behind him, I could see smoke billowing into the hall. 'You did, though,' Alessandro said. 'You hurt her hand once. I remember. You slammed her hand in the piano. She couldn't play for weeks.'

'Alessandro, for God's sake, come to your senses. Run and get Massimo. We can talk about this later. Chiara, come here at once!'

For a moment, Alessandro remained still, as though trying to decide, then ran pale-faced from the room, taking Zefiro with him. Chiara remained by my side. I saw flames flicker in the hallway and I pulled myself up and took hold of her arm. 'Chiara, we need to get out.'

She was not listening to me, however, but staring at her father. 'You killed Mother,' she said again. 'I saw you pull her by the hair.'

'I didn't kill her. She fell. And you're best off without her, do you hear me? She meant to leave, break up our family. Now do as I goddamn tell you or, by God, I'll make you sorry.'

He rushed towards Chiara, but at that moment she rose up,

260

screaming, and a huge lick of fire flared in front of Dante, seeming to stretch out towards him like a hand. He stared at it, mesmerised, horrified. In that moment, I was quite sure that it was Chiara's trauma, her anger, powering the fire, powering all of it; the buried memory of what she'd seen bursting forth as dark fury to destroy the world around her. But there was no time to think. The fire, I realised, had taken hold on the bottom stairs as well, running up the wallpaper, snaking up the carpet. We were trapped. We were going to die here. I could hear the shattering of porcelain and crystal as the fire ripped through the upstairs rooms.

'The bathroom,' Chiara said, and we ran, spluttering, coughing, shutting the bathroom door against the smoke. Dante, cut off by the tower of flame, was unable to follow. Behind us, I could hear him shouting.

Struggling through the smoke, I managed to get the window open and crawled out onto the roof. 'Chiara, give me your hand.'

'But Father!'

I glanced back and could see only fire. More cracking and tearing as parts of the house gave way. 'Chiara, please. You have to save yourself. Now, before it's too late.'

She hesitated only a moment, then grabbed tight hold of my hand.

We made it outside just as a whoosh of fire took hold of the bathroom rug and I heard a tremendous crashing sound, which I thought must be the stairs. I clambered down the outside ladder, Chiara coming after me, both of us shaking, coughing, dropping the last few feet to the ground.

There we found Alessandro, his skin glowing red in the reflection of the flames. He was carrying Bruno in his cage and Zefiro was cowering next to him. 'Did you go for Massimo?' Chiara asked.

Alessandro shook his head. 'No. Someone had already called the fire brigade. Is Father still in there?'

'I think so, yes.' She put her arm around him.

Various neighbours had emerged from their houses in night-gowns and slippers. Others stared from windows. We moved further back and watched with them as the fire spread, running up the house, the flames rising towards the roof. I kept thinking that Dante would emerge, broken and blackened, but alive. He did not. Instead, the fire took everything – the windows, the shutters, the roof tiles. I still had my bag, though: my bag with some money, and the gold watch, and the passports that Adelina had obtained.

Alessandro, I saw, was sobbing. I thought of being a child in Trieste, watching the world I knew burn to the ground and I knew for him it was worse. Not only was he losing his father, but realising he represented a lie. I tried to comfort him, but he pushed me away, wanting only his sister and Zefiro.

More and more people joined us standing in the street. Some neighbours draped a blanket over Chiara and Alessandro. I stood holding Chiara's hand. The fire brigade arrived, and the police. Was anyone inside, they wanted to know? Yes, I said. Yes, I think there is.

It was as I was watching them douse the still-burning build-ing that I felt Chiara's hand tighten on mine. 'Over there,' she murmured. 'Look.'

Following the direction of her gaze, I saw Massimo, talking to the carabinieri, gesturing. He turned around to stare at us, the fire casting flickering shadows on his face, then turned back to the officer. What was he saying to them? What would he think? What exactly would he do?

I reached for Alessandro's hand and this time he didn't shake me off. He must have realised there was no one else. That he and Chiara were now alone. I said: 'I have to leave now. It's not safe for me here. I think you should come with me. I think I know where to go.'

Chiara and Alessandro looked at one another and seemed in that long moment to agree, to understand that they had to trust me. We took Bruno and Zefiro and we slipped away, leaving the flames stretching into the sky.

Epilogue

Nice, 1945

'*Comment allez-vous? Comment allez-vous?*'

It was one of the phrases the children taught Bruno on our arrival in the south of France and, six years later, he's still saying it, along with a variety of ruder phrases.

How do we do? Well, we are still standing, which is more than can be said for much of Europe. We've risen from the ashes and remade ourselves in another country, helping the Resistance abroad, as many Italians have. We are part of the *fuorusciti* – the exiles, the outsiders. Not as brave as those who stayed in Italy and liberated Naples, who fought in the hills against the Nazi occupiers, who inscribed their names in the walls of the Gestapo's interrogation chambers, but we made some difference, we saved some lives, we kept the small flame of humanity burning. With Mirella, we've been helping Jews in Italian-occupied France, trying to hide them, help them escape, or procure them false papers. This is how Mirella herself has survived.

I haven't returned to Rome since the war ended. I can't face the destruction, the buildings turned to rubble, the columns ground to dust, the businesses and homes blown apart. Nor

264

have I any wish to be reminded of my former self: the one that chose to believe the lies of Dante and Mussolini and the rest of them. If I hadn't, then Ettore might still be alive; Ettore, a bright light in the darkness, who taught me that friendship – a link based on a sense of understanding and belonging – was more important than homeland or nation. I wrote often to Pietro. After his release from *confino*, he continued his work for the Resistance and the underground press until, in 1943, he too was killed, shot down by government forces during the fighting in Sicily.

I've not heard again from Greta, though I tried to locate her in Milan. So many people have dispersed or disappeared. I often wonder what became of her, and of how much she knew of what had happened to Adelina. Did she suspect, but never speak? Is that why she thought it was Adelina's ghost that stalked the Cavallera house?

Myself, I will never be quite sure what caused the things I saw and heard. At the time we left Italy, I feared that the happenings were a product of Chiara's suppressed memory and trauma, perhaps added to by my own suffering, perhaps even with an echo of Adelina's: a violent surge of repressed anger and hurt that had to find an outlet. But then I was distraught, unwell, confused. I'd just read an article which appeared to give me the answer. When I look at it now in the cold light of day, it sounds entirely implausible.

Chiara has not wanted to discuss the happenings at all, and Mirella theorises that they may have been Alessandro, acting out his anger and distress by breaking, smashing, burning. I don't want to accept either of those theories, for if the fire was caused by one of the children, then it was they who killed their father. I prefer to think of it as the house itself, or the force within it, rising up to swallow him – and what he stood for – whole.

It didn't entirely leave us in France. For over a year, there were moments when something peculiar would happen – when a door would slam or a cup would smash – for no apparent reason. But there was never any fire again, nor wasps, nor faces; never anything terribly frightening. I came to accept these small disturbances as an echo of what had gone before. And though the phenomena had seemed so terrifying, so awful when they were happening, they paled in comparison to the things that were to come. In July 1942, the Fascists created concentration camps for Slavs, the most notorious on the island of Rab. Thousands died, starved to death, my uncle and some of my cousins among them. In October 1943, 1,259 people, mainly members of the Jewish community, were rounded up from Rome's ghetto at the Portico Octavia and sent to extermination camps in Germany: men, women and children all lined up and shipped out. So too were most of the remaining Jews in Italy, located using Italian records and helped by Italian forces. Mirella's parents got out, managing to bribe their way into Switzerland, but many of her family did not escape in time. Some of the children I taught music perished.

For the survivors, life goes on and we try to use the pieces of our fractured past to build a better future. Chiara works with Mirella and me, as a piano tutor, but also for the Resistance press, for she is a brilliant and passionate writer. Alessandro is studying engineering; his love is now not guns, but cars. He has a propensity to steal them. For him, the move to France, away from Fascism, was the most difficult, for he had grown up believing it – and his father – entirely. At times, he has hated us all. He has been in some trouble with the police, but so far we've avoided anything more than words, largely thanks to Mirella's interventions. He is surprisingly gentle with my son, his half-brother, Gabriel, who is now nearly six years old.

What is Gabriel like? Well, sometimes I see a touch of his

father in him — in the flash of his dark eyes, or the tilt of his head — and for a brief moment I am afraid. But I remind myself that he is only partly his father. He is also partly me, and partly the product of our community, our era — part Slovene, part Italian, part French, part person entirely of his own making. He has inherited some of my musical ability and is already playing the piano. Sometimes he sits between Mirella and me and we play a simple trio. Then I remember how we practised with Ettore in that dusty schoolroom, our laughter echoing down the years.